STUFF DREAMS ARE MADE OF

ALSO BY DON BRUNS

Jamaica Blue

Barbados Heat

Death Dines In
(contributor)

A Merry Band of Murderers
(editor & contributor)

South Beach Shakedown

Stuff to Die For

St. Barts Breakdown

STUFF DREAMS ARE MADE OF

A Novel

DON BRUNS

Oceanview Publishing

IPSWICH, MASSACHUSETTS

ISBN-13: 978-1-933515-16-8

Published in the United States by Oceanview Publishing,
Ipswich, Massachusetts
www.oceanviewpub.com

2 4 6 8 10 9 7 5 3 1

PRINTED IN THE UNITED STATES OF AMERICA

This book is dedicated to Edward Stratemeyer who invented the Hardy Boys. His juvenile mysteries were my first foray into the genre. Nancy Drew, The Happy Hollisters, The Bobbsey Twins, Tom Swift, and The Rover Boys were all products of his fertile imagination. Skip and James are grown up Hardy Boys, and I think that Edward Stratemeyer would be proud.

ACKNOWLEDGMENTS

I'd like to acknowledge my support group, Mike Trump, Don Witter, Jay Waggoner, Mike McNamara, and my brother Dave. Thanks to my wife, Linda, who edits all my work, and to Maryglenn McCombs who is the best publicist in the business, and getting better with every book. Mary Stanton, my good friend and advisor, thank you. Bob and Pat Gussin, Susan Greger, Mary Adele Bogdon, George Foster, Susan Hayes, and the rest of the staff from Oceanview, you make the product look and read like a million bucks!

STUFF DREAMS ARE MADE OF

CHAPTER ONE

I was fifteen years old when I found out my Uncle Buzz's name was really Clarence. Not that it mattered that much. Despite the name Clarence, Buzz was a very cool uncle, ten years older than I was, and on my fifteenth birthday he picked me up in his 1987 Mustang convertible and promised to take me places I'd only dreamed about and show me things I'd never seen.

Dad had left home four years before, and my mother had pretty much washed her hands of any serious parental control, tending to be bitter about her lot in life and distant in her relationship with me. I waved to Mom and my little sister as we pulled out of the driveway, and Buzz burned rubber at the end of the street.

Leaving Carol City for the weekend was enough of a treat, the urban blight of that depressed area leaving real stains on my outlook on life, but Buzz had promised the excitement of Miami, Ft. Lauderdale, and maybe a trip down the Keys as an added bonus, and I was on a true emotional high.

I still remember the hot Florida sun washing over us as he cruised down I-95 and the sweet bite of Coke and Jack as we pulled from the silver flask he'd brought for this special occasion. Jack was my new best friend and my head was in the clouds.

"Gonna be a weekend to remember, Skip. Honest to God, a weekend to remember."

We met with God that night, sitting on dew-damp grass on a slight rise watching a full-scale tent revival with a black preacher, gold Bible in hand, regaling his flock with stories loosely borrowed from the Bible. About three hundred parishioners swayed and chanted with the preacher and when they sang it was as if the sky had opened and the Lord had unleashed all of his unruly angels to shout his praises.

"People get worked up for a lot of reasons, Skip," Buzz sipped his Jack and Coke, watching the proceeding with the eye of a skeptic. "I used to get worked up because of my name. Imagine. Upset about a little thing like that."

"Buzz? What's wrong with your name?"

He passed the flask to me. "That's not my name, Skip. It's Clarence."

I smiled. There was no room to laugh. With the name Eugene haunting me for fifteen years, I knew the stigma.

"Clarence. Both of our moms had a sense of humor."

Buzz laughed. "That show down there, those people when they get worked up could accomplish anything tonight. Do you believe that?"

I shrugged my shoulders.

"Right now, Skip. They could move a mountain. No, they could. They could go from here and raise a million dollars in the next hour. They could heal the sick and raise the dead. Raise the dead, nephew. They could do it. But when this show is over they go back to their miserable existence. They return to their drab, humble shacks, their cheating spouses, their screaming litter of kids, and their sham of a life. When it's over, the only thing to look forward to is the next revival."

I thought about that. I wasn't quite sure why we were there, except he was fulfilling his promise. He was taking me places I'd never been.

"So what's the point, Buzz?"

"It's gonna be a weekend of revivals, Skip. The only thing we have in this world is looking forward to the next revival."

He put a twenty in the collection box when the pretty little black girl stopped by our resting spot. Then, as we stood up and walked away from the thundering voice of the gospel choir, he offered me a cigar. We puffed away in the steamy night and in my foggy state of mind, the booze and the thick smoke swirling in my head, I realized Buzz may be onto something. Life was a constant search for the next adventure. My uncle was right.

But he was wrong about the capabilities of the faithful. If that crowd could have raised the dead, seventeen-year-old Cabrina Washington would be alive today. As it is, she's in a grave, and the last adventure she had was the tent revival near Miami.

CHAPTER TWO

"Think of it as an adventure, Skip." James was into his selling mode. "Come on pal, it won't interfere with work and we'll make some good money. Tell me you couldn't use a little extra scratch!"

The truth was, I could. And James had outfitted the truck with two gas grills, a small refrigerator, and a stove. He could cook, I'd sell and collect the money, and it would all happen after our regular working hours. The one-ton box truck was a regular kitchen of the road. He'd cut a window out of the side, where we could let the air and light in, and he'd cut a hole in the top to vent the greasy smoke. He'd fixed up a makeshift counter next to the small grill at the rear of the vehicle so I could sell the food and hand it down to the lines of hungry Christians. Adding an aluminum step-up to the rear of the truck so customers could "rise" to the occasion was the final modification. It wasn't perfect. I would have to lean down to give the masses their meals, but it was doable. I stalled, taking a swallow of beer and gazing down the row of apartments with their postage-stamp concrete porches.

"Skip! Amigo! You know I can make this happen."

I put my hand up, silencing him for a moment. "The last time you told me this truck would make us some money, we got ourselves in a world of shit and you almost got beaten to death!" There had been an international incident that we didn't bring up very often.

"This is strictly selling food, Skip. No more terrorists or international plots." The last idea he'd had, we'd both been in life-threatening situations. "We start at six p.m. and work until about eleven. There are supposed to be fifteen hundred to two thousand people at this tent revival every night. My God, we could make a fortune." He tapped his cigarette, dropping ashes on the stained cement. Wine, beer, and some stains I can't explain.

James was convinced we'd both be worth a fortune by the time we reached thirty. I had my doubts. As small children growing up, we had dreams. By the time we were seniors in high school, James had decided he would study culinary arts and I would major in business and we could open up the greatest restaurant on South Beach. It didn't happen.

College loans, personal debt, family problems, and two dead-end jobs later we were struggling. James was a short-order cook at Cap'n Crab, a fast food restaurant, and I was selling home security systems in a community where no one had anything to secure. Carol City does not appear on the Miami Chamber of Commerce list of must-see places. It's a secondhand city, urban and poor. We've got a couple of old run-down malls, one decent restaurant, and a handful of old stucco gas stations, which have been converted into nondenominational churches with names like Church of the Lamb, or Salvation Congregation. There's Hallelujah Station (a converted grocery store) and a strange building a couple blocks from our apartment with a faded sign outside that simply says "Welcome Sinners." James and I have often said that that's the one we'd pick if we were to pick any of them.

But the revival was in a tent, at a fairgrounds outside of Miami, and this wasn't Salvation Congregation. Nope. This was the reverend Preston Cashdollar who headed up the largest church in the Miami area and boasted a congregation of fifteen thousand members, growing every Sunday. I swear to you, that's his name, Cashdollar. And to have fifteen thousand members in your congregation? I couldn't even fathom that.

"What do you say, pard? I'm figuring we lay in a supply of ground beef, brats, corn on the cob, and potatoes and we're good to go. There's a chance we could take home two or three thousand a night, Skip."

"Two thousand dollars a night? How do you figure?"

"Jeez, you're the business guy. We get two hundred customers a night, sell 'em a meal for ten bucks and —"

"You're gonna sell a hamburger, corn, and potato salad for ten bucks? My God, James, those people won't have anything left for the collection plate."

"Listen, Daron Styles says that —"

"Daron Styles? Why would you quote that reprobate?"

"All right, he wasn't the most trustworthy kid in our class, but he's done this revival meeting. He says it's a license to steal."

"Daron Styles 'did' this revival meeting? What does that mean?"

"He had a booth. Sold religious stuff like small Bibles, pictures, silver crosses, statues and stuff. He says the followers come with money to spend. I believe he did quite well."

"Styles is sleezy. Is that the kind of person we're going to be working with?"

"He's not with the meeting anymore. He's working in South Beach, but Skip, who the hell cares? Listen, pard, we're in the middle of a campground. These people have been dancing and singing and whatever they do at these revivals and they are hungry, Skip, with nowhere else to go. Ten bucks a meal covers our gas, our time, and our supplies. We can make some good money, pal. Come on, would I steer you wrong?"

He paused, waiting for me to jump at the chance. If this was such a good idea, why had Daron Styles left? And would James steer me wrong? Of course. No question. He'd steered me all over the place since grade school. "James, there has to be a tariff. They're not going to let us just make that kind of money off of their congregation without some sort of fee."

James smiled. His charming smile worked on a lot of people, but we went back much too long for it to have any effect on me. "Skip, Skip. I can't pull anything on you. You're my amigo."

"Can it. How much?"

"Five hundred a day."

"Jesus!"

"That's why we're going, son. For Jesus."

"And if we don't make five hundred dollars a day?"

"Well," he studied me as if to gauge my reaction to his next *charming* statement, "we still have to pay. It's up-front money."

"Oh, well let me get my wallet out. I've got three days worth of five hundred dollars right here. No problem." I probably had nine bucks if I was lucky.

His charm went out the window. "Look, damn it. We can make twenty-five hundred a night off this thing. I've met with one of Reverend Cashdollar's business guys, Thomas LeRoy, and he assured me we could do at least that well."

"Thomas LeRoy?"

"Thomas LeRoy. He handles Cashdollar's business affairs. His title is," James pulled a crumpled piece of paper from his jeans and opened it up, "Deacon Thomas LeRoy, Division Head of Financial Affairs."

"Jeez, James. The whole thing sounds suspect." And then another thought hit me. "And how many other food vendors are there at five hundred bucks a pop?"

"I don't know. I'm thinking maybe two or three."

"And where did you think we were going to come up with that kind of cash?"

"I've already got it. We just have to pay her back."

"Who?"

"Brook. She took five hundred out of her savings account."

"I've got to hand it to you, James. You've gone out with her, what, six times? And you've already floated a five hundred dollar loan."

"Charm, Skip. Obviously something you need to cultivate."

I studied the hot midday sun, the cracked and pitted concrete porch that we sat on in our cheap, faded, plastic lawn chairs. I scratched at the label on my cheap off-brand beer and considered the fact that I didn't have any idea better than my roommate's.

"Three nights?"

"Three nights, bro. Thursday, Friday, and Saturday night. We come back here after each dinner shift, and Sunday after the big finale, we pack it in. Comin' home with some real cash."

"And all we have to do is pay one night at a time?"

"Pay as you pray, brother."

"And you trust this Thomas LeRoy? Division head of whatever?"

"As much as you can trust anyone. He's a very professional businessman. Suit, tie, very organized, and he's got this personal organizer with him. I'm talking to him, he's keeping notes on this thing. I was impressed. We're going to have to get one of those things eventually. A personal organizer. Pretty cool." He swallowed the rest of his beer and stood up, his tall lanky frame towering over me.

"James, you've already got a personal organizer. And sometimes I get a little tired of being *it*."

He didn't smile.

"And I'm not sure Styles is a good reference."

"Like him or not, Daron Styles did the show and said it's a good way to make a nice chunk of change. Skip, a lot of life is just looking for the next adventure. Look at this as our next adventure."

I'd heard it before. From Uncle Buzz. "You don't see Styles doing it again, do you?"

"He had a run-in with a couple of the other vendors."

It didn't surprise me at all. Daron Styles was always having a run-in with somebody or something.

"That was it? He had a run-in with somebody?"

James was quiet for a moment. "Look, it doesn't matter. Somebody was killed the weekend he worked at the revival. And maybe Styles was implicated. I don't have all the information, but it was a one-time thing. No biggy."

"Somebody was killed, and it's no biggy? Killed on the campground?"

"Come on, Skip. It had nothing to do with us."

James was full of bullshit. He could say that now, but when I got involved with him, everything had to do with us. "And Styles?"

"Never arrested, never convicted as far as I know."

"Who was killed?" He was stalling.

"I shouldn't have mentioned it."

"But you did."

"Damn it, pard. It's not important."

"Who was killed?" I could hold out as long as he could.

"Are you in or are you out?"

I thought about it for a minute. Sixty seconds can be a long time when you're under pressure. Finally I nodded. James already knew my answer. And I hated that. "All right."

He raised his empty beer bottle, toasting the venture. "We're gonna make some serious jack, Skip."

"Who was killed?"

"May have been an accidental death, amigo."

"Who?"

"A vendor. A food vendor. Okay? You happy?"

I just shook my head. Why was I always letting him drag me into these things?

I remembered my last revival. I remembered meeting the attractive seventeen-year-old black girl as she walked up to Buzz, basket in hand.

"The Lord took a few loaves of bread and a few fish, multiplied them and fed five thousand. Will you help in the Lord's work?" she had said.

Buzz reached into his pocket and pulled out a twenty. In the few times I'd actually been inside a church, I'd never seen anyone give more than a five dollar bill.

"See how far this will go."

"Thank you," the girl smiled bashfully.

"I'm Buzz and this is Skip. I was just telling my nephew about the power of your revival meetings."

Her face lit up as she took the bill and put her hand on his. "I'm Cabrina. Cabrina Washington. The Lord will bless you for this."

The next day we heard it on the radio, driving Buzz's Mustang down A1A to the Keys. Cabrina Washington was found strangled to death in a grove of pine trees about one hundred yards from a group of camper/trailers inside the campgrounds. To my knowledge they never found the murderer.

"You'll be surprised at how powerful these revivals can be." James smiled, and took a drag from his cigarette.

"No, I won't be surprised at all." I popped the cap on another beer and prayed that this would be much less eventful than the last revival I'd attended eleven years ago.

CHAPTER THREE

The truck was James's. He'd bought it with a twelve-thousand-dollar inheritance from an aunt he didn't even know. In the last month I'd made a few more security system sales than usual so I chipped in to help buy the kitchen appliances. The stove and two small grills worked off propane gas, the refrigerator off of a generator. As I said, James cut out a window in the side of the truck, hinging the cut-out metal so we could breathe fresh air and see daylight. Then he'd cut a hole in the top of the vehicle, and we ran stove pipe to vent the grills. The aluminum step-up folded down when we parked, and our hungry patrons could step up to the makeshift counter, where I would hand them their plates. It wasn't pretty, but it was functional. Everything was used and cheap, including my cast iron skillet, and I figured the worst that could happen would be that everything would break down and we'd be out $500. It turns out worse things can happen.

James shopped for supplies and we loaded up the truck. The meeting started Thursday afternoon, and when we pulled into the fairgrounds about six o'clock that night, I did a double take. It wasn't the hundreds of cars, campers, and trailers that crowded the sprawling acreage, and it wasn't the size of the massive yellow canvas tent. It wasn't the throngs of people or the rows of portable toilets that threw me. It was the row of food vendors lined up on one side of a gravel drive. There were fifteen trucks, carts, vans, and booths offering pizza, donuts, chicken tenderloins and wings, burgers, onion rings, hot dogs, and barbecue.

"James?"

"Uh-oh."

"Reverend Cashdollar gets seventy-five hundred a night and we do all the work?"

"Ah, Skip, there's still going to be plenty for everyone. Let's not go crazy. You saw all those cars as we drove in."

Our place was clearly marked with a wooden sign: #15 **MORE OR LESS CATERING**. It was James's idea, not mine. His name is Lessor, mine is Moore, so he thought it would be clever to — well, it was his idea. We pulled in, leaving the rear of the truck facing the drive. James had a table to set up in the back end of the truck and I'd serve from there.

"Honest to God, James. You should have checked to see how many vendors were going to be here."

"Yeah, but look at our position, dude. We are number one when you come out of the tent. Right next to God's door, amigo."

I stepped out of the cab and almost knocked down the older balding guy with the pink apron standing right outside the truck door.

"Hey. You're the new guys, huh?"

"Yeah, I guess. It's our first time here. So you've been doing this for a while?"

"Bruce. Bruce Crayer. I'm the donut guy in the next trailer. Just wanted to introduce myself. Yeah, been coming to Cash's revivals for about three years now. Every year they grow. We do real well, yes we do. Four years ago, there was maybe five or six vendors, and now just look. Enough for everybody though." It was as if Bruce Crayer and James had set this up ahead of time.

"I'm Skip Moore and —" I motioned to the cab as James came around the truck, "this is my partner James Lessor."

Crayer seemed to notice the lot sign for the first time and chuckled. "Sure. **MORE OR LESS**. Well, we'll be neighbors here for the next four days and three nights. These nights are something. Lots of things going on at night let me tell you." Crayer rubbed his hands on his colorful apron. "Water hookup is right in front of your cab. You can just hook up your hose." He pursed his lips and let his gaze roam up and down the two of us as if he was measuring us for a suit.

After an awkward silence, I finally grabbed his hand, shook it heartily, and looked him in the eye. "Thanks for coming over and saying 'Hi,' Bruce. I assume we can ask you if we have a question about anything."

"Sure. You just ask for me. A little later some of the full-time vendors play a little poker down at Stan's place. He's got the pizza booth where you first drove in. You're welcome to join us."

He walked back to his trailer and James shook his head. "We just got here and already we've got a game."

"Bruce said he's been coming here for three years, and the nights get pretty interesting."

"Oh, I'm sure," James squinted, leveling his gaze at me. "Pard, where I come from, this is either a revival meeting or a craps game."

"Poker, James."

"*Titanic*, Skip. Nineteen fifty-two or three. Thelma Ritter."

James watched far, far too many old movies. "Obscure quote, James."

"It fit the bill, amigo."

"I say this tent revival meeting can't be that interesting."

But it was.

*   *   *

The first night was chaotic. Our setup was fast, since we'd prepared everything ahead of time. We had about five hundred burgers preformed and seasoned, and James had boiled the brats so all we had to do was finish them on his grill. He'd arranged the brats and burgers on waxed paper in cardboard boxes. I cooked the onions and peppers on my small grill and in my cast-iron skillet, always keeping them simmering, and we were off and running. About a quarter till seven the meeting broke up, and what had been a slow parade of diners turned into a torrent. Two thousand people poured out of the huge yellow tent, and they swarmed over the vendors like biblical locusts. I couldn't keep up, and we lost dozens of customers who grew tired of our inexperience.

"Skip, I could use a little help back here!" James yelled from his grill covered in smoky burgers and brats.

"Join the crowd, buddy. I'm a little jammed up here at the moment."

The line grew and grew and some people who got impatient just walked away, several who had paid their ten dollars. They just walked away from ten bucks.

The sweat ran off my face, the heavy smell of grease was nauseating, and a dozen customers at a time yelled orders up to me.

"A brat, two burgers, and make sure there are plenty of onions on the brats."

"I said no onions on the brats, young man."

"Kid, excuse me, but I gave you a twenty. You owe me a ten."

"Peppers? I don't want any peppers, can you take them off?"

"Lady, take the peppers off yourself!" Thirty minutes into our maiden voyage and I was about fried.

"Skip, I'm out of peppers. Why aren't there more on the grill?"

"Because I'm a little busy up here, my friend, with the friendly Christians."

And then it got to be a pattern. I could get most of the orders, tend to the onions, peppers, and the fried potatoes, and James started organizing the meat grill so we were actually ahead of the game. From time to time I'd see him flip the burgers, and press them to the grill to hurry the cooking process. He'd stack them, then I'd grab them and place them in buns, spoon on the onions, peppers, and potatoes and serve the meal on a cheap paper plate.

The gray, smoky haze hung everywhere and we observed the operation through tear-filled eyes, wiping at our faces with stained shirtsleeves.

"For ten bucks, can't I get a decent helping of potatoes?"

"Did someone even cook this meat?"

"More onions, please."

"I said no onions."

They offered up the worn, paper money, some of them digging for quarters and the last of their change. Grabbing the greasy food, they'd start tearing into it before they'd even left. As ravenous as this crowd was, they may have eaten the paper plates too.

And finally, it was over. Finally the line evaporated, disappeared, and we just stood and looked at each other, shaking our heads. I'd smell like this for the rest of my life. There was no way a shower, deodorant, or cologne would ever get rid of the cloying, greasy smell of fried meat and onion. And I didn't know if I could ever go through this another night, much less two.

It was eight thirty. We'd been jammed for a full hour and forty-five minutes. Not much time in the scope of eternity. "James, I don't think I've ever worked that hard in my life." I wiped my face with the sleeve of the white cooking coat, noticing the sleeve was more damp than my face.

"Man, Cap'n Crab is never this busy. I didn't think we were going to keep up."

"I don't want to depress you, but we didn't."

"Wow. It just never seemed to stop."

"James, I don't think I want to do this again. That was crazy."

He stooped over his boxes, lifting and sorting.

"James did you hear me?"

"I heard you, my friend. Have you counted the money?"

I hadn't. It was jammed into the cash box, and I'd taken some out and dumped it into a large canvas bag that sat on the floor.

"Well, if your cash deposit matches the food we sold —"

"Yes?"

"We did about thirty-eight hundred ninety dollars tonight. Minus the rev's five hundred."

"Thirty-three ninety? Not bad. Not bad at all."

He had a big grin on his face. "Still want to bow out?"

I shook my head. "No, I think I'll be here tomorrow night."

"Great. Bring the dog, I love animals. I'm a great cook." I had to think for a minute. Obscure as it was, it came to me. "Glenn Close in *Fatal Attraction*."

He wiped his wet, greasy hands on his dirty apron. "You know your movies. I'm proud of you, pard. Proud of you."

CHAPTER FOUR

The fairground restrooms had six public showers, like a college dorm. The cement block facility smelled sour, like ripe laundry, and as I washed off the stench of the grease and onion, I wondered which was worse. The running water echoed off the block walls and I scrubbed for all I was worth.

We cleaned up as well as we could, glad that we'd brought a change of clothes, and we put on less offensive jeans and T-shirts and walked down the path.

James found Stan's pizza wagon. If it involved cards, a scheme, a business idea, or making and losing money, James could always sniff it out. The vehicle was painted like a circus wagon, with bright colors, big fake wooden wheels, and a huge slice of pizza painted on the side to look like a clown's face. Two slices of pepperoni for the eyes, an olive for the nose, and a slice of red ripe tomato for the mouth.

They'd already dealt a hand and cracked their first beers by the time we arrived, and my nose told me that one or two of the six had not yet showered.

"Pull up a chair, boys." Bruce Crayer waved, motioning to us to sit, so we watched the game close-up. The folding table sat outside the wagon, and an assortment of bugs buzzed the lights strung from Stan's pizza emporium. Some of the six players had tossed a handful of poker chips in the center of the table and we watched as the game unfolded.

No one said another word to us. There were glances, each of the players secretly sizing us up. Occasionally Crayer would look up and smile at me, but the others kept stern looks on their faces. I wondered if the rest of them were as interested in our participation as Crayer had been. The one thing they did know was that we'd made some good money in the last couple of hours, and I assumed they were ready to take it away from us. Twenty minutes later, the first game was over and after a whispered sixty-second conference with a cigar-smoking ringleader, two of the players left.

"Sorry, guys." Crayer nodded to us. "Should have introduced you, but the first game we play every year is all seriousness. Kind of sets the tone for the rest of the weekend. Stan, this here is Skip, and this is James." He introduced us to the cigar smoker, who checked us out through squinty eyes. "They got the number fifteen booth up there. Burgers, brats. By the looks of things they did well tonight. Right, boys?" There was no recognition of the other two unknown players.

"We didn't know exactly what to expect." I glanced at James. "I'd say we did very well."

Crayer smiled. "Well, what you made, we'd like the chance to take away. Are you boys in?" I knew it. For a couple of bucks we'd be accepted about anywhere.

We played the first few hands and broke even. The conversation centered around the reverend himself. A guy I knew very little about.

"Well, another season and more pickin's for the rev." Bruce

Crayer settled back in the rickety wooden folding chair. "The rubes are out in number."

"Rubes?" James looked up from studying his cards.

"Cashdollar's flock," Crayer said. "He has them all believing that if they follow his lead, they'll be rich. 'Course, he makes sure that he gets rich first."

Stan, the pizza man, leaned back in his chair, keeping his cards close to his chest. Lighting another cigar, he studied us, not hiding his hard look. It was as if he was gauging our reaction.

"And he's back at it, pickin' his targets." A big mouthed guy who'd been silent up to now leaned back in his folding chair. He waved his hand at me. "The rev. Every campaign he picks a different target. Tonight he was working on this right-wing Miami talk show host, Barry Romans."

"He'll get him, Mug. End of this tent meeting, Romans won't know what hit him."

James sipped on his beer, holding his cards tightly. "I've heard Romans on the radio. Like a local Rush Limbaugh."

"Bigger than local." Stan, the pizza man, took a puff off the fat cigar. "He's got stations that carry him all over the state. Some even up in Georgia, I believe. So you boys are aware of him, huh?"

The big-mouthed man referred to as Mug continued. "It's gonna be brutal. Rev's gonna accuse him of being the Devil, get his congregation all riled up."

"They'll picket this Romans," a tall skinny guy with thick glasses spoke for the first time, "and send hundreds of letters of protest to the newspaper, the radio stations."

"And," our neighbor Crayer gave us all a broad grin, "we make more money every meeting. Right, Dusty? Cashdollar's loyal following love to blame somebody else for all the world's evils. Yes, they do."

I couldn't help but smile too. More money was just what I needed right now.

James added to the pot, apparently sensing a big win. It didn't happen.

For some reason I needed to know the outcome. "So does the reverend get his man? Does he bring down the target?"

"Sometimes." Crayer shuffled the deck.

"What happens to Barry Romans?"

Mug ran his hand through his unruly, greasy mop of hair. "The rev's nailing him for being a racist, for being a card-carrying member of the NRA, for being anticivil rights, and a whole bunch of other stuff. I think he was just makin' shit up this afternoon, just to get more reaction. He gets a good reaction when he threatens right wingers. Even a better reaction if something happens to them."

Mug laughed, almost like a rumble deep in his throat. "Make stuff up? The rev?"

"And?"

Crayer looked around at the five of us. "And? If the rev gets three or four thousand people riled up, they take Romans on. Tear him down."

James was engrossed. "Is that what you mean about 'something happening to them?' You mean he influences that many people?"

"Kid," Stan was puffing like a locomotive, "he'll influence maybe ten thousand people just this weekend."

"Wow."

"You remember what happened to that talk show host, Don Imus? He made some comment about some black college girls, and got fired inside of a week, from TV and radio." Stan took another puff on his cigar and a spiral of smoke climbed high and disappeared in the dark. "Reverend Al Sharpton took him on.

Crucified him. Kid, ministers and public opinion are powerful forces. They can bring down mountains."

Everything got quiet, and I was aware of the warm, humid night air. The cloying odor of old grease, stale beer, cigar smoke, and sweat was getting to my stomach and I realized, with all the food we'd cooked, I hadn't eaten anything.

I lost three hands, folded quickly, and was down about forty bucks. James had won his first hand, raking in over $300. And then, in typical James fashion, he promptly lost the next two hands and ended up down $200. I'd locked our newfound money in a small closet in the truck, so thank goodness he had limited funds. Knowing James, he could have blown the entire night's take.

"More beer?" Crayer pulled a couple of long necks from the aluminum cooler by the side of Stan's trailer. We'd already swallowed three, and I pushed myself away from the table.

"I'm going to have to decline. I've got work tomorrow, and then *this* again tomorrow night."

"Skip, couple more hands here. I can win this back and we can really go home with a stash." James gave me a pleading look.

I grabbed him by the shoulder, and he shook my hand off. "Come on, amigo. One more hand." He twisted the cap off his beer and played another hand. Now he was down $500. It was obvious they could smell blood. Stan, Bruce, Dusty, Mug all pleaded with him to stay in the game.

James looked down at his dwindling stake, shoved the few paltry dollars back in his pocket and sadly shook his head. "Got to take Skip home, guys."

Stan pointed up the lane. "Girls comin' in half an hour."

James and I both perked up a little. "Girls?"

"Thought maybe Bruce told you. Where there's loose money, they'll find it."

I glanced at my partner, his big smile dwindling. "Working girls?"

The guy with the big face and shaved head named Mug, laughed out loud. "They'll be workin' their asses off once they get here. We set 'em up in a small tent over by the Intracoastal Waterway." He pointed off to the right, behind a stand of trees, where the state had built a series of shelters that looked out on the man-made waterway. Working girls. Another fine use of the Florida taxpayer's dollar. A tented whorehouse.

"Uh, I think we'll pass."

"Tomorrow night," Stan the pizza guy jammed his finger into my chest, "you stay late. There's a special little treat goin' on and I think you young guys would enjoy it. Stay late, got it?"

We said our good-byes and Crayer said goodnight as well. The three of us worked our way up the end of the dirt road.

"I'm stayin' in a little trailer just over there." Crayer pointed to a spot in the distance where a scattering of dim lights shone from tents and trailers. "Most of the guys you met stay there."

"What about the other vendors?"

"Most of the others are like you. They're local and they go home in the evening. Got families and stuff. We're on the road. If the rev's got a gig, we do that, but we spread out and do shows all over the country. Fairs, carnivals, sometime even other revival meetings with other guys."

"Well, we're driving the truck back to our apartment. We'll see you tomorrow night. Thanks for showing us the ropes." I shook his hand.

"Hell, you guys were goin' like gangbusters tonight. You got the hang of it right away."

James nodded. "Tell me something, Bruce. When Cashdollar brings all this force to bear on somebody like Barry Romans, you're telling me he can get him fired? That's pretty serious power. What's happened in the past?"

James was obsessed with it. Power, money, making something happen with his young life. He wouldn't pass up any chance for a learning experiece. My best friend, the entrepreneur.

"I've been doin' this little circus for a lot of years. Three years with the rev, but lots of years on different circuits." Crayer ran his hand through his thinning hair. "I've made enough donuts to circle this world a hundred times, so I've got a little background."

"And?"

"The rev started out like a lot of them, with fire and brimstone. God's gonna getcha' if you don't straighten up."

I remembered the revival meeting Buzz and I had gone to many years ago. Somewhere, I remembered, not too far from here. I had no recollection of who the preacher was. I just remember he marched around his platform with a Bible clutched in his hand and he was angry. Angry at the Devil and just about everyone else.

"And I believe that he changed people's lives. I do. But it's a different world out there."

"How's that?" James was leaning in, eagerly hoping for some business advice he could use.

"People want to blame somebody else for all the problems of the world, and the rev honed in on that. First of all, he got into the 'God's gonna make you rich' thing. He got people dreaming. That's doing really well for him. Collections doubled, tripled. But he really saw his fortunes start to climb about three years ago when he nailed that senator from Nebraska, Long I think his name was."

I drew a blank.

"Guy was antigay, anticivil rights, and he made a couple of statements that struck the rev the wrong way. Very right wing. May have even used the N word. Rev went after him and Cashdollar was getting national press — cover of *Time* magazine — and the money was rolling in."

"And what?" I asked. "They ran this Long out of office?"

"Not exactly. The rev got the national media behind it, got the newspapers and television networks to go after this guy. Rev was on Larry King and a lot of left-wing talk shows. He started a letter-writing campaign, phone banks, blogs on the Internet, and stuff you couldn't imagine."

"He's that powerful?"

"More powerful than even that."

"How much more powerful can you be?" Now I was intrigued.

Crayer folded his hands over his ample stomach and in the dim light gave us a hard look. "I was there when Fred Long got killed."

All of a sudden he'd remembered the senator's name.

"Somebody shot him in cold blood on the streets of Washington D.C. And boys," he stopped for a moment, looking off into space, "boys, you don't get any more powerful than that."

CHAPTER FIVE

James drove, and when he'd occasionally hit the brakes we could hear the kitchen equipment rattle in the back.

"What do you think he meant?" James hadn't said much since we left the fairgrounds.

"Well, I don't think he meant that Cashdollar actually shot the man." I was thinking how Crayer had not been sure of the deceased's last name, then all of a sudden had come up with the full name. No question, he knew the story.

"I don't know the story, pally, but Jesus! That's some serious charge." James took a long drag on his cigarette and blew a stream of smoke out the driver's window. "Think about it, Skip. Enough clout to have somebody whacked? What would that feel like?"

"Feel like? It would scare the hell out of me. I don't want that kind of power. I mean, I really don't want someone killing a senator or anybody, because of something I said."

"And Crayer says when Cashdollar attacked, the money came pouring in." James was all about finding new ways to make money.

I thought about Crayer's accusation. It would be easy enough to find out if Fred Long had died. And, it should be easy to find out how he died. Maybe Cashdollar's constant hounding did bring about his death. Or maybe the shooting was totally unrelated. Or maybe, just maybe somebody in Reverend Cashdollar's congregation actually killed Long. "And the other thing he said —"

"What was that?"

"I was there when he was shot."

"He must have been living in Washington at the time. They eat donuts in D.C. too."

"And then, what about Barry Romans? I mean, is his life in danger?" James turned to me. "Imagine, Skip. What kind of business is that? One where you actually try to bring somebody down?"

"James, you're actually showing some compassion?"

My roommate rolled his eyes. "Hell, no. I was thinking about what Bruce said. Something about absolute power. Getting someone killed? I'm with you. I don't want to kill somebody, but I just wonder what it would be like to have that absolute power."

"Let's hope you never find out." Sometimes, James scared me.

"Absolute power, bro. Like God."

I thought about the senator. And about the food vendor who may or may not have been killed, right there on the park grounds. And I thought about Cabrina Washington, who'd been strangled at a revival meeting. These events seemed to be somewhat scary. Somewhat suspect. We didn't talk the rest of the way home.

James and I share a computer. And we pay for high-speed access, which is a considerable cost since neither of us makes much money. When we got to the apartment I ran a Google search and found about 15,000 hits on "death of senator Fred Long." How we could have missed the story, I don't know. I guess the news in South Florida isn't exactly the news of North Dakota or Washington, D.C.

"Here's the short version, James."

He'd stripped down to his baggy boxers and lay on the sofa sipping on his fifth or sixth beer of the night. I'd at least stopped at four. "Give it to me, pard."

"He was shot."

"Short version, sure enough."

"In broad daylight. He came out of an office building in Washington, was headed for a place he frequented for lunch, and somebody shot him."

"Jeez. He's just walking to get some lunch and they nailed him? They got the guy, right?"

"Not in the last three years. No one was sure where the shot came from or who the shooter could have been."

"Mmmm."

"Short-range shooting. Five or ten feet."

"Well, that's got to be a Federal crime, wouldn't you think?"

"I would."

James belched. "So was there speculation? Did they have any suspects at all? Must have been some thoughts."

I scanned the news story, finally finding some theories. "Yeah. Everyone figured it was a nutcase, but there was a lot of speculation that it was fueled by the pressure from Cashdollar."

"Wow. Some guy in the senate gets killed and Cashdollar gets national press."

"I'm not sure that's a good thing."

"But, dude, think about it. You want to get rid of somebody, but you don't want to do it yourself. Think about the power the rev must have. Think about how much money he makes. All those people who want to buy into his aura."

"It says here that Cashdollar disavowed any knowledge of the shooting."

"No shit."

"And that he considered it a vile act. However —"

"However," James echoed.

"He did make reference to the fact that God often takes matters into his own hands."

"He did what?"

I refocused my attention on Cashdollar's quote. "The reverend Preston Cashdollar said 'While we are a peaceful people, while we do not tolerate violence, the Lord, in his own way, often takes matters into his own hands. And this may very well be one of those times.' "

James stood up, stretched, and tossed the empty beer bottle into the trashcan in the kitchen, about five feet from the sofa in the living room. Our apartment is cozy. "So God took this matter into his own hands and shot the senator, huh? God is a marksman. Something I never knew."

I nodded. I didn't even know Cashdollar, but here was a man of the cloth who found his fortunes rising when a prominent statesman was murdered. It was twisted and I had a hard time getting my mind around it.

"A T-shirt slogan for Cashdollar, Skip. 'Guns Don't Kill People. God Does.' "

"I've got to get some sleep. I'm supposed to be in by eight tomorrow morning. Some sort of training."

I wondered how I'd ever gotten involved in a situation like this. James was my best friend. Almost like a brother. But when his sales pitch started with — "There may have been a murder," then I should have turned the other way and run as fast as I could. But no, James is my buddy. Couldn't do it.

"Tomorrow, amigo. You and me. We're going into the tent."

"James, I'm not up for it." The upcoming training meeting was already draining my energy.

"I want to hear what he says about Barry Romans. If he's

going to crucify him, we should hear how he does it. Come on, pard. Should be good for a laugh. And we'll have something to talk about when we play cards tomorrow night."

I thought about it. It had been a while since I'd attended any organized or unorganized religious service. Living the way I did, I suppose it might be good for me. Of course, after what I'd heard about Cashdollar, I wasn't sure he had the answers. In my case, I wasn't sure there were any answers.

CHAPTER SIX

The training session amounted to a royal chewing out from our new director of sales, Norbit Bronder. Honest to god, the guy's name was Norbit. He looked like a Norbit. I don't know where they get these guys, but they're all pencil-pushing geeks who must think they are on the way up. Why else would anyone else take the job of director of sales in Carol City? I mean, Carol City is not exactly the city you want to be working in if you're upwardly mobile. In fact, I would think our burg would be a real career roadblock. It's an urban, blighted suburb of Miami, that tends to go further downhill every year. Cinder-block row houses, faded old stucco buildings that sit deserted on every street corner, empty malls, and a crushing sense of depression at every turn. That and our pathetic apartment complex. Rows of tiny stucco residences with crumbling facades and deteriorating interiors. Other that that, Carol City was okay.

Norbit lit into the three of us who actually tried to make a living in the community.

"You know your job depends on selling more security

systems, but *my* job also depends on *your* selling more security systems."

Now *there* was a real reason for us to try harder. So Norbit could keep his job! I'd hate to be responsible for Norbit losing his exalted position.

After the meeting I drove over to Esther's, a great little local restaurant, and had some sausage gravy and cornbread. Not the most healthy meal going, but I felt I needed some comfort food. I looked around for Emily, a girl I've dated off and on since high school, but I knew she wouldn't be there. She hadn't talked to me in three months. I did run into Rick Mosely, an old buddy from high school who worked for the fire department.

"How goes the sales job, Skip?"

"Not exactly lighting any fires, Rick."

He frowned. Firemen don't like jokes about their job. "I talked to James last week. Said you two were moonlighting with the revival meeting over at Oleta River Park."

"Yeah. Last night was the first shift. Interesting evening."

Rick took a long swallow of mud-brown coffee and shoveled some barbecued pork into his mouth. He chewed, looking at me thoughtfully. In a muffled voice he said, "You know, there are stories about this Cashdollar character."

"I heard some last night."

"Cashdollar. Somebody said that's his real name."

I buttered the cornbread. The stuff was like nectar from the gods. Sweet, so sweet and it would melt in your mouth.

"And he's got these people believing that if they follow him, they'll all be rich."

"After they make him rich?"

Rick nodded. "He's been at this game for a long time. Do you remember back, oh about —"

"Three years ago?" I asked. "The senator from North Dakota?"

He looked at me with a puzzled expression. "No. About ten years ago."

"What happened?"

"He was holding a revival meeting, same place. And some young girl who worked for him ended up dead, right there on the grounds."

I almost choked on the cornbread. "That was Cashdollar?"

"Sure was."

"Wow! I was there that night."

He laughed. "You?"

"No, really, I was. My Uncle Buzz took me. It was sort of a guys weekend, and —"

"You were really there?"

"I was. I didn't remember the minister's name, but I was there. I met the girl. She came around with a collection plate." I could picture her, smell the night itself, and I could see Buzz dropping the twenty in the plate and her big smile afterward.

"Well, my friend, the story was that she was Cashdollar's underage girlfriend."

"She was what?"

"Cashdollar's underage girlfriend. And he was married at the time. Still is."

"No shit?"

"No shit."

"So, was he ever implicated in the death?"

Rick wiped up his sauce with a piece of white bread. "I don't remember, Skip. I mean, the guy's out there on the circuit so it couldn't have done much damage to his career. From what I hear, people are still dropping money in the guy's collection plate."

More than ever. "Still —"

"Yeah, that's what I'm thinkin'. What were you talking about, this senator stuff?"

"Never mind. Just a story I heard." I'd finished half the sausage gravy and found out that I'd lost my appetite. I wasn't in the mood to eat anymore. I said good-bye and drove back to our crappy abode. I wasn't in the mood for selling either.

James came home about three, begging off early so we could get to the park.

"I ran into Rick Mosely at Esther's today."

"Rick? I saw him last week. Told him about our gig with the rev." James walked to the refrigerator and grabbed one of my long necks. We were fifty-fifty on expenses, but my fifty was usually about seventy-five or eighty.

"Yeah, well he told me something I'd forgotten."

James pulled a brick of cheddar cheese from the fridge and took a bite off the end. My cheese, his germs. "And what was that?"

"About ten years ago, I took a weekend with my Uncle Buzz."

"I sort of remember that. You came back and raved about the pleasures of Jack Daniels. Hell, I thought that he was your new best friend."

"Buzz and I went to a revival meeting."

"And?"

"And, the girl who took collections from us was murdered. They found her body the next morning in the park. She'd been strangled."

James took another bite of cheese and washed it down with my beer. "You forgot that?"

"No. I think I probably told you about it."

"Yeah. I'm sure you did."

"However, I forgot that it was in Oleta River Park. And

even though I was at the revival, I never really knew who the minister was. It was Cashdollar."

"So what's your point?"

"Rick said she was Cashdollar's underage girlfriend."

"That's it? The underage girlfriend?"

"What do you want?"

"I don't know. It lacks any passion, romance, or decadence."

He had a point.

"So Rick was insinuating that the rev killed the girl?"

I joined the party and pried the top off a long-neck beer. I decided against the cheddar cheese. "Rick said he'd never heard anything about that. He figures that if Cashdollar is still on the circuit, it must be because no one ever accused him."

But, man, Cabrina Washington, Senator Long, the food vendor, and who knows how many other deaths — all happening under the shadow of Cashdollar's tent.

"Man, we've got to go into the tent. We'll leave now, set up the truck, and we can catch an hour of this guy's spouting before we have to serve the starving masses." James swallowed the last of his beer. "Help me get the stuff organized. I went out and got more patties and brats. I think we've still got enough peppers, onions, and potatoes to feed a Third World country for six weeks."

"And once more, tell me why we really care what the reverend has to say. Why do we even want to involve ourselves in the dreams and schemes of a man who may have been implicated in two murders and a mysterious death?" The food vendor that James had mentioned — it bothered me.

My partner was silent for a moment. He tossed his beer bottle toward the kitchen trashcan, it missed with a thud, and rolled across the cheap linoleum floor.

"Why do you want to do this, James?"

"It's not so much the intrigue of foul play at the revival

meeting, amigo. It's not that I want to see how he's going to bring down the talk show host, Barry Romans."

"Then what is it?"

"He's successful. I think we need to explore success, whenever the opportunity arises."

It sounded like James. Always trying to find the next get-rich-quick idea. "Okay, I'll go with you. We'll see what this man has up his sleeve. But, James, I can't help but believe the guy is a little crazy."

"And I make it a rule to never get involved with possessed people. Actually, it's more of a guideline than a rule." He gave me a wicked grin.

"So you're breaking your rule and —" and then it hit me. "Bill Murray, from *Ghostbusters*?"

"Let's do the tent, compadre. Let's see what makes a possessed man tick."

CHAPTER SEVEN

James was my best friend. We'd known each other since we were in grade school, and we balanced each other well. James was a little headstrong, I was a little cautious. I'm not saying that the balance stopped us from making some pretty big mistakes, but we did have a good relationship.

I also used to have another good relationship. My on-again-off-again relationship with Emily. Emily was what I affectionately call my "Rich Bitch." Her father was a wealthy contractor in the Miami area and she didn't do too badly herself. She worked for the old man as they built multimillion dollar mansions in the tonier sections of Miami Beach. Em kept the books and invested the spoils for the old man as he continued to expand his empire. She and I had been through some really good times and some really bad times. Good times when we could laugh, talk about the future, and I could dream a little. Bad times when she found out she was pregnant. It turned out to be a false pregnancy, but she left town for about three months and I hadn't heard from her since she got back. I knew she was back. I saw her flashy red T-Bird convertible at her condo on Biscayne Bay. I drove by the condo about every other day. The T-Bird just appeared two days ago. I'd driven by only about twenty-two times to make sure it was hers. Twenty-two or thirty, who was counting? I figured she'd call eventually, maybe today or tomorrow.

She had issues to work out. She was back, so I assume she's worked through them. Of course, I was probably one of the issues and if she didn't call, then I assumed she'd worked that issue out as well.

I could talk to Em. I could talk about things that I can't even broach with James. And I miss her company, in every way.

I thought about her as we drove from Carol City to the park. She'd be the first person I would talk to about Cashdollar and the odd assortment of people he collected as vendors. She'd sit back and listen, study the situation, then suggest that I back off. She'd tell me that James was a bad influence, and I was better off distancing myself from anything he was planning. And, of course, I wouldn't listen to her. Maybe that's why I'm an *issue* with her.

Oleta River Park is right off 163rd street, the Sunny Isle Causeway that runs down to A1A. A1A runs down to South Beach. Distance-wise nothing is that far away. Traffic-wise, it can sometimes take forever. Friday afternoon for some reason the traffic was light and we got to the park a little before four. James parked the truck in our great up-front spot, hooked up water, plugged in our refrigerator, and I sorted out the plates and plastic utensils.

I'd been here before. With Emily. It was a great place to visit, lots of things to do like hike, explore, kayak, and visit the butterflies. *CSI Miami* and other TV shows and movies shot here on a regular basis, and Florida's largest urban park had a sense of familiarity. "Could be another big night, Tonto." James laid out his stained apron. "Look at all the cars."

"So the meeting starts at five —"

"And we can visit the tent from five to six. We didn't do much dinner business until about seven."

I glanced next door. There was no sign of Bruce Crayer or any of the vendors. Cars pulled into the paved lot, a steady stream of vans and trucks, Cadillacs and SUVs, all depositing the faithful where they could walk to the faded yellow salvation tent.

"Apparently the early birds get salvation." James watched the parade. "Lots of Cadillacs, Skip."

James's dad died several years ago. He'd been an entrepreneur, just like his son, but he'd run into a partner who skipped out and left Mr. Lessor with a whole bunch of tax and other financial liabilities. Between prison and cancer, his old man was beat to death, but his biggest regret was that he'd never driven a Cadillac. That defined success for the man. We all have our own definition of success. I watched James, nodding his head up and down almost in respect as every Cadillac rolled past our truck. I knew exactly what he was thinking.

Silently we walked up the path, following the disciples to the open flap. Most of them carried Bibles, and they were dressed in shorts, jeans, Sunday finery, suits, and even bathing attire. It was as if some of them had come straight out of the lagoon, off the beach, or maybe they'd just been kayaking the Oleta River. Em and I had taken that tour one afternoon just last year. I had fond memories of the place.

"You can't stereotype this bunch. Some look like they're already rich and famous." James pointed to a couple of men in suits and ties.

"And then there are all those who look like us." I looked at James with his one-day growth, his Jimi Hendrix T-shirt and jeans, and me with my cutoffs and uncombed hair.

"The Lord doesn't care who you are, Skip." James gave me that big grin. "As long as you come with an open heart."

"You're gonna go to hell, James."

"I go to work there every day, pardner. I'm used to it."

We worked our way through the thickening crowd, looking for seats on the aisle so we could make a fast getaway when it came time. Halfway to the big stage we found the perfect chairs.

"Look at that stage." James was staring in awe at the mammoth structure in front of us. It rose probably ten feet in the air, and was maybe sixty feet wide. The stage was covered in a shimmering gold cloth that caught the colored spots from above and reflected blinding patterns of light into the crowd.

"There are three semis parked out to the side of the tent that must carry that thing everywhere." I glanced up and in block letters probably five feet tall I read,

YOU WILL BE MADE RICH IN EVERY WAY SO THAT
YOU CAN BE GENEROUS ON EVERY OCCASION.
— 2 CORINTHIANS 9:11

"One truck just to carry the message." James whispered it to me as the throng milled about.

Three podiums graced the glittering stage, each one with a large cross on the front and the two monster screens were mounted on either side of the stage. The Reverend Cashdollar's huge face and toothy smile covered the screens.

"Wonder how much it takes to fund this extravaganza every night?" James kept staring at the spectacle.

"We're helping pay for it."

"Yeah, but think about how much we're making."

I *had* thought about it. We owed Skip's girlfriend Brook $500, we owed the cost of our basic food products, the money every night to the rev and his crew, cost and maintenance of the truck and equipment, and whatever James was losing in poker. It never seems as good as it seems, if you know what I mean. Or maybe I should be an optimist and think positively. As Tim Holt said in *Treasure of the Sierra Madre*, "You know, the worst ain't so bad when it finally happens. Not half as bad as you figure it'll be before it's happened." Then again —

The congregation provided a pretty good sideshow, but as James said, "in the house of the Lord —" The appointed time grew near and the wooden folding chairs were full as far as the eye could see. It was warm and whatever breeze blew outside was certainly not available under the hot canvas tent. I remembered a song, from the sixties I think, by a guy named Diamond. Neil I believe it was. Something about a hot August night and a revival meeting. A traveling salvation show. That was it.

"Pard, in the wings over there." James pointed to the side curtains where I could barely make out two figures huddled just off the stage. "I swear that's the pizza guy. I can tell by the gut hanging out."

"Stan?"

"Yeah. The guy who had the poker game last night."

"I can't tell."

"I think it's him. I guess if you've been with the rev long enough, you get to go onstage."

I shook my head. "That's what I aspire to. Being on stage with the rev. Who's with him?"

James squinted. "That's our finance guy. The one who gets the money, Thomas LeRoy."

I could make out the well-dressed man talking to Stan. The guy would talk, nod, then glance into the palm of his hand. Talk, nod, glance into his hand.

"Thomas LeRoy," James said it like he was very impressed. "You can see he's going to his organizer there, making notes or whatever."

It appeared that Stan was doing the same thing. These two guys didn't need to carry on a conversation. They could just punch their words, numbers, or thoughts into their organizers and read them.

"Skip, we've got to get one of those."

"What?"

"An organizer, pard."

I ignored him. "And LeRoy is in charge of all the financial doings of this organization?"

"Son, you're going to be our business manager when this whole thing gets off the ground, and you'll make more money than Thomas LeRoy ever dreamed of."

"Yeah. But you're the one that's going to buy me an organizer or a BlackBerry—something so I can look important."

"I'll do it, pard."

There was a hush as the spotlights went dim, then they came up full force, flashing off the gold stage and dancing in wild patterns. From somewhere, a huge organ chord thundered through the tent and a line of men and women wearing multicolored robes paraded onto the platform. Black, white, Oriental, they kept coming until there must have been forty of them. They faced the rear of the stage and, with one unseen command, spun around. Then, in one loud vibrant voice they all started singing with an up-tempo gospel beat.

> Free up your spirit, free up your heart
> Give to the Lord, get a fresh start.
> It's all in the giving, it's what you must do.
> Rewards from your Father, it's all up to you.

I remember the lyrics, because I heard them over and over again throughout the hour. Every time the rev wanted to emphasize a point, he'd bring the choir back in for a reprise.

And then, I swear to you, the stage started filling with that phony fog that they used to use in discos back in the seventies. I

41

saw movies of it. It is cheesy and if you're too close to it the stuff gets in your throat and makes it all scratchy. But it started rolling across the stage, like smoke from a fire, and you could hear over one thousand people gasp. The organ was building to a thunderous volume and through the billowing fog this large black figure in a flowing robe came walking to the front of the stage. The lights hit him perfectly for a moment, a wind machine blowing his robe, and it seemed as if he was the anointed savior. All things considered, I was quite impressed. I glanced at my roommate and saw he was mesmerized. This was so James.

"Impressed?" The voice came from everywhere. Speakers must have been placed in numerous locations, because I thought the voice belonged to someone in the next row.

"Well don't be!" If God has a speaking voice, this had to be it. It boomed. It rocked.

The congregation started applauding. The man held up his hands as the wind died down and the fog slowly drifted out into the tent. He gripped a gold-covered Bible in his right hand. I could feel my throat tickling already.

"God doesn't believe in fancy entrances." The word entrances echoed from speaker to speaker. "God doesn't believe in noisy announcements. God brings his message to the world from a stable, from a manger in that stable. *Man* believes in fancy entrances. *Man* believes in noisy announcements. *God* will quietly enter your heart, and make a true believer of you. Quietly."

A slight cough all the way in the back of the tent was the only sound to break the silence. Everything was very quiet. This guy had made a knockout entrance. He'd made an entrance to rival all entrances, then told us all to ignore that entrance. What a performer. Cashdollar tossed off the robe, and was now dressed in a tailored black suit that hid his ample girth. He accented the look with a simple red tie. Walking to the podium on the left of the stage, he held that gold Bible tightly.

"I have a message for you tonight. A message that will set your hearts free. A message that could help you move mountains. Ask me what that message is. Let me hear you say 'What is the message, reverend?' Let me hear you!" He stepped back and put his hand to his ear. The response was deafening.

"What is the message, reverend?"

"I can't hear you, friends."

I figured the guy must be deaf, because they'd about blown my eardrums out.

"What is the message, reverend?"

If this guy didn't believe in fancy entrances and noisy announcements, I must be crazy.

"It's a very simple message." He shouted back at us. "God wants you to be rich. God wants you to have an abundance of everything. Do you believe God's message?"

Like a well-rehearsed group, the several thousand people screamed, "Yes."

"Do you believe that God, your Father, wants you to be rich?"

"Yes."

Cashdollar turned and pointed with his Bible to the huge letters that hung above his head. "Let me read to you *why* your God wants you to be rich."

The air was sprinkled with a light smattering of excited applause.

"You will be made rich in every way, so that you can be generous on every occasion. Do you understand? Do you?"

The resounding answer was "Yes."

"God wants you to be rich, but demands that you be generous with your wealth."

The choir sang their four-line song again, and Cashdollar smiled. A video camera picked up his face and flashed it on the big screens. The wide smile, the gleaming teeth.

43

"Be serious about your generosity and God will be serious about your riches. We will start off tonight with a free-will offering. Can I please have the ushers pass the plates?"

Dozens of dark-suited men stepped off the far end of the aisles and started passing collection plates down each row. James dug into his pocket and pulled a five and some ones.

"What are you doing?"

He looked at me through squinted eyes. "I've never given a dime to any religious group. What can it hurt?"

"Never one to take any chances, are you?"

"Skip, it's like insurance. You never know when you might need some riches, right?" He dropped the money in as the plate passed and I saw a look of contentment on his face.

CHAPTER EIGHT

We stayed for another fifteen minutes, just before they asked for collection number two, and right after the choir had reprised the song about three more times. Cashdollar mentioned that this collection was the serious one. I found out later there were two more during the service.

"There are those people who give and there are those who take away. Do you know who I'm talkin' about? Do you understand the people who would stand in your way to the riches that God will give you?" He'd moved to the center podium, and he was working up to fire and brimstone, pointing his left index finger at the crowd. On the huge screens you could see his hand and the huge diamond ring on his ring finger flashing under the spotlight.

"You have a man who lives in your community, a man who eats in the same restaurants as you, who sends his children to the same schools you send your children to, a man who drives the same streets as you," and with each "who lives," "who eats," "who sends," and "who drives" he got louder, and angrier, "but a man who does not, does not, my brothers and sisters, get his riches from the Lord. This man is a racist." Now he was roaring.

Another gasp from the crowd. It was almost as if it had been scripted.

At the top of his voice he shouted. "A racist, a coward, a man who believes that the downtrodden deserve, do you hear me, they deserve to be kept in their place. He wants the poor to remain poor."

The word poor seemed to bounce around the cavernous arena. The glint of perspiration on his face was brilliant on the large screen. This was one of the best presentations I'd ever witnessed.

"He wants the weary to remain weary."

The crowd was murmuring. Who was this terrible individual?

"And he wants the sufferers to keep on suffering."

Now they were shouting back at the stage. Cashdollar moved to the next podium, held up his hand, and the camera zoomed in on his eyes. Black on the screen. I'd expected animation, a sparkling flash. The eyes appeared to be empty and soulless. But then, hey, this was television. I could have been wrong.

"This man, this instrument of the Devil, has access to your home, your car, your place of business. He comes in and takes control. Every day." Cashdollar held up his watch and somewhere a camera zoomed in and the watch with its ticking hand exploded on the large screens beside the stage. "Somewhere, at this exact minute, this man is talking to thousands of people, spreading his brand of venom and hate."

Again there was a hum in the air, voices from the assembled, buzzing, talking to each other, and getting worked up.

"Barry Romans! You know him. Barry Romans. The man is evil, and he stands for everything that we oppose. If you believed in the gospel according to Barry, you wouldn't be here right now."

Spontaneous applause, a session that was punctuated with whistling, shouts, and screams.

"What does he say? He says 'The welfare problem is caused by the blacks.' That's right, the blacks. I'm black. Do I appear to be part of the problem?"

They shouted back to the stage. "No."

"He says 'We are all ruled by fear. This love thing, this getting along together is a crock.' He said that, people."

James leaned over and shouted "This is what keeps 'em coming back every night."

"Yeah, and the idea that if they agree and give him the change in their pocket they can inherit a fortune tomorrow."

He scowled at me.

"James, I say we get out of here. It's going to be noisy, ugly, and I'd just as soon not be a part of it."

He looked at me, his eyes dancing back to the stage. "All right. I don't know how far this guy is going to go, but I suppose we should get ready for the crowd. They're really going to be worked up tonight."

We worked our way up the center aisle, and I half expected to have the rev call us out and ask us where the hell we thought we were going. It wouldn't have surprised me.

I looked over my shoulder and immediately worried about turning into a pillar of salt. Some Bible story I'd heard when I was a kid. Cashdollar was waving that gold Bible in his hand and everyone around us was opening theirs. He was asking them to refer to another scripture.

"This is our scripture. In this book, right here. We don't buy into the gospel according to Barry. No, this, this is the word of our Lord. God's action is inside this book!"

We made it to the tent flap, and two men in dark suits and matching lapel pins held it open for us. As we stepped outside, I heard the first clap of thunder and the skies opened up. We made a beeline for the truck.

CHAPTER NINE

They stayed in the tent. We could see them from our truck, even through the vented window that James had cut in the body of his precious money maker. We could see them through the sheets of rain that poured down outside our little kitchen. They would huddle right on the inside of that huge tent and then a group would make a mad dash for their car. Their van. Their SUV. Their truck or their Cadillac. Then another group would dash to the community of tents and trailers, and then another group. Pulling towels, sweatshirts, anything they had, over their heads. Some of the planners had, of course, brought umbrellas. There was a muddy trail leading from the tent to the paved parking lot, and more than one person slipped and ended up on his butt. It got to be a contest for James and me to see which one would go down.

"The girl in the blue shorts and white blouse." James pointed as she and a young man came dashing out. "She's got those floppy sandals. She'll never make it."

"My money is on the fat little guy. He's got on those nerdy white tennis shoes."

And sure enough, the fat guy went down. Embarrassed, he picked himself up, covered with mud from the waist down, and ran a little farther, slipping again.

"Damn. How much am I down?"

"Seven thousand, James."

"Shit."

Then we saw the black limousine pulling around the side of the tent. The windows were tinted, but the license plate told the tale. CSHDLR 1. There must be more where that one came from. The limo inched its way around our truck, and headed down the narrow road that led to the causeway. I remembered the line they used to use when an Elvis Presley concert was over. "Elvis has left the building. Elvis has left the building." This Cashdollar guy must be richer than Elvis.

"Permission to come aboard." I looked out the back of the truck, and Crayer stood there, umbrella open and a yellow slicker covering his short body.

"Come on in."

He jumped up from the step-up, throwing water into the truck, scooted around my serving table, and looked out our side window. "Playing who slips first?" He dripped all over our wooden floor.

James gave him a glance. "It's actually a real game?"

"Ah, you do enough of these things, everything becomes a game."

I pulled up a stool and offered it to the wet donut man.

"Boys, I've got some very bad news."

"How bad?"

"Tonight is gonna hurt."

The rain beat a tattoo on the metal roof of the truck and James stared glumly out the window at the mad dash of worshippers running and sliding to their cars. "I kind of had that feeling."

"Cash has a saying—"

"Yeah?"

"The Lord giveth, the Lord taketh away."

"Yeah, I've got a saying." James put his hand out the window, letting the steady downpour soak his palm. "You win some, ya lose some."

"Well, there's gonna be taketh and lose tonight."

I studied our neighbor. "Bruce, you said I could ask you anything, right?"

"About this operation? Sure. Fire away."

I sat on the edge of my table/counter, a pan of peppers next to me that would probably never see the grill tonight. Heavy rain beat down on the truck and I spoke up to be heard. "Ten years ago, Cashdollar was here, at the park, doing a tent service and a young girl was killed. Were you here then?"

Crayer looked at me carefully, then slowly shook his head. "I came here three years ago, full time."

"You'd never worked for Cashdollar before?"

He was quiet, his mouth drawn in a tight line. "Yeah, actually I did. Off and on for a couple of years. I don't see why it's any of your business, but I could have been here that year. I've worked a lot of shows, a lot of carnivals. I can't remember all of them."

"So, did you know anything about it?"

"What?"

I gave the situation a two-second review. It couldn't hurt to ask the man what he knew.

"A seventeen-year-old girl was strangled. And just a couple of years ago, a food vendor died, right here. Do you know anything about these deaths? Just wondering, Bruce."

He paused. Confusion colored his face. "Are you thinkin' about what I said yesterday? About the senator getting killed?"

"Well, it struck me that Cashdollar has been mentioned in three different killings."

"Three? I mentioned one, for God's sake." Crayer backed up a step, gazing at me with a puzzled look on his face. "Ah, what I said. I meant nothin'. I think somebody took Cash too seriously and maybe shot the senator. But I didn't really mean that the rev had him killed. Don't ever get the idea I said that."

"What about the girl?"

"That was a while ago. Like I said, I don't remember much about it."

"Skip was there — here. Right, pardner?" James jumped in.

"Yeah. I was. I met the girl."

Crayer's eyes got a little brighter. "Oh? You met the Washington girl?"

I studied him for a moment. He'd perked right up. "Yeah. Her name started with a C I think. Do you remember?" I waited for him to finish it for me. Instead, he shut down.

"No. It was a long time ago."

"Cabrina. Cabrina Washington."

He avoided my look. Instead he shook his head again. "I don't know, okay?"

"I've got a friend who says she was Cashdollar's underage girlfriend."

Crayer gave me a brief look of recognition, then shrugged his shoulders. "A lot of craziness goes on in a place like this. Not all of it involves the Lord's work, believe me."

"So you don't know if Cashdollar was ever implicated in her death? Or the death of the food vendor?"

He frowned and shook his head. "Hell, no. Why would you say such a thing? Listen, the vendor? It was accidental. I don't know what you heard, but nobody was involved. A pure accident. And the girl? I told you, it was a long time ago." The donut man stood up, adjusted his rain gear, and stepped down from the truck. "There's nothin' to that. Okay? I've got a couple of years on you, son. I don't think you come into somebody's home or business and start asking questions as if the person is a criminal. At least we don't do that where I come from." He stared at me. Almost a pleading in his eyes. Then he turned and started back toward the donut trailer. Almost as an afterthought he shouted over his shoulder, "Oh, and by the way, there's still gonna be a game at Stan's tonight and you're invited."

There was a pounding on the side of the truck and James stuck his head out the vented window.

"Can we get a couple of burgers?"

James gave me a frantic look. "Uh, sure. Let me get some meat on the grill. We just didn't think with all this weather that —"

"Hey," the young man stared up at him, water streaming from his long blond hair and down his face. He motioned to the young pregnant girl by his side. "People still got to eat."

CHAPTER TEN

"Nice guy, Bruce." James was cleaning up the burger flipper, his big long fork, and wiping his hands on his apron. We'd sold about fifty sandwiches. Paid for the space, minus the cost of meat, peppers, onions, buns, plates, gas, potatoes, and, oh yeah — our time.

"Why? Because he invited you down to get your ass kicked again in poker? I thought he was evasive and not that nice at all. What he wanted to do was distance his comments about Senator Fred Long."

"What do you mean, distance his comments?" James gave me a funny look.

"I brought up the murdered girl, and he immediately wanted to tell me that he hadn't meant anything about his comments the other night. I mean, he practically accused Cashdollar of killing Fred Long."

James continued to wipe his hands. A little soap would have helped. "Now that you mention it —"

"So I'm thinking that's one of the reasons he came over here."

"What? To tell us the rev was not the killer?"

"Yeah. And he made a big deal of telling me that the vendor death was an accident."

"Oh, come on. It came up, pardner, that's all."

"And when I asked him about Cabrina Washington, he said he didn't remember much because it has been so long ago."

"So?"

"And right away he remembers her last name. He says 'Oh, you mean the Washington girl?' Like it was on the tip of his tongue. I thought that was a little strange. And he doesn't want to admit he was working the revival show back then. And finally, he almost warns me about asking too many questions. Did you hear that?"

"Maybe he was right, pard. You were coming down pretty hard on Cashdollar. Was he ever implicated and all that? Maybe it's best to just drop it."

"It was a question. That's all it was. And I never even asked him what he meant when he said 'I was there when Long was shot.' What did that mean? Was he there, standing right there? Was he in D.C.?"

"Skip, what's the last movie you and I saw?"

I stared at him for a moment, thinking. "What the hell does that have to do with the current conversation?"

"Just humor me. What was the last movie we saw, pard?"

"We rented *Disturbia*. And we were talking about it and—"

"Yeah, kind of weak."

"— and you decided to rent *Rear Window*, the Hitchcock movie. You said *Disturbia* was a really weak copycat movie of *Rear Window*."

James smiled, shoving his utensils in a drawer beneath the stove. He latched the drawer, took off his apron, and sat down on an upside-down plastic bucket that previously contained thousands of pickles. "I like the fact that you're one of only three people in the world that like pizza-flavored chips."

Stupid quote, stupid movie. "*Disturbia* had some weak quotes. I'll give you that."

"But *Rear Window*—I love that movie. Jimmy Stewart, Grace Kelley." For a moment he was lost in his James world.

"They're trying to convince themselves that the lady has been murdered and Lisa says to Jeff, 'What's a logical explanation for a woman taking a trip with *no* luggage?' "

I had no idea where he was going with this scenario, but I did know Jeff's next line.

"That she didn't *know* she was going on a trip and where she was going she wouldn't *need* any luggage.

"And Lisa says—"

We both said it together. "Exactly."

"What's the point of this exercise, James?"

"I've got to get you to more comedies, son. You're taking this conspiracy, this clue thing way too far. The guy is our neighbor. He's just being friendly. Hell, you're replaying *Rear Window* and trying to make somebody a killer. You're spooked about a girl who died ten years ago and a senator who could have had hundreds of enemies. Come on, Skip. Take it easy, my friend."

"I was there. The night Cabrina Washington was killed. Right here."

"So?"

"You told me the story of Daron Styles and the food vendor. My God, James, a vendor, just like us, died. Right here."

"Oh Christ. Give it up. Come on, amigo. They were stray moments. We aren't a part of that scenerio."

I nodded. "You're right."

"We'll rent *The Producers*. The original, with Zero Mostel. We'll drink some beer and laugh our asses off. Man, you are getting way too serious, amigo."

I saw him approach the truck from the corner of my eye, his

stomach preceding him. He was puffing on a big brown cigar and carried a beer bottle in his hand.

"Hey, boys."

"Stan." James nodded. Stan had quite a bit of James's money from last night and I could tell from just the way he said "Stan" that James was thinking about getting that money back.

Our poker buddy leaned on the back of the truck, studying us. "Heard you went into the tent this evening."

James looked at me. "We did."

"Who told you?"

"Hey, kid, don't take offense. Thomas LeRoy noticed you in the crowd. Wanted to know who the new guys were and how you were doing."

"Tell him we're doing fine." James smiled.

"So, you saw the rev. Pretty good show, eh?"

"Well," I watched him take a swallow of beer and realized we didn't have any. What the hell were we thinking? "we didn't stay for much of it."

"Still, you saw some pretty powerful stuff. You make sure you come down to the trailer in 'bout half an hour. We're playin' some poker and I think you'll have a good time."

More free beer? Sooner or later they'd make us pay for the privilege. Of course, the way James played, the beer wasn't free.

And, of course, James had the same thought I did. "We'll be there. Looking forward to it."

Stan kept his elbow on the truck bed, watching us and blowing out puffs of gray smoke from his cheap cigar. It smelled somewhat like wet rags in a trash fire. "What do you boys do when you're not selling food?"

"You mean for fun?" James asked.

"No. What are your day jobs? Some of us do this full time. I travel with the rev. Crayer pretty much works with the rev full time. Now Dusty, he's a retired school teacher if you can believe that, and Mug is a three-time convicted felon who has his own catering business. You don't want to fuck with him. Is that what you boys do? Cater?"

"No, sir." James got off his bucket and stepped to the rear. "I work for a seafood restaurant and Skip here sells security systems."

"And neither of us is a felon," I added.

James nodded. "Not yet."

Stan pursed his lips and frowned, almost as if he didn't believe us. "That's what you do, huh? A little sales and food."

"Yes, sir."

"Bruce tells me you had some questions about the rev and this operation."

I could feel James's eyes shift toward me. "Just heard some things and wondered."

"You got questions, ask me." Straightforward. The horse's mouth so to speak.

"They weren't important. I'd just been here a while back and remembered an incident —"

"The Washington girl?" He said it in a low, guttural voice.

"Yeah."

"Sad story. They never found the killer. Reverend Cashdollar," he paused, "and his wife felt terrible. You know Gwena? Anyway, any time someone in this unit has a problem, the rev and his wife get personally involved. He even paid a private detective to look into the death, but they never got the first clue."

I was tempted. I wanted to say, "Hey, I heard she was Cashdollar's girlfriend," but I didn't. There was a menacing tone to Stan's voice and I didn't even want to go there.

"You listen to me, kid. I've been here longer than anyone. Got it?" He puffed on the cigar.

"Got it."

"Michael Bland, he was a druggy. Guy overdosed. It's on the record, so you can drop your questions about him."

"Michael Bland?"

He stared at me, his eyes burning holes in my retinas.

"He was a vendor. Just like you." There was a long silence.

"Ah."

"I just think it's better if you get a straight answer from someone who knows what's going on."

I nodded. "I'm sure you're right."

"Well boys, I hope you do well in your day jobs, that sales and fast food thing, because this right here is a tough racket. And to be honest, we don't need more competition."

I waited for him to smile. He blew a puff of smoke at me, and didn't. "Just so we understand each other."

I'll admit I was puzzled. "I'm not sure we do."

"You think on it, boy." He spun around and headed back down the path.

As he walked away I said, "Nice guy, that Stan."

"Oh for Christ's sake, lighten up, Skip." James glared at me. "All he said was he didn't need the competition. And as for the questions —"

"James, I think there was a veiled threat in there somewhere. Not really veiled."

"Skip, Skip. He's right. If you're going to go around talking about the possibility of Cashdollar being involved in a murder, you probably should talk to someone who was here when it happened. Pal, I'll always defend you, but you were a little out of line. And our cigar chomping buddy just wanted to let you know."

"What about his line 'Just so we understand each other?' When someone says something like that, it's a threat, James."

I could see him replaying the conversation in his mind. "Like I said, Skip. He doesn't like the competition. So we take a hint and don't come back next year. Hell, if we make it big, we won't have to."

"Maybe that's all it was." I didn't ever want to come back. Ever. So I wasn't going to argue with James.

He lit a cigarette and took a slow drag. He let the smoke out through his clenched teeth and stared down the trail at the line-up of competing trailers and trucks that sold the food. The donuts, the pretzels, the onion rings, and pizza. "I mean, the guy did invite us down for poker."

I saw two guys carrying a heavy crate to their pretzel van, and two doors down somebody was dumping a bucket of soapy water from the back of his trailer. One old man walked by our trailer, his shoes sucking mud as he hefted two cardboard boxes of frozen french fries on his shoulders. The vendors were getting ready to close up shop.

We pushed the temporary counter back into the truck, folded up the aluminum step-down, and pulled the sliding door down. I snapped the padlock. "Poker and free beer." I had to admit it.

"Oh yeah, we can't forget the beer."

"It doesn't pay for the losses, but it makes them tolerable, eh, James?"

"Ah, yes. Beer. Now there's a temporary solution." James gave me a wide-eyed stare.

I had to think. Finally it came to me. Homer Simpson. You've got to love Homer. Beer, a temporary solution.

CHAPTER ELEVEN

We showered in the cement block building, ignoring as best we could its sour odor of rotting garbage and soiled laundry. I changed into another pair of jeans and a T-shirt. I kept thinking about Em's car being back in her parking lot. Maybe somebody brought the car back and she was still wherever. Or maybe something had happened to her and they just brought the car back, but she was laid up somewhere or worse. You know how you start thinking some bad thoughts and they just get worse and worse? I've never had good thoughts that just got better and better. Does that happen to everyone?

"Skip, let's tap a couple bucks from last night." James pulled on a Bob Marley T-shirt and walked out of the building. I ran to keep up.

"James, we talked about this, man. If we're going to run this like a business, then —"

He turned, and with a very sober expression said, "Poker is a business too, Skip. The kind of money those guys were playing for? Come on. Five hundred dollars."

I took a very deep breath. "It comes out of your share. No questions about it when we do the split."

"Do you realize how upset you're going to be when I win big tonight?" He gave me a sad look.

I wasn't too concerned about how upset I might be. I'd had a feeling that the regulars weren't quite playing fair the last time. I believed there was a little cheating and sleight of hand going on. Even the shuffle and deal seemed a bit off, but then, James had put eight bucks in the collection tonight and Cashdollar had promised him a return. I'm sure I heard the reverend say something about "if you give, God will make you rich." I was probably blowing a perfectly good chance to make a lot of money.

I opened the truck and reached back to get our cash. I'd transferred the cash box to the small closet behind the passenger seat. Pulling it out, I opened it. Nothing.

"James. You took the money?"

"No, man. Not me."

"James?"

"Skip?"

I looked again. Then I looked back in the closet. I leaned in and ran my hands along the wooden floor, picking up a sharp splinter. I jerked the sliver of wood out of my index finger.

"Skip, what's the problem?" He stood behind me in the wet grass.

"There's no money in the box, buddy."

"Don't *buddy*, me, Skip. I don't have it. I didn't take it."

"No?"

He gave me a stern look.

"Damn."

"Dude, how much did we lose?"

I'd put in $500 for change, plus the $500 we made. "A grand."

"Jesus. That hurts. Had to have happened when we showered."

I sat down on the passenger seat and rubbed my eyes. We didn't know these people, we didn't know anything about these people. I remembered when I was really young and my dad took me to a carnival. Probably the only carnival he ever took me to. Some guy with greasy hair, a bright red scar on his cheek, and two or three teeth in his mouth ran the Tilt-A-Whirl. I did not even want to get on. Not because of the ride, but because the guy was so scary. Dad laughed and said, "He's a carney, son. A carney. He's a guy who works for a carnival. They're all scary. And you can't ever trust 'em, but don't worry. I'm right here to protect you."

Dad didn't stick around a whole lot longer to protect anyone in our family and I have never trusted carneys since. I was guessing the same guys who worked carnivals worked traveling salvation shows as well.

"We can't afford to lose that money, James."

"No we can't, pard."

"So we're out of the card game."

"Are you kidding? I've got to win that grand back. I've got a hundred right here. I was just hoping for a bigger stake."

I watched him pull a one hundred dollar bill from his shoe.

"Ben Franklin, here I come."

"James, are you crazy? Think about it."

"About what?"

"Chances are very good that someone in this group of food vendors stole the money."

"Skip, we'll never find it. There's nothing we can do."

"Not my point."

"The point is?"

"That same person may be playing poker tonight. And

things are not necessarily as they seem. The game may be fixed. You may lose more than a grand tonight."

"Ain't gonna happen, amigo."

He lost fifty bucks in the first five minutes. Another fifty in the next ten.

"Hey, pard. Lend me twenty. I know you've got it."

"Beer money, James."

My roommate gave me a pleading look. I gave him a twenty. My last twenty. Our last twenty. I wasn't sure what we were going to use for tomorrow. Maybe James could hit Brook up for another five hundred dollar stake. And I had no idea where we were going to get more beer money.

"So you're in?" Mug shoved some chips to the center of the table. He had a big head and a jowly face. His cheeks kind of bulged and when he talked it was as if he had a wad of cotton there. I wondered what the three felonies entailed. I remembered what Stan had said. You don't want to fuck with Mug.

James matched the chips.

"You boys do any business tonight?" Mug smirked.

"Matter of fact, we sold a little." I defended our meager night. Meager, hell. With the theft, it was a total loss.

Stan squinted at me. "I told you, you can't be a weekend vendor and make any money. It's a full-time commitment. You take Henry over there." He pointed to lemonade-and-hotdog Henry. "Henry, how long did you go before you were full time with the rev?"

Henry studied his cards, moving them around, never looking up. " 'Bout a month."

"See, Henry worked in a tool and die shop, did this part time, but he realized he needed a full-time commitment." Stan reached out and touched Dusty's arm. "Tell 'em I'm right, Dusty."

"Right as rain." Dusty looked up, apparently realizing he might anger the rain god again. We all looked up. The god remained quiet. The former schoolteacher let out a sigh.

James took the pot. With two pair. And just like that he was up $150. Then he took another one and he was flirting with $400.

The rain had washed the grease smell from the air, and had hosed down some of the more offensive odors of two of the poker players themselves, so I could smell pine trees on the cooling night air. A hundred feet or so away, I could hear the soft lapping of the Intracoastal Waterway, and there were murmuring voices coming from the community of tents, trailers, and campers where the faithful and the vendors lived for the weekend.

I looked around while James played, and I tried to figure out if one of these full-time vendors had taken our money. Stan and Crayer, with their cryptic threats, Mug, who may have done jail time for theft, Dusty the school teacher who didn't look like he could hurt a fly, Henry the tool shop guy, and the silent man sitting to my right. Any one of them could have done it. All they had to do was pop open the truck, bang the door behind the passenger seat, and it usually popped right open, even when it was locked. There's a false wall there and a narrow closet. I'd just put the cash box there. If someone had seen me do it, stealing it would be a snap. It could have been any one of these guys, but I had suspicions about Crayer. He was right next door, and he'd probably seen me open that little closet several times. I watched him, thinking maybe I'd see something. A glance, a guilty look. Obviously, I'm not a detective. I had no idea what to look for.

The night grew quiet and I could hear crickets. Crickets and the sound of someone walking down to Stan's pizza wagon. The footsteps made a faint sucking sound, as the soles of the shoes walked through the wet dirt and gravel left after the day's downpour.

Somebody called from the dark. "Yo."

Stan stood up and walked out onto the dark path. The game came to a halt and I could see James's eyes darting around. He was on a roll. Don't fuck with Mug? Heck, don't fuck with James.

I struggled to see who the man was in the dim light. Taller than Stan, someone with a jacket on.

In a minute, Stan walked back to the table. "Men, the collection tonight was pretty good."

James and I looked at each other, wondering how Stan knew.

"Share was a little up from last time." He held a canvas bag in his right hand. "You see boys," he looked hard and long at James and me, "for the full-timers among us, Cash shares the wealth. Like he says, if you give, the Lord will give back."

The assembled, as one, murmured, "Amen."

I knew who the visitor was. Thomas LeRoy.

James looked at the bag, then up at Stan. "How much?"

"Tonight? About $800 per man."

"No shit?"

Stan stared down at James. "No shit." He held James with his eyes, as if daring him to make another comment. Just a little tension, bubbling beneath the surface. Stan didn't seem to like us too well.

"Bruce," I looked at the donut man sitting next to James, "you never told us about this."

"Are you ready to be full-time vendors?"

We spoke in unison. "No."

"Then there was no reason for you to know."

"Will somebody deal?" Obviously irritated, James had lost all patience.

Henry dealt the cards and James won the pot. Three more times. I know it sounds crazy, but we walked away from the table with $620 in cash and three free beers for each of us.

Stan stood up, stretched, and picked up the canvas bag of cash. "Gonna get some air." He reached into the bag and pulled out prewrapped bundles of cash, handing them to the full-timers. No one bothered to count it. They just shoved the bundles into their pockets as if someone gave them $800 every day of their lives. Stan surveyed the assembly then pulled a silver-looking palm-sized item from his shirt pocket. He used his thumbs like he was text messaging, nodded, and put it back in his shirt. "Well," he nodded to the guys, "right now I need to get rid of some of this beer." He walked away from the group, heading up the path toward the row of portable johns.

The others stood, picking up chips and counting their remaining money from the poker table. Crayer, Dusty, Henry, Mug, and the guy who had been stone-cold silent both nights. I could barely make him out in the dim light.

Crayer tapped James on the shoulder. "Got kind of lucky tonight, didn't you?"

"I've played a lot of poker. When I should have been working, when I should have been studying." James smiled. "I hope it was more than just luck."

"Yeah. Well, we'll see how it goes tomorrow night, okay?"

"It's a date." It would have been like stopping a runaway train, trying to get James not to show up.

"We'll see you guys tomorrow," Mug mumbled.

Finally, James turned to me. "I'll make up the other five hundred tomorrow night, pardner."

"James, did you notice Stan, after he handed out the cash bonuses?"

"What about him?"

"He pulled out a pocket organizer and punched some stuff in."

"Yeah? So what?"

"He and Thomas LeRoy. They really depend on those."

"It's like I told you, we've got to get us one of those."

"I just thought it was a little strange that they both use the same —"

"Skip," he jumped in, "I swear you are worrying this thing to death. Just drop it, man."

I thought about the night. Maybe he was right. Maybe I was paranoid. I felt like we were surrounded by crooks, thieves, and murderers. And I was even wondering about the card game. All I had done was watch, but it just didn't feel right. It was as if they were setting him up, hoping tomorrow he'd lay it all out. So they could take it all away. Because when James thought he was hot, no one could convince him he wasn't.

"Okay, you're right. I'll get it under control. And by the way, quite a comeback, James." I nodded. At that point, I didn't want to burst his bubble. Tomorrow night would be a different story.

"I'm the comeback kid, Dude. Remember that."

And in some ways, he really was.

CHAPTER TWELVE

We walked back up the muddy path, past the pasta wagon, Henry's hot dog stand with the picture of a pooch in flames, the Freedom Fry cart, and other assorted grease traps.

"So all the poker players down there are full time except us?"

"There's what? Six? Must be." James still had the cash in his hand, rubbing his thumb over Franklin's face.

"James, I'd put that money away. Somebody here is not above taking it away from you."

"But there are people who are also giving it away. How about that cash bonus down at Stan's?"

"Yeah. Cashdollar pays them back when the collection is good? What's that all about."

"Well, if you think about it," James said, "he needs these vendors. Without us, he wouldn't keep the flock. Knowing there's food, a little community can stay here for three or four days."

"Yeah. Just seems strange. I wonder how the congregation would feel if they knew that the money they gave to Cashdollar went out to the food vendors who are overcharging like hell for their product."

"Take notes, amigo. Cashdollar is a smart cookie. He knows what he's doing, and obviously he knows how to get loyalty."

"Yeah. Buy it." It took money to make money.

"Unusual group of guys."

"You know the story on Mug? Three felonies. What do you think they were for?"

James thought for a moment. "Well, they weren't for cheating at cards. I cleaned Mug out tonight."

I heard the pops about halfway to our truck. Four of them. Pop, pop, pop, pop. It sounded to me like someone had set off some of those small firecrackers that you light on the Fourth of July.

"Skip, did you hear that? Like a banging?"

"Whatever. I heard it."

Everything went quiet. We kept walking, finally making out the truck in the faint moonlight.

"Thank God we don't work tomorrow."

"Actually, James, this is more work than my day job."

"Yeah, but if the weather holds tomorrow, think of the money we'll make."

He was right. If the sun shone, we would have lunch and dinner. Could be one heck of a day. And then I saw it, up ahead. My business partner was not going to be happy. "Oh, no. James, this is not good."

"What's the problem now, pardner?"

"You don't even want to know."

"It's not . . ." He stood there with his mouth hanging open. I couldn't even look back at the truck.

"Who the hell would do this?"

"Carneys?" I ventured.

"Who?"

"Never mind."

"My God, Skip, do you know how much it's going to cost to

get someone to come out and replace all of these?"

"I can guess. About six hundred dollars."

James just kept shaking his head, staring at the four flat tires on our traveling kitchen.

CHAPTER THIRTEEN

Crayer showed up two minutes later, as if he knew. "Boys, I am sorry to see this, but you can't go callin' the cops."

"No?" James was wired. He unlocked the padlock on the back of the truck, slid the big door up, and climbed in. He fired up the stove and began heating some coffee, something he seldom drank. A couple cups of strong black coffee along with the beers we'd had was exactly what we needed. We'd probably go out and kill someone.

"No." The voice was forceful. "You've got to remember where you are. This is a spiritual revival meeting. Any sign of crime or interest by law enforcement would send the wrong signal to followers."

James shook his head. "I thought they were *rubes*. Isn't that what they were last night?" He spit sarcasm with every word. "I believe you called them rubes. Now, all of a sudden they're *followers*? All of a sudden you become pious? You need to get your terms down, Bruce."

Crayer gave him a hard look. "Look, boy, you don't want to fuck up a good thing." He shoved his right-hand index finger into James's chest. "I'll get Stan to cover your tires. New tires, rookie. Got it? By tomorrow afternoon, you'll be ready to roll, but don't screw it up. No cops. Do you understand?"

James never backed down. He didn't move an inch, which is surprising for James. And Crayer didn't have a clue how much James distrusted cops. Four flat tires and the mention of cops is enough to send James over the edge.

"I'm not sure I do understand." James was treading on thin ice. He usually backed off when the action got a little rough. But the truck was his dream, his way into the big time. And somebody had screwed around with his dream. "Shove me with that finger again, and I'll break it. I'll break your finger, understand?"

"I'm asking you, son. Leave it alone. Finish your shift here tomorrow and Sunday, then go back to your day jobs. No complaining about your truck here. I'm serious. Please. You'll save yourself a lot of pain. Please. You don't want to mess with what you don't understand." Crayer spun around and disappeared in the direction of Stan's pizza wagon. We watched him, until he disappeared into the dark.

"Nice guy, that Bruce. Eh?"

"Skip?"

"Yeah, James."

"Shut the fuck up." He walked over and kicked one of the flattened tires as hard as he could. He let out a yelp and lifted his foot, massaging the toe of his shoe.

"So what do we do?"

"I want to flatten the tires on every single wagon on this path. That's what I want to do. I want to run every one of these assholes out of here. Look at this, look what they've done. If I had a pop gun, I swear I'd shoot out every tire on this row of junk food peddlers." He took the coffeepot and poured himself a cup in an old mug with a faded blue logo. Never even offered me one.

"James, Crayer said he'd get Stan to arrange for the tires.

Look at it this way. You get new tires. For free. Free, James. Brand new tires. Not too bad, huh?" I poured myself some coffee in a chinked-up faded red cup that we'd found in the apartment when we moved in.

"Well then, why didn't we tell him about the theft? Why didn't we tell him about somebody breaking into our cash box and taking the change plus tonight's profits? Maybe they would have given us new money. Maybe fucking Stan would have given us our one thousand dollars for *free*."

"James. Settle down. You accused me of being too uptight. Just look at you."

He sat down on the edge of the now-lower truck bed. It was surprising how low to the ground the truck was. I thought about it for a second. It would be a lot easier to serve our food from this elevation. Even with the step-up, I was stretching way down when the tires were inflated.

"Skip, somebody's trying to run us out. Why?"

"You've seen too many *Rear Window* movies, James."

"Screw you. All right, maybe you were on to something. Okay? I'm sorry about accusing you of being a little conspiracy crazy."

"You're not sorry." He wasn't.

"Hey, I'm telling the truth. Even when I'm lying, I'm telling the truth."

I knew the line. Al Pacino in *Scar Face*. James was going to be okay.

We lay down in our clothes, using some old towels under us, and our arms as pillows. The floor of that truck bed was harder than rock.

"Could have called a cab." James shifted and I could feel a slight sway in the truck.

"Probably fifty bucks easy."

"For the chance to sleep in our own beds? I could make that up in five minutes tomorrow at the poker game."

I wanted to tell him. The game was fixed. But I figured he'd had enough anger in his system for the evening. I shifted. Sleeping on the ground might be more comfortable. Wet, but comfortable.

"Cashdollar isn't sleeping in the back of a truck." I closed my eyes and pictured that limo — number one — sliding by our truck on its way to wherever he lived.

"No. I read he owns a twenty-thousand-square-foot mansion, somewhere south of here."

I'd read the same thing. And *People* or some other rag reported that his bedroom had a walk-in closet that dwarfed our apartment. Of course the magazine didn't mention *our* apartment. I just superimposed our modest dwelling into his bedroom. And supposedly he owns like one hundred suits. I didn't own one. Neither did James.

"Skip, we'll have a good night tomorrow, and I've figured out how to beat these guys in poker."

I could feel a little breeze blowing into the truck, and the smell of a small campfire drifted into our cramped quarters. "James, I don't think we're doing the poker thing tomorrow."

"Yeah?"

"You heard Crayer. Just finish the shifts and get out of Dodge."

"Skip?"

"Yeah."

"What was that he said about 'don't mess with what you don't understand?'"

"Yeah. That's what I consider a threat."

"But, dude. He said please."

"Nice guy, that Bruce."

"I'm serious. He said please. He was trying to be nice. But

74

he followed with something about saving ourselves a lot of pain."

"Here's what I really think, James. For some reason — either my questions or the fact that we're not full time, or they don't think we fit in with their country club set — one of these guys is messing with us. And they pushed it a little too far. Now, they just want to call off the dogs so we don't call the cops. They're going to make it all right tomorrow with new tires, we can stay through Sunday, and everything is all right. Just a fraternity hazing. Sort of. Nothing to worry about. Okay?"

"Just a fraternity hazing?" He grunted.

Somebody whistled as they walked up the muddy path. I looked at my watch in the pale moonlight. Eleven p.m.

James was quiet and I thought maybe he'd drifted off to sleep. Finally, "Is that really what you believe? Fraternity hazing?"

"No. That's not what I believe." And it wasn't. I was pissed. "I don't know, James. There's obviously a body of politics here that we're not part of." I lay on the truck bed, acutely aware of the unevenness of the plywood floor. "Man, we should get some sleep."

"Yeah. Listen. Do you know when all this shit started? The robbery? The flat tires?"

"About three hours ago."

"No, I mean think about what happened."

I thought for a moment. "When you put eight bucks in the collection plate?"

He mulled over my sarcastic remark. "Maybe. But I think this whole thing happened when you asked Crayer about the Washington girl's death. When you mentioned the death of the food vendor, Michael whats his name."

"Bland." He was finally understanding that the questions might be responsible for the destruction of his tires. "Oh, come on."

"You think about it. You mentioned the girl's death. You

even suggested Crayer might have been working for Cashdollar at the time."

I thought my sarcasm was obvious, but he never once picked it up. "For Christ's sake, James. I asked how long he'd been with the show. Of course I never insinuated anything else. Not me."

"Doesn't matter. He immediately responded with a retraction of his statement from the night before."

"You see?" I raised my voice, rolling over on the hard surface and pointing my finger at him. "I try to tell you this and you tell me I'm crazy, but now that it's your idea —"

"Crayer was worried. You mention the Washington kid, and he defends with the senator." He was quiet for a long time. "And he makes a big point of telling you that the food vendor, Michael —"

"Bland."

"Yeah, that he had an accidental death. You might be on to something, pal."

"I told you that several hours ago."

"Crayer is trying to protect someone. My guess is, it's Cashdollar. And who the hell shot our tires out? I mean, who would do something like that?"

I'd told him that before too, but he hadn't listened. Carneys. "James, I'm tempted to say let's hit the road tomorrow. Once they get the truck fixed —"

"I'd like to finish what we started, Skip. We've got two days, and if the weather holds we could make another six, seven thousand dollars. That is so huge. Do you really want to walk away from that?"

"It's just the money?"

"Mostly."

I could tell from the tone of his voice it wasn't. "What else? What could make you stay in a place like this? Where people take potshots at your truck and steal your money? Where people basically threaten you? Where people die? Huh?"

"It's a whole lot of things, Skip. It's the money, okay. More money than you and I've made in a while. It's that, and some of it is that I'm pissed. I feel like going down to Stan's wagon and whipping somebody's ass."

"You couldn't whip anyone's ass."

"Not only that, I wouldn't know whose ass to whip."

We both laughed.

"But it's a little more than even that. I'm watching this little business venture, with Cashdollar, Thomas LeRoy, the full-timers, and his cadre of suits—"

"Cadre?"

He hesitated. "Wrong word?"

"No. I just didn't know you threw around words like that."

He shot me a nasty look. "Anyway, his *cadre* of suits and employees, I'm watching these guys. And I've got to tell you, pal, I'm impressed. They may be doing the wrong things for the wrong reasons, but there's a lot of business tips to be had. This is like a dream, where everything this guy touches turns to gold."

"Are you serious?"

"I am. I've never worked for, or with, an organization like this, and besides the money, besides being somewhat pissed, I say we stick around and get an education. And let's face it, Skip, we'd be stupid to leave two more days of money on the table. Saturday and Sunday could be huge. Am I right?"

I was a college graduate, with a finance/business degree. And James was right. There were lessons here that we'd never learned at Sam and Dave University. Was I crazy? Yeah. I was. I must have been because I said, "You're right. It's too good to pass up. But we watch each other's backs. Somebody's screwing with us and we've got to be aware of that."

"I'm with you, pally. I didn't tell you, but Brook is coming in tomorrow. She offered to help a little — maybe spell you for a while."

"We have to divide the profits?"

"Amigo," I could hear him sigh, "she did bankroll the entrance fee. I'm thinking a couple hundred bucks for the day?"

"What the hell."

"You know, Skip, there's something about Cashdollar and these three deaths. You mentioning it just seems to have started this whole chain of events."

"Yeah. And James —"

"What?"

"We've got to start watching more comedies. I say we rent *The Producers* and drink some beer and laugh our asses off."

"Skip, fuck you. Go to sleep."

At that very moment my cell phone rang.

CHAPTER FOURTEEN

I checked the number. I knew it by heart. "Em."

"Hey, you."

I didn't know what to say. I'd thought about what to say for three months. I'd talked it out in my head so much that it was almost real. And then when she finally called, I didn't have a clue.

"Skip?"

"I'm here."

"I'm back."

"Yeah. I kind of knew that."

"Been checking up on me?"

"What do you want me to say?"

"Maybe that you missed me."

"I missed you. Are you okay?"

"I am. Where are you? You sound funny."

I glanced over at James. He was sitting up, and even in the dark I could see he was watching me intently. He knew what I'd been going through. James was the only other person in the world who I'd told about Em getting pregnant, and I knew he was worried about how her return would affect me. "I'm in the back of the truck. James and I are doing this food thing out at Oleta River Park and there's this revival meeting and we're staying over because the truck has some problems and—"

"Whoa. You lost me in the back of the truck."

"It's a really long story."

"Where will you be tomorrow at nine?"

"Morning?"

"Morning."

"Oleta River Park. The place where they have the kayak tours? Right on the Intracoastal. Em, we took a kayak trip last year, remember?" We'd done something else there too. Back in a private grassy area by a picnic table. I was pretty sure that was still in her mind.

Silence on the other end and I thought maybe I'd lost her. "Of course, I remember."

Actually we'd been to the park a couple of times. We'd found a place where we could be all alone and—then they have a little outdoor restaurant that serves great burgers. She loved them.

"By the causeway? With the picnic shelters? That's twenty minutes from here if the traffic isn't bad. Why don't I pick you up and you can tell me all about it over breakfast?"

I closed my eyes and said a silent thank you. "Why don't you do just that."

"You're buying, Skip."

James had $600 that he made off of my $20 stake. He could at least give me breakfast money. "You're on."

"Hey, for what it's worth, I missed you too."

And then she was gone.

He didn't say a word. "No comment?" I asked.

"No."

"I'm doing breakfast with her tomorrow morning. I'll need sixty bucks."

"Yeah. South Beach breakfasts aren't cheap."

"It's funny, man. It's like three months never happened."

"I'm happy for you, dude. Truly happy. You need a little Em in your life."

"In light of everything that's happened tonight, you gonna be okay by yourself?"

"Hey. I assume someone will be here to work on the truck. Who's gonna fuck with us at nine in the morning? Besides, Brook is coming in sometime in the a.m."

"All right. That does it. Want to do shifts tonight, stay awake and watch for trouble, or do you think we're safe?"

"Nah. We're safe."

But I stayed up half the night. Coffee, beer, being robbed, having the tires blown out, being threatened by a carney, and thinking about my breakfast with Em, I couldn't clear my head.

About three in the morning I took a slow walk down to Stan's wagon. Everything was still, quiet, and the grass was wet from the rain. A night bird let out a low moan. Maybe an owl, maybe a dove.

"You got business here?"

The voice scared the hell out of me. A tall, skinny, shadowy figure stepped out from behind the tenderloin truck parked one up from Stan's.

"Ah, you're one of those kids who played poker with us, right?" It was Dusty, the retired schoolteacher. He'd reminded me of a math teacher I'd once had. Slim, glasses, and his remaining blond hair going gray.

"You scared me to death." I could make out his silhouette in the moonlight, and it looked to me like he was carrying a pistol in his right hand.

"Some of us take turns as night security. That way we don't have to hire off-duty cops. We just take care of our little community by ourselves."

81

I wondered how many of them had guns. "How many are *some of us?*" My guess was the six full-timers.

"Do you need to know?"

I was wired, and probably a little mouthier than I should have been. "Where was someone when somebody broke into our truck and stole today's receipts? Where was security when someone shot out the tires on our truck? It doesn't sound to me like your security is very effective."

The slight man was quiet for a moment. "Didn't say it was a perfect setup. What is? You'll get your truck fixed."

"And the money?"

"Grow up, son. You paid to play. Accept the consequences."

He seemed to be totally aware of the situation. Even though we hadn't told a soul.

It was the beer talking, two cups of coffee keeping me awake past my bedtime, and the thought or maybe the dread of seeing my once-upon-a-time girlfriend for the first time in three months, but I decided to push my luck. "Dusty, how long have you been with Cashdollar?"

"Why do you need to know?"

"I don't *need* to know. No. But I'm curious. How many years? Come on. I know Crayer has three years. I get the impression that Stan goes back further than that."

"Five years."

"You? Five years full time?" Full time seemed pretty important to these guys.

"Yeah. Full time." He hesitated.

"Cashdollar isn't on the road twelve months a year. So full time is what? Whenever he's doing his revival meetings?"

I could barely make him out in the darkness, but I could see his arm swinging the pistol back and forth.

"And there are six full-time vendors who share in Cashdollar's success?"

I could see him shake his head. "There are six now. Full time is when the rev needs us. Now go back to your truck. Like I said, this is none of your businss."

"What does that mean 'when he needs us?'"

"I said it doesn't concern you."

"Can't you answer a simple question?"

"What did I tell you? Mind your own business."

"Dusty, just because it's been a really crappy twelve hours, humor me and answer me one more question. Have you ever heard any rumors that Reverend Cashdollar was in any way involved in the murder of Senator Fred Long, or a seventeen-year-old girl named Cabrina Washington?" Stan had warned me. Don't go to anyone else with your questions. What the hell could he do to me in the next two days? "What do you know about Michael Bland, the vendor? Did he die in some strange accident?"

His voice quivered and he raised the pistol and pointed it at me. "Go back to your truck. Now. I'm not supposed to talk to you. Do you understand? Go."

"You're not supposed to talk to me? There's an edict out on this?"

"I don't think you get it. Leave."

I did. My blood pressure was up another notch and I was shaking by the time I got to our flat-tired moneymaker. James was lightly snoring in the truck, and I lay down on the rain-damp ground and stared up at the stars, the water seeping through my T-shirt and jeans. The clouds had cleared and the Big Dipper looked like it was ready to spill something all over me. I couldn't get the image of the former math teacher out of my head. He wasn't supposed to talk to me? Someone actually told Dusty that? James and I were just trying to make a couple of bucks. That's it. And people were told not to talk with us? It made no sense.

I watched a shooting star and tried to make a wish but it was much too fast. The wish would have been that Em and I could pick up like nothing had happened. Or, the wish could have been that James and I would make a million dollars. Or, the wish could have been that the recent run of bad luck would stop. By the time I decided, the star was a distant memory.

CHAPTER FIFTEEN

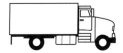

The camp woke up about six a.m. I could smell wood smoke, and a couple of the tents had grills fired up for an early breakfast. By seven, one of Cashdollar's assistant ministers was in the tent with a Saturday morning service. I wandered to the opening and watched for about fifteen minutes. This was a wake-up service, and this minister didn't tote a gold Bible. Even though there was a mention of God making you rich, I didn't hear anything about Barry Romans. However, there was one constant in the service. They took up a collection. And when it was over, they took up another one. Maybe he needed to give his employees a raise. Or maybe he needed a bigger closet or a couple more suits.

The sky seemed to be rained out, and what appeared to be a cloudless pale blue canvas stretched out above us. James made some more of his really bad coffee, and he fried a couple of beef patties and had what passed for a morning meal. I sipped the coffee and watched the park grounds come alive. Already you could feel the heat and humidity.

The early risers walked from the parking lot to the shelters spread out by the Intracoastal Waterway, watching the Saturday boaters who were already out. I could hear the engines as they slowed down for the "no-wake zone" on the narrow channel.

"Hey, pal. When you and the ever-lovely Em have your expensive breakfast at News Café or wherever, see if you can find a couple of six packs of beer, would you. This breakfast would have gone down a lot better with a little cold beverage."

"I'll do it."

I watched the distinguished black man come walking from the tent, the sharp crease in his gray trousers, a pale blue shirt with button-down collar, and a well-tailored jacket giving him the appearance of someone of great importance. I knew him before he got to our truck.

"Skip, do you know who that is?"

I did.

He approached us and nodded, giving a brief glance to the four flat tires. "Boys, I'm Thomas LeRoy. I handle the finances for Reverend Cashdollar."

With my coffee in my left hand, I extended my right. He made no effort to take it. You always feel so stupid when that happens.

"I've authorized an emergency vehicle to be here in —" he glanced at what appeared to be a solid-gold Rolex watch, "half an hour. They will replace the four tires on your truck."

He barely looked at the truck. Maybe he'd seen four flat tires before, or maybe he'd already seen the damage. He reached into his jacket pocket, pulled out the organizer, and struck several keys. He stared at the screen for a moment, then shoved it back into his pocket.

"I keep a record of what happens here. Oftentimes it comes in handy."

We nodded.

"Reverend Cashdollar and I are truly sorry this happened to

you during our event, and I hope you find the rest of your stay less eventful." LeRoy paused, stared right at me and said, "I hope this will end any questions, concerns, or problems that you may have." He paused, looking me in the eyes. I don't think he ever blinked. "Do we have an understanding?"

"An understanding?"

LeRoy pursed his lips, and I detected an underlying tension. "An understanding. We're taking care of your concerns. You have no reason to go any further with this." The finance director nodded, turned, and walked away.

"Very officious." James sat on the back of the truck.

"Four new tires, James."

"Four free tires, amigo."

I nodded. "Stan must carry some weight."

James lit a cigarette and with a couple of days' growth of beard, his tousled hair, coffee in one hand and a cigarette in the other, he looked like a poster child for juvenile delinquents. "I was thinking the same thing. They really didn't want us going to the cops. LeRoy himself comes out and tells us that it's going to be handled? That's pretty heavy."

"And, James, there was a pretty momentous occasion a minute ago."

"What was that?"

"We're now in the famous organizer."

"Yeah. There's that."

"Listen, this morning, about three, I took a walk. Dusty, the school teacher comes out of the shadows with a gun."

James took a short breath. "Jesus. The school teacher? With a gun?"

I nodded.

"Like in the gun that someone used to shoot our four tires?"

"He had a good excuse for this gun. He says that some

of the full-time guys double doing security at night. When I started asking questions about security and Cashdollar and the two deaths —"

"Pard, you weren't supposed to be asking questions. Remember?"

"Yeah. I follow the rules about like you do. Anyway, he tells me that he's not allowed to talk to us."

James took a long drag on the cigarette. "He said what?"

"He said he wasn't allowed to talk to us."

"What the hell does that mean?"

"I don't know. What do you think it means?"

"First of all, I think it means that Stan is probably going to be pissed you're still asking questions about Cabrina Washington. He gave you the official story on questions. But no, my good buddy has to keep prying."

"Fuck you, James. I actually enjoy prying. Maybe I'll approach each of the fabled six and ask them individually."

"There's only three left that you haven't asked. Henry, Mug, and the quiet dude."

"Yeah."

"My friend, this is a very strange adventure we're on."

"A movie quote?" If it was, I couldn't place it. Maybe *Bill & Ted's Excellent Adventure*.

"No, just the truth. Somebody shoots out our tires, somebody steals our money, you have someone tell you that he's not supposed to talk to us, and," he reached into his pocket and pulled out a piece of paper, "then we get this." He handed it to me, folded.

I opened the paper and read it out loud.

We know who you are, we know why you're here. It would be best for all concerned if you left now. The next time, it might not be the truck.

"You were thinking of telling me about this?"

"Of course, pard. It was laying on the truck bed when I woke up this morning. I needed some time to process it in my mind."

"Jesus, James. We're getting new tires, maybe we should just hit the road."

"And I think we should stay. I'd like to know who's shooting out our tires. I'd like to know why people can't talk to us, and I'd like to know who we supposedly are and why we're supposedly here."

"Isn't it enough the person who wrote the note knows those things? *We know who you are and we know why you're here.* Come on, James. There's no reason we have to know the answer too."

He smiled. Not a laugh, but a smile. "Free tires, pard. There's always a silver lining, eh?"

I needed time to process it too. Last night I'd agreed to stay. Now, someone was threatening our lives. That didn't sit well at all.

"Come on, Skip. I don't think they mean it. They're not going to kill us, for God's sake, and they really don't have any reason to run us off. Do they?"

"You know, James, everyone was being so nice, then you had to spoil it. You had to go and do it."

James's eyes got wide. "What the hell did I do to spoil it?"

"You don't even know?"

"You tell me."

"You won at poker last night." I was only half kidding.

He flicked his ash in my direction. No smile. "Yeah. Maybe that's it. But my guess is it's something to do with you asking too many questions, pardner. In fact, I'm sure that's exactly what it is."

"Maybe. But what aren't they supposed to be talking to us about? And was that a threat that they might shoot *us* next time?"

"It beats me, pard. I just want to make enough money to get this little business venture on its feet."

"And now there are full-timers with guns walking around the grounds."

James smiled a grim smile. "Yeah. Let's hope Mug doesn't do guard duty. A three time felon with a gun. Scares the hell out of me."

"And what were the felonies?"

The repair truck showed up on time, and with power jacks and two able-bodied men, they had our truck re-tired in half an hour. James couldn't stop smiling. It was the most expensive repair on his pride and joy so far, and it hadn't cost him a penny. In James's world, this was nirvana.

It was closer to nine thirty when I saw the red T-Bird working its way down the narrow park road. I'd figured maybe she wasn't coming, then I thought she might have had an accident, and finally I decided if she didn't show up, it was just as well. But there she was. I checked my pocket one more time for the money and walked out to meet her.

CHAPTER SIXTEEN

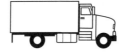

She sat across from me looking fresh, blond, and wonderful. The News Café was bustling, with a steady stream of walkers and gawkers parading up and down the sidewalk. We sat by the street, feeling the morning heat starting to steam the place up, as cars lined up, going nowhere very slowly, and the sideshow that is South Beach played out for us in every direction.

"You haven't said four words since I picked you up."

Twenty minutes, driving A1A through ethnic villages, past big hotels and ritzy shopping areas, by Indian Creek where the elite rich live, and down to South Beach. She'd asked how I was and I think I answered "okay." Then she'd talked about her father and how she was working for him again, although she'd really never gone off the payroll. Then she asked how James was, even though the two of them do not like each other, and I think I answered "okay." The other two words I don't remember.

"Skip, what are you thinking?"

It came spilling out. "That you left. That I know you needed some time to work things out, but I was stuck here with everything closing in on me, and I missed you and needed to talk to you every day and you weren't here." It wasn't what I wanted to say. Not even close. I wanted to hold her, ask her if things were back to normal, and ask her to never leave again. I know it sounds sappy, but I really care for this girl. It just didn't come out right.

She stared at the sidewalk and the review marching by. Overweight tourists in T-shirts and shorts, girls in bikinis, half the gay population of Miami Beach, and two dogs as big as horses being walked by a midget. Finally she looked at me. "Well, I asked, didn't I?"

"What do you want me to say? I don't know what you went through. You thought you were having our kid, then found out you weren't. I guess you needed some space, but *I* thought you were having our kid, then found out you weren't. And I guess I didn't get any space. Maybe I needed some space too."

She turned and looked into my eyes. She took my hand, covering it with her own. With a slight smile she said, "I've got the answer."

I took my free hand and picked up my cup of coffee. "I'd love to hear it."

"You take off. You go away for three months. Whatever harebrained scheme James is working on, I'll take your place while you get the space you need. Okay? I'll fill in with James, and you get your space."

Just the picture of that made me laugh out loud. If she only knew what James and I were into. "I would pay to see that. I really would."

"Now, can we get past the self-pity? I'm ready for a new start." She laughed too.

I was ready. "I'm working on it, Em. And I suppose you're not too far off with the harebrained scheme that James has hatched."

"Oh, Jeez, I was hoping it was something halfway decent."

"I think it started out that way, but things have a way of —"

The waiter brought two steaming plates of eggs, hash browns, sausage, and English muffins to the table.

"A way of what?"

"Things have a way of not working out."

"Are you in trouble?"

"We may be. It's too soon to tell."

"Skip!" She was looking at me like she didn't even know who I was. "What are you thinking? Get a real job. Quit buying into your roommate's dreams and find something that works for *you*. Have you noticed how many of his ideas turn into nightmares?"

I told her how he'd turned the truck into a traveling kitchen. I told her about the carneys, Cashdollar's message of wealth, dreams, and destruction, about the poker games, the threats, and the flat tires. I told her about Crayer and Stan, Henry, Dusty, his gun, and Mug. I think I left out the silent partner. Again, everything came pouring out of me. I'd wanted to talk to her, tell her exactly what was happening, but never figured the situation would present itself. And now that it had, I unloaded. All concern for our relationship, my hurt feelings, whatever, disappeared for the moment. I told her everything. When I was done she was stone-cold silent. Neither of us had touched the eggs, hash browns or bacon, and breakfast was cold.

"You know, this is a novel. Fiction. No two guys stumble into this much crap, just by accident. Either you are making half of this up," she paused, "no, two-thirds of this up, or you are the most unlucky son of a bitch that ever lived. I should not only keep you at arm's length, I should move to another state, west of the Mississippi. Tell me you're messing with me, Skip. Please, tell me."

"Come on, Em. You know I'm telling you the truth."

"Jesus, Skip. You're nuts if you stick this out with him."

"Easy for you to say. How much do you make? How much money do you make? My God, Em. I make nothing. We stand to clear two to three thousand dollars apiece when this is all through. To me, that's a fortune."

She was quiet. She was breathing deep through that cute little nose, and I marveled at how perfect her face was. Even the teeth, straight as an arrow. I figured the teeth had been worked on, but not the nose. She was *so* out of my league.

Finally she reached for her untouched coffee, took a sip and made a face. "Cold."

I caught a waiter's eye and he replaced the two coffees. She nibbled on a piece of cold, greasy sausage and stared past me.

"Look, we're seeing each other for the first time in a long time."

"We are." I agreed.

"When I left the last time we were both in a lot of trouble."

"We were."

"And now—"

"I'm in trouble again. Or on the verge of trouble."

"Skip, this doesn't make the relationship very stable."

I looked into her eyes. There was a lot here worth saving. "No, but it certainly makes it interesting."

She squinted, a frown gracing that lovely face. "Is that supposed to be funny?"

"Maybe. But there's a grain of truth to it. I've got an uncle named Buzz, and—"

"Buzz?"

"Buzz."

She shook her head. "Buzz is not a name. It's the sound bees make. It's a condition."

"Like getting a buzz on?"

"Yeah."

"My uncle Buzz, he told me something about life."

"Oh, jeez, a life lesson from Uncle Buzz. I can't wait to hear this one."

I ignored her sarcasm. It had been an hour and she was already down on me big-time.

"Buzz said 'the only thing we have to look forward to in life is the next big revival.' "

Em sipped her warm coffee, leaning back in her chair and staring up at the clear blue morning sky. "So Buzz was a philosopher?"

"Well, we're all philosophers sometime in our life."

The morning sun crept under the shade of our umbrella and Em reached into her purse and pulled out her Ray-Ban sunglasses. I couldn't read her eyes, but I could hear the sarcasm drip from her voice.

"The next time you see Uncle Buzz, please tell him for me that life is a little more than looking for the next buzz."

"Think about it, Em. What else is there? I mean, I'm trying to get to the next level. That's what he was talking about."

"And how does that fit into *big trouble* at the yellow tent?"

I knew how it fit in. I'd spent half the night, looking up at the stars, thinking about it.

"I'd like to tell you. But some of it involves you. And some of it involves James. That's a mixture that never seems to go well together. And some of it involves me."

"Well at least tease me. Give me a hint." She had picked up her spoon and was softly tapping it on her napkin. Irritating.

"James gives me some vision. Some dreams."

She shook her head, her streaked blond hair shimmering in the light. "Dreams? James?"

"*You* give me some dreams."

"We'll table that for now."

"Cashdollar gives me some dreams. He says that if you give generously, you will be rewarded."

"And you believe that?"

"I'd like to." I hesitated. She wasn't buying this. "James

95

thinks the Cashdollar machine can teach us some things, about how a business organization should run. I can't argue that this guy is a huge success. He's got more money than —"

"God?"

"It would seem."

"Oh, please."

"Do you want to hear this or not?"

"Okay. And," her annoying spoon tapping sped up, "where does all this trouble fit in?"

"Getting to the next level — with James, with you, with Cashdollar's philosophy — doesn't just happen. I think it's a struggle to get there."

"What? And you're telling me that the truck, the tires, a threatening letter, the girl getting murdered, a vendor having an accident, and the senator getting shot are all things that *you* have to overcome? These are your problems so you can get to the next level?" She whipped the sunglasses off her face and her eyes were wide and bright. "Skip, have you completely lost your mind?"

I buried my head in my hands. It had all made sense last night, or early this morning. In a twisted sort of way I'd figured it out. And now, when I needed this concept to save a relationship, to get to the next level, it had escaped me. It sounded stupid.

"Can you forget it? James and I have some trouble. I'll get through it."

I looked across the street, toward the beach. A big limo was moving slowly in the heavy traffic, and I thought about Cashdollar and his trappings. The staff, the gold Bible, the limo with the tinted windows. Then there was a break in the traffic and I caught a glimpse of a man, standing in the grassy area. He immediately turned and ducked behind a passing car. When the line of vehicles finally passed, he was gone.

"I'm sorry, Skip. We've just seen each other after three

months, and I have no right to come down on you like this."
There were tears in her eyes. "I want to start over. I'm not going
to argue with you, okay?"

"Maybe you're right. Maybe this is all just smoke."

"No. You've got to figure out what your dream is. I'm all
right with that. And," she wiped at her eyes with her hand, "I'm
glad I give you dreams. Really."

I looked into her eyes as she wiped them with her hand.
Then I scanned the grass on the other side of Ocean Boulevard.
He'd disappeared. The man had gone over the dunes, run to the
beach, walked across the street, maybe even jumped into a car.
But there was no doubt about it. The short stature, the thinning
hair, it was the donut man, Bruce Crayer. And he'd been staring
right at us.

CHAPTER SEVENTEEN

By the time we left it was eleven a.m. I knew that James was planning on serving lunch, but Brook was coming in so he should be covered. Em and I drove over the Venetian Causeway and we ended up at her condo in the Grand Condominium complex. She's got a sky-box view of South Beach and I'm always both glad to be there and envious at the same time. We didn't talk much because there wasn't much to say. I didn't ask where she'd been and she didn't volunteer the information. She didn't ask what I'd been doing; I'd already told her. If she'd had any affairs while she was gone, I didn't want to know about it. And since she didn't ask me about the past three months, I decided she already knew. I'd pretty much been celibate. I'd been out with James's cousin Gail one night. So, as I said, I'd been celibate.

We took the elevator up, and for the next hour we still didn't talk. We looked out the window at the causeway with its stream of cars and trucks, the marina with its sailboats and yachts, and we viewed the islands and the buildings of South Beach just a little over a mile away. No talk, just the occasional grunting and groaning that come with the physical act of sex. At about twelve fifteen she rolled over, looked at me, and said, "Well, that was fun. We should do it more often."

I agreed.

As we pulled into the park, the clock struck one. The story was breaking at the top of the hour.

"Controversial talk show radio host Barry Romans, a syndicated right-wing conservative staple in the Miami area for the past ten years, was gunned down in South Beach this morning just two blocks from the former Gianni Versace mansion on Ocean Drive."

My eyes locked on Em's. We'd been two blocks from the huge, gated mansion ourselves.

"Romans remains in critical condition at Mount Sinai Medical Center. Personnel at the hospital refused to comment any further. Romans's assailant remains at large and police are asking for anyone with information to please call the Miami-Dade Police Department."

"Does this have anything to do with your story about the reverend Cashdollar's call for action against Romans?"

I thought about telling her. I thought about Bruce Crayer being in the exact location at the exact time. I thought about our previous conversation, where she said that my being in trouble didn't help a stable relationship. I didn't want to go there again.

"No. It has nothing to do with any of this. There are a lot of people who disagree with the guy. You've listened to him. I'm sure he's a regular target for the lunatic fringe."

Em kissed me on the lips, I stepped out of the car, and before she'd disappeared from sight I was on a dead run to the truck. James had to hear this one.

He was wiping his hands on his apron, the lunch crowd having disappeared. I motioned him down from the truck and told him my story. James glanced up at Brook, in her tight shorts and halter top, and she waved down at us. She was covering the pans of peppers, onions and potatoes.

"Jesus, Skip. It doesn't necessarily mean that—"

"James," I was whispering loudly. "I told Em, it could have been anyone. I mean this guy Romans agitates on a daily basis."

"Yeah," he copied my hushed tones, "but it does seem to be an added coincidence that it happens as soon as Cashdollar starts ranting against him."

"And this thing with Bruce Crayer."

"But Skip, he had every right to be there. It's stranger than hell, but maybe he's thinking the same thing."

He'd lost me. He did that sometimes. "What?"

"Crayer comes back here and hears the same story about Romans getting shot. So he remembers seeing you at almost the exact location."

"And he thinks that Em and I shot Romans? Give me a break."

"Dude, it makes as much sense."

"Not to me." I glanced at the donut wagon. "James, this guy didn't want me to see him. He ducked down, like he was trying to hide. Remember what he said about being there when Senator Long was shot?"

"Yeah, but—"

I glanced over at the donut wagon.

"Was he open for lunch?"

"Yeah. There was a long line. I didn't notice who was running the show. He might not have been there. I didn't have time to see. Hell, we were swamped. I'll bet we did a couple thousand dollars."

"James," she'd moved to the edge of the truck bed and sat her pretty butt down, letting her perfect, tanned legs swing over the edge. "I think everything is put away."

"Hey, babe, thanks. Skip was just saying that he is very appreciative of your taking over lunch today."

"Uh, yeah, Brook. It was great of you."

"Well thank you, Skip. I'm glad you got to spend a couple of hours with Emily."

"Yeah. Thanks. It was nice."

"Mmm, I'll bet it was. And we did some serious business of our own, didn't we James?"

"We did." He grinned at me. "We also did a good lunch."

I didn't even want to think about what went on in the truck before lunch.

"You see. My investment was a good one." She hopped down from the truck, walked up to James, and gave him a big kiss. "You'll be back at the apartment at ten?"

"Should be."

"I'll meet you there." She spun around, batted her eyes for me and said good-bye.

"Nice girl." I watched her wiggle as she walked away. All of a sudden everything had a sexual feeling about it.

A couple of vendors from down the row walked by, nodding to us and heading for the portable johns. The whole idea of this setup and what it stood for was foreign to me. It was like a summer camp, and your parents were going to pick you up Sunday afternoon. There was almost a feeling of make believe in the air.

"Skip, I don't know what to think. After your story about last night, the gun and everything —"

"Yeah. I know. And the note this morning? But this thing with Bruce Crayer has me confused. I mean, he's the one who told us how powerful Cashdollar could be. Then all of a sudden he's in the exact location of a shooting?"

"Let me borrow your cell phone."

I handed it to him, hoping he wouldn't use many minutes.

James dialed the number, waited, left a brief message, and handed the phone back to me.

"Daron Styles is going to call back." He put his hands on the truck bed, lifted himself up, and walked to the front of the truck. He came back with two cold green labels and jumped down.

Daron Styles? I started to question the rationale of calling the con man, and then I remembered. "Oh, man, I forgot to get the beer." I shook my head.

"Brook didn't forget. Look. Foreign stuff." He handed me a bottle and I took a long, slow swallow. God, it was good.

We sat on a wooden bench about fifteen feet from the truck.

"Money is safe?"

"We're watching the truck aren't we?"

"I guess."

"I put it in the air filter."

I'd waited long enough for the avoided explanation. "And what is Daron Styles calling back about?"

"I told you. He's one of the reasons we're here. He told me about this gig and how well he did selling religious statues and crosses and stuff. Daron worked for this road show, and he may be able to give us some insight."

"Insight? Into what? How he was involved in the death of a vendor?"

"Into what's going on." He shot me a hard look. "Insight into these clowns who work here. I've got a lot of respect for Styles's instincts. You may not approve of the businesses he runs, but he's got a good head."

"What's he doing now?"

"He works right near the Versace mansion. You know, he sells stuff. Watches, purses, DVDs, scarves, stuff like that. The guy has his ear to the ground. His eyes on the world."

I'd heard he was selling stuff. "So he knows what happened?"

"He knows the players. It's a chance to pick his brain. He'll at least have some ideas. I think it might be a good idea to have someone else helping us."

I had my doubts. Daron Styles was a sleazy son of a bitch with a highly inflated ego. He'd never held a steady job for more than a couple of months, and the last I'd heard he was selling counterfeit merchandise out of his trunk. It matched what James had said about him.

"Maybe we don't want to know something. Maybe we want to ignore this entire story, make our money, and go home."

"And maybe, Skip, maybe we've already asked too many questions, and someone isn't going to let us just walk away."

"What the hell are you talking about? Are you crazy? You're now the one doing this conspiracy theory thing and it makes no sense."

"You believe the same thing. You know there's something very strange going on here. You've told me the story about you and your uncle Buzz a couple of times. I thought about it, and I remember you said how you met this girl and the next day she'd been murdered. You've questioned this situation for ten years. Aren't you the least bit interested? Don't you want to take this just another step forward and see what's going to happen next?"

I drained the beer. "We've got more of these?"

"We do, thanks to the beer goddess."

I got into the truck and took two more bottles out of the cardboard carrier in the refrigerator. I carried them down to the bench.

"Skip, it's better to be informed. Let's see if we can figure out if any of our vendor group was responsible for the shooting. Let's find out who messed with the truck. Let's find out who stole our money. Let's find out who is sending us threatening mail. They're threatening to shoot us, Skip. Come on, dude, don't you want to know who it was?"

I did think there were some serious problems. I didn't trust any of the full-time vendors. I didn't trust their businesses, their security system, or their poker game. I even wondered if James had won just because they wanted him to stick around. I know it sounds paranoid, but I wondered.

"Skip? I'm not crazy. I think we need to do a little investigating."

"I know, I know. It's a good chance to make some serious money, and it's a good chance to see how Cashdollar makes his millions."

"Yeah. All that too."

"Jesus, James. The last time we did this —"

"The last time we did this it was because *you* wanted to investigate a situation and I went along with you."

He was right. And James had taken a severe beating because of it. We'd almost lost our lives. And it had been my pigheadedness. I'd talked him into it.

"So you want to look into this?"

"I do. I really want to. I'd like to say you owe me, pard, but I won't, because you don't. Good friends don't owe each other. Am I right?"

I should have hit him.

"I'd like to know if we're hanging out with a bunch of murderers. I'd like to get the guys who tried to sabotage our truck. I'd like to find the person who told us to leave, because, pardner, I have no intention of going anywhere. There's still money to be made."

"James, I think you're crazy. But I'm in, because you're right. You're an asshole, but I do owe you."

I could see a smile trying to form on his face. He'd won, but he didn't want to gloat.

"Nah, I shouldn't have said it. You don't owe me anything, Skip. Seriously. You want to take a hike, hell, I'll drive you home right now. On brand new tires. I'd like this to be an equal decision. Somebody is messing with us. We've stood up for each other since we were kids, am I right?"

He was.

"We're in this together, amigo. Tell me I'm right."

Selling his ass off, and I wasn't even sure why. The thrill of the adventure, the stupidity of youth, I don't know for sure what it was. "You're right. I'm in."

As we sat there sipping our second beer, the phone rang.

CHAPTER EIGHTEEN

"He's going to pick us up."

"Why? Where do I want to go with Styles?"

James looked around, as if to make certain no one was listening. "He said he's got some information we might find interesting."

"This guy is a scam artist. He was a crook in school, and I will bet he hasn't changed."

"Skip, he needs our help. He said he had a little favor and, if we help him, he'll help us."

I didn't want to go anywhere with Daron Styles. The last time we'd met with him, he'd treated us to breakfast at a Hampton Inn on Collins Avenue in Miami Beach. I'd been impressed—eggs cooked to order, bacon, toast, coffee, juice—until I found out he'd stolen a room key and was using it to get free breakfast two or three times a week.

"And I come back at four and get free cocktails. It's a sweet deal, Skipper."

First of all, I hate it when people call me Skipper. Skipper sounds like a ten-year-old kid in a sitcom, who is still looking for a best friend. Second of all, his scam to get free food and free booze pissed me off. Maybe because I hadn't thought of it. Now, I pictured the punk, coming to get us in his big Buick. He wore his hair shaggy, down around his collar and always wore a flowered shirt and cargo shorts. James liked him because he was an entrepreneur. He was the wrong kind of entrepreneur. He sold illegal merchandise and financed his business with scams like the Hampton Inn deal, but, in James's mind, the guy was a sharp businessman.

I had James get the money out of the truck. I didn't know where it was in more danger, in the truck where it could be stolen or in the Buick where Styles could get his hands on it. James put it in a small canvas bag and tied it to his belt. Somebody would have to have a pretty sharp knife to take it off.

When the Buick arrived, I knew why James's favorite con man drove it. The trunk was a mile wide and almost as deep. Jeez, you could pack watches, silver crosses, stolen Coach purses, and a small army in there and still get the trunk closed.

"James. Skipper." He had a two-day growth, the flowered shirt, and a funny round porkpie hat that made him look like Kid Rock. And he still called me Skipper. "Hop in, boys. I've got a brief stop to make at the airport, then we can grab a cup of coffee and talk."

Styles and James bullshitted each other for twenty minutes, talking about girls and schemes, and generally catching up. I kept quiet and thought about Em being back in town. Twenty minutes later Styles pulled off onto the access road and parked in front of terminal H.

"You guys hold down the car, I'll get Aunt Ginny and be back in just a minute." He left the engine running, jumped out, and popped open the cavernous trunk. I watched him stroll into the terminal. James and I looked at each other.

"Aunt Ginny?"

"Hey, James, he's your friend. Did he say anything during the trip about picking up his aunt?"

James shrugged his shoulders and we waited. Maybe three minutes later he came bustling out, an overnight bag strapped to his shoulder, and two large suitcases that he pulled behind him. His pace picked up as he approached the car, and he tossed the three pieces of luggage into the trunk, slammed it closed, and stepped into the car. He closed the door, hit the gas, and shot out onto the access road.

"Daron."

"Dude."

"Didn't you forget something?"

"What?"

"Aunt Ginny?"

He shook his head. "Nah. That's just for airport security if they asked you why we were parked there."

I glanced at James. "There is no Aunt Ginny?"

"No. I just needed you guys to cover the car. There's no security on the luggage carousel. All you've got to do is go in and grab a couple of bags off the belt. If someone says you're taking their bag, you apologize, tell them they all look the same, and put it back. Ninety percent of the time no one says a word."

"What? You steal luggage on a regular basis?"

He pulled out of the airport, checking the rearview mirrors.

"Depends on what you mean by regular. When I can get someone to watch the car. You'd be surprised what you find in people's luggage. There's usually something that you can sell. I bet I average fifty bucks a bag. One trip to the airport, you can make one, two hundred bucks."

James smiled. I closed my eyes. Now we were accomplices to a crime. Hanging with James was always an adventure.

"I sold a GPS for four hundred bucks last week. It was right on top of this lady's underwear. And that stuff was pretty kinky. She had a vibrator in the suitcase too. I couldn't sell a used vibrator."

Ten minutes later we were inside a coffee shop named Miles's. Styles sat across from us, breaking open multiple packets of sugar and shaking each one into his creamed coffee.

"I told Skip that you used to work for Cashdollar's traveling circus."

"I did. Nice little business. I sold cheap little crosses, some Bibles that I got from China, wooden charms, wall plaques, and statues. You'd be surprised what kind of junk is made for the religious trade. Christ, napkin holders with scripture engraved on them, flower vases that look like the tomb Jesus was buried in, and everything in the world in the shape of a cross."

"Good money in those things?"

"A gold mine, my friend. And speaking of that, I found out about the gold Bible that the rev always carries with him. He's rumored to never go anywhere without it. So I got some little keychain gold Bibles and those sold like hotcakes."

"But you're not with him anymore? Even though you made good money?"

"Obviously, no."

James and I waited. Finally, my roommate asked the question. "Why?"

He hesitated. "Couple of reasons. I guess the best is it wouldn't have been a good business decision. The rev works these things about six times a year, mostly in the South. If you want to work for him you've got to commit to full time."

There it was again. Full time.

"When you get called, you show up."

"For his shows, right? Six a year?" James was eagerly eating it all up.

"His shows, and whatever else he wants."

James looked at me. I looked at Styles. "What else does he want?"

"I never found out." His eyes left us and he stared over my shoulder, out the window.

James took a swallow of his coffee, while Styles kept stirring his sugary drink with his finger.

"Daron, what the hell are you talking about?"

It took him a long time to answer. I figured he was going to make something up, or it was difficult for him to talk about it. Finally, "There were seven full-time guys with him three years ago. All I know is that I heard they could get a call at a moment's notice, and they'd all have to drop whatever they were doing and meet with Cashdollar, or Thomas LeRoy. You've met LeRoy?"

James nodded.

"Thomas LeRoy has the exact location of all the full-timers. He keeps it in this personal organizer he carries with him."

"He knows where all these guys are?"

"Seems to be important to the operation. Me, I can't figure out why you need to know where a pizza guy is at two in the morning or a hot dog guy on a Sunday afternoon. Unless you're at the ballpark and you want a dog or some pizza." He sipped the sweet coffee. "Anyway, LeRoy has his organizer and if he wants you, you drop what you're doing and show up. I wasn't ready to do that."

"So LeRoy is more than just finance?"

"Yeah. He's the business manager, you know? And I tell you he's a guy with no personality. I'd play with him a little, tell him I was having an off day and see if I could get a deal on the day's rent. Man wouldn't even smile or appreciate my attempt. I learned you don't mess with him."

"Some people just have no appreciation."

"Oh, he'd just frown and walk away. But the donut guy,

Bruce, came down and told me to either shape up or they'd ship me out. Apparently they thought I was trying to run a scam on them. So I learned that Thomas LeRoy gets some of the boys to do his dirty work."

"Imagine that," I said.

"So you got threatened?" James leaned halfway across the table. "We did, too, dude."

"It was some stuff I did, and some stuff I thought I saw. It's a long story and kind of confusing," said Styles.

"You want to tell us exactly what it was?" Here was a guy who'd been asked to leave. Maybe he could give us a clue.

"Not right now. It's something I haven't talked about. Not a big deal, just better left unsaid."

"Something about the accidental death of a food vendor?"

Styles frowned and gazed at James.

"What the hell happened?" I needed to know.

"I really don't know. I heard stories, but—" His eyes drifted off to a spot on the far wall.

I shrugged my shoulders. Sooner or later.

"Daron, what could be so important that you'd have to be that available twenty-four-seven? I mean, Cashdollar has a nice business, but why would the vendors have to be on call all the time?"

James sipped his black coffee.

"I don't know, boys. I told you. I never went full time."

"Well," James stroked his chin, "it's a big business. I mean, if he needed to meet with the vendors and get their take on setting things up, I mean—"

I swirled a mouthful of Miles's coffee, understanding why Daron had put so much sugar in his cup. The strong, acrid beverage almost took the enamel off of my teeth. "You said there were seven full-timers?"

"There were."

"There are six now."

"I heard. They never replaced Michael."

"What happened to number seven?" I was still trying.

"Michael Bland. Nicest guy you'd ever want to meet. He'd had a sandwich shop in Denver. He sold it and came to Florida. Guy was about sixty-two years old, seemed to be well adjusted, then, supposedly" he leaned on the word supposedly, "up and died of a drug overdose."

"Wow." James shook his head. "You usually think of drug overdoses with younger guys."

"That's what a lot of people thought."

"When did this happen?"

"The weekend I was there. The Saturday night of revival."

"Any idea that he was on drugs?"

"I think it surprised everybody. Well, except Stan. Stan claimed he knew all along that Bland was on something. Used to call him a —"

"Druggy?" I remembered Stan's comment.

"How the hell did you know that?"

I said nothing.

"Any investigation into the death?" James jumped in.

"Oh, there was. They never proved anything and I know they never found the money."

"What money?"

"A couple of hours before he died he'd won a pot load at the nightly poker game. They figured he'd used it to buy the drugs, because no one ever found the cash."

CHAPTER NINETEEN

An old weather-beaten, white-haired man in a tattered gray jacket sat down at the counter. Fishing in his shirt pocket, he came out with a bent cigarette and tried to light it with a pack of matches that had seen too much moisture. I watched him as the waitress came down the seats, shaking her finger at him.

"Sir, sir, you know there is no smoking inside restaurants. Sir."

His hands shook as he tried to strike the third match. There was no chance the older gentleman would ever get the thing lit.

"So you've got Stan—" James was writing on a napkin, making a list, "—Bruce, Dusty, Mug, hot dog Henry," he paused. "Who the hell else is there."

"Invisible Sailor." Daron smiled. "I always called him 'IS'. Sailor is a real quiet dude, just sits there and quietly plays. Wins some, loses some, you never know. He blends in."

I'd been down there twice, but I couldn't put a face on Sailor. I'd seen him, but he was a shadowy individual and I hadn't paid much attention.

"So that's six. Any murderers in the group?"

Daron took a swallow of his creamy, sugary, caffeinated beverage. "One of the guys has some felony convictions. They're upfront about him. Mug, I think. I would guess that some of the others have some felony convictions, too, but the rev doesn't exactly do background checks on his vendors."

I'd never considered that. Murderers, sex offenders, muggers, robbers, and rapists, after they'd done their time, what did they do with the rest of their lives? Work in a car wash? Fast food? Or work for somebody like Cashdollar? Because you'd almost have to move from your hometown, and you certainly couldn't work for a bank, teach school, work as an accountant, or for that matter, much of anything else. Maybe you'd have to — and then it hit me. Maybe you'd have to sell security systems or work at a place like Cap'n Crab. Well, hell. We were both on the bottom rung of the ladder with murderers, sex offenders, muggers, and the like. That was encouraging. As far as I knew, no one had ever done a background check on me, or James.

"You know, there are some people like Cashdollar who have backgrounds in murder. I mean, celebrities usually skate on something like that. They don't do any serious time. Don King, Phil Spector, Snoop Dogg. Major celebrities who've been implicated in murder. I mean, look at Robert Blake, O.J. Simpson — it hasn't stopped most of them from going on with their lives."

It hadn't. As far as I knew. Of course, you only know what you read, see on TV, or hear on the radio. And I wasn't sure that I should believe everything from the media.

The old man at the counter had laid his head down and appeared to be asleep, the cigarette and matches lying on the vinyl surface.

"Sir, sir, you can't sleep here." The poor waitress was shaking that finger and I was afraid she'd jam it in his eye.

I half listened to James and Daron speaking intently about the full-time players. I wondered what was happening to the people who were standing at the airport terminal's Delta counter, asking about their missing luggage. I worried about Em, who was trying to figure out if I was full-time material, if I was worthy of being a husband, a father. I thought about Bruce Crayer and the attempted murder of Barry Romans on South Beach, and I kept thinking about James, the truck, and whether I wanted to get myself into another jam.

"What do you think, Skip?"

I hadn't been listening enough. Damn.

"Well," James was staring at me. "Should we have Daron spend tonight and tomorrow with us?"

I'd missed the turn in the conversation.

"Huh?"

"Skip! Give me a sign, amigo. I think Daron could help. He could be our eyes, our voice, and he knows the players.

Putting it to me, right in front of the guy himself.

"We had a good lunch, we'll have a good dinner. Let's say we pay Daron a couple hundred bucks," he glanced at Daron and got a nod, "and he gives us a hand."

I had no idea where this was going.

"Maybe we ought to kick it around? You and me?"

James frowned. I was embarrassing him in front of a business associate. Well, excuse me. I had an investment in this too.

"Skip, dude, Daron is going to help us." And that was that.

I watched the counter, as the waitress patted the white-haired man on the head. She patted, then shook his head. He made no attempt to respond. Either he was passed out or dead.

"All right, James. Daron is part of your team. But his salary comes out of your half." And *that* was *that*.

CHAPTER TWENTY

We snuck into the tent for the late afternoon show. Cashdollar, resplendent in a maroon tux and black cape, came storming out from the wings, the wind machine kicking into high velocity.

"Impressed? Well, you shouldn't be." And he went into his opening act for twenty minutes.

"He's going to mention Romans. You just wait. What was it he said about the senator this morning? God takes matters into his own hands?" James was positive. Positive about the negatives.

Cashdollar worked the crowd, pacing back and forth on the huge stage, working up a personal sweat and a fervor in the faithful as they shouted "Amen" and clapped their hands. The choir chimed in at the appointed moments and when the reverend pointed to the banner behind him everyone screamed.

"Say it with me," he shouted. "Say it with me." The voice boomed over the speaker system. "You will be made rich in every way so that you can be generous on every occasion!"

As he thrust the gold Bible at them, waving it in the air, they said it, over and over again.

"Did *I* say it? No. Did *you* say it? No. Who says it, brothers and sisters? The *Bible* says it." He shook the book. "The Bible. God's holy word says it." Now the gold book was the featured visual on the huge screens. "It's in here, my friends. And not just my Bible, but your Bible. God's word. God says it. In his very own book. People say 'reverend, God never talks to me.' Well listen! Listen. God says, from his lips to your ears, you will be made rich, but there's a catch. There's a catch. You must be generous on every occasion." He paused. That was the important part of his message. "You must be generous on every occasion."

I glanced at James to see if he was planning on putting any more money in the collection plate. I figured he wasn't going to be quite as generous this time. After all, we'd paid Brook $200, and he was about to pay his good friend Daron another chunk of change for hanging around. I was right. As the collection plates were handed down the aisle, James's hand never dipped into his pocket. Daron and I followed suit.

The organ music was loud and shrill and the choir fought to rise above it with a spiritual sounding song. All I knew was, the collection plate was going to be minus by a little more than $8.00.

Cashdollar walked back out with two burly men by his side, both of them wearing coal black suits and looking very somber. In contrast to his slicked-back hair, these two men had shaved their heads and Cashdollar's rather rotund figure was almost dwarfed by the six-foot-five muscular sidekicks.

"Some of you may know that we've been rallying against the forces of bigotry. We've been shouting down the voices of evil and those who would stand in the way of the Lord's work. Some of you may know that."

There were scattered "amens."

"Some of you may know that I pointed a finger," he held up his index finger. James raised his middle finger, but kept his hand down low. "I pointed a finger at a local radio host. Barry Romans.

A voice that is filled with hatred, filled with evil venom, filled with intent to do harm." His voice was hoarse, gravely, and filled with passion and emotion.

More "amens."

"Barry Romans speaks about the gospel according to Barry. He is a racist, a bigot, and he spews his poison on the airwaves of our nation."

Loud amens and booing.

Cashdollar held up his hand, and we could see the creases of his palm on the big screen TVs. "What many of you do not know is that Barry Romans was gunned down today, not ten miles from where we are at this very moment."

A hush fell over the crowd. Then there was a low murmuring of voices that got louder by the second.

"My brethren, we preach change through peaceful actions. We preach change through peaceful means."

There was a pleading tone in his voice. It amazed me how he could change the entire tone by just the modulation of his speech.

"It is not our intention to bring an end to a violent life with violence. So we pray for the recovery of Barry Romans. We pray that he may live another day to understand the sins he has perpetrated on the public's airwaves. A moment of silence please, so that we all may pray that God's will be done. Whatever God wills, we pray that it be done."

A hush fell over the congregation. Daron, still wearing his porkpie hat, leaned over and whispered loudly, "As long as God's will is the rev's will." A woman in the next row turned and stared daggers at him.

Cashdollar picked it up again, the two men standing very close to him.

"We wanted no physical harm to come to Mr. Romans. And we will not tolerate physical harm to anyone, even those who would possibly try to harm us. Jesus suffered the cross and never fought back. We are Christians. Therefore, we are peaceful people. Let me hear an amen."

The crowd gave it to him with a resounding shout.

"But you know what God says. The Bible clearly states, brothers and sisters, that the Lord says 'vengeance is mine.' The Lord will take matters into his own hands and it is out of ours. Amen."

"Where the hell is this going?" James shook his head.

"Mr. Romans is in the hospital, recovering from this dastardly, cowardly act. And now, *we* have received death threats. Yes, my people, I have received a threat on my life."

There was a cry from two thousand plus people. A cry, followed by a gasping. James even made a guttural sound.

"It is necessary for the next few days for me to have these two — deacons — at my side. They will seek to protect me from anyone who would attempt to physically harm me."

James whispered. "What about the Lord's prerogative?"

"The Lord spoke to me."

"Ah, there it is."

"And after much prayer, after soulful, heartfelt prayer, I know that the Lord asked me to protect myself from the slings and arrows of others that would try to bring me down."

Now there was a loud din of voices, screams, and shouts. There were even a couple of shrill whistles. Here was the man who was going to show us the road to riches, and now he was about to be assassinated. Another cry from the masses and a conversational murmur of voices as people turned to their neighbors and expressed disbelief.

"Jesus."

"Funny how you would bring up his name. Cashdollar was just talking about him, James." Daron tugged the brim of his porkpie hat.

I was in the presence of greatness. I was watching a true master of the arts. Here was a self-professed man of the cloth who had taken the attempted assassination, the near death of a media celebrity, and turned the entire focus on himself. All in a matter of seconds. The magician David Copperfield had nothing at all on Reverend Preston Cashdollar.

The crowd was stirred up. They'd all come in the hopes of becoming wealthy, and now there were shootings and death threats. This couldn't be a good thing. The voices of two thousand plus people in an enclosed area can be just plain loud. And it was.

"My people, please." Cashdollar held up his Bible, calming the crowd. "We will work through this."

The noise diminished. Slowly, but surely, they turned their attention back to the man who'd brought them together.

"Let us remember the message we've all come to share. You will be made rich in every way. Say it with me."

And the crowd chanted the message, reading from the banner the scripture that was burned into their minds. The two bodyguards melted into the curtains and the Reverend Cashdollar held the congregation spellbound in the palm of his hand. After all the crap, he had them right where he wanted them.

"Let me bring out two people, just like you, who heard this message three years ago. Brethren, welcome brother Steve Olean and brother William Riley."

There was light, scattered applause. The names sounded vaguely familiar, but I couldn't place them.

"Brother Steve Olean and brother William Riley both believed this message. They prayed on it, they came to our revival meetings, they met with brother Thomas LeRoy our director of finance, and they met with me."

Two young white guys walked out on stage, dressed in casual slacks and knit polo shirts.

"Ladies. Gentlemen. I give to you the founders of *Meet and Greet*, one of the Internet's biggest meeting places."

James grabbed my shoulder. "Oh, my God. Do you know who these guys are?"

"He just told us, James."

"Skip, amigo, these guys were just on the cover of *Rolling Stone*. They're like rock gods of the tech world."

I knew who they were. You'd have to be in the Stone Age not to know the business they started. Started, and sold to one of the big networks for something like a billion dollars. Maybe two billion. James even has a personal page on *Meet and Greet*, just like *My Space*, complete with his picture and a doctored history. Believe me, I knew who these two guys were.

"My friends, these two gentlemen would like to tell you their story. Do you want to hear it?"

There was a frenzy of screaming and applause. This was the meat and potatoes. This was what the Cashdollar experience was all about. Two very rich white dudes who owed their success to God — and to Preston Cashdollar. The two men spoke for the next fifteen minutes, telling their story very well. They spoke of their belief in a higher power, they referred to the banner in an almost choreographed manner. Olean and Riley owned the big yellow tent.

"Do you have a dream?" Riley, a thirty-year-old, short, Tom Cruise-looking guy took the lead. "Do you?"

There was confusion in the ranks. Shouts of "amen" and "yes, brother" followed.

Olean leaned into the microphone. "If you have a dream, you can make it happen. If we did it, you can do it."

The crowd screamed. Shouted. They stood up, and as

strange as it felt, as cynical as I was, I stood up with them. We had a dream. I wanted it to happen. And when they were done, they asked the congregation to repeat the phrase. It came back louder than ever.

You will be made rich in every way so that you can be generous on every occasion.

During the next passing of the plate, James put in ten bucks. I put in five. I didn't want him to feel totally alone. Daron Styles smirked and shook his head.

CHAPTER TWENTY-ONE

Is it me? Is it the people I hang out with? Is it the society we live in? Is it the American way? One minute I'm totally bummed out. The idea that someone, maybe in the Cashdollar camp, tried to commit a murder. The idea that someone has threatened Cashdollar himself. My feeling that Cashdollar is a slimeball. And then, in an instant, I find myself sucked into a scam. I know it's a scam, but I want to believe it. I want to believe that *you will be made rich in every way*. What is wrong with me, with the people around me, that our belief system can change in a nanosecond? What we believe one second can totally change due to greed.

I'm not what you'd call a religious person. I believe in a God, but only because there's got to be something out there. I don't buy into this primeval slime that we supposedly evolved from.

So all of a sudden, I'm investing $5, betting that God will make me rich. And I already know where that $5 is going.

"You guys know where your money is going, right?" Styles had cocked the hat back on his head and, back at the truck, he was eating a burger that James had cooked for him as he prepared for the evening rush. The bun was loaded with pickles, peppers, relish, onion, mustard, and whatever else he could find.

James sat on his upside-down pickle bucket, his apron on, waiting for the crowd to come piling out of the yellow tent. "Yeah. Some of it goes to the full-timers. But you know, damn it, you see two guys up there who are worth a billion dollars, and you've got to wonder."

Styles sat on the rear of the truck, dangling his legs over the edge. He sipped on one of our expensive green labels and kicked his feet back and forth. "Yeah, you're right, James. You've got to wonder how much Cashdollar paid them for that testimonial."

I hadn't thought of that. I was up by the grill, precooking potatoes, onions, and peppers. "What do they need the money for? They're worth billions?"

"Boys, read the *Time* magazine article on them. Read the *Rolling Stone* interview. See if they mention Cashdollar one time."

James took a long swallow of the good beer. "You mean, they don't mention him at all? It's a hoax?"

"Hell, I don't know. I don't read that crap. But I'll bet they don't mention him. I'll bet they don't say a word about how Cashdollar was responsible for their wealth and fame."

"So, what could he pay them? My God, they're billionaires."

"Look," Styles finished the beer and pointed to the refrigerator. James, the obedient lapdog, brought him another. We were almost out.

"I'm not saying these guys didn't attend one of the rev's meetings. And I'm not saying that they didn't contribute some jack to his fund. And, I'm not saying that they don't believe that Cashdollar and the scripture had something to do with their wealth."

I was tired of him already. "Then what are you saying? Man, you talk in circles."

"Maybe there's a grain of truth there. Maybe Cashdollar had something to do with their success, but you've got to remember, Skip, this is a show. It's a circus, a carnival. Remember that. It's set up to get money from the locals any way possible. These people are entertainers. Entertainers pure and simple. They get paid depending on how well they entertain. It's no different than the hucksters that paraded around at the turn of the century selling swamp water in a bottle to cure all our ills. It's a business. An entertainment business, and that's all it is. The minute you forget that, you become a sucker. Listen. James drops ten in the pot, two thousand people put ten in the pot, they've got three collections per service, that's what? One hundred twenty thousand dollars for Thursday and Friday. Saturday and Sunday, we've got *two* services. Count 'em, two. That's two hundred forty thousand dollars per day. That adds up to," he paused, working the figures in his head.

As a business major I could have told him, the trick is to do the math as the story unfolds, not wait until the end.

"Three hundred sixty thousand dollars."

He'd gotten it right.

"And son," he continued, "there are a lot of people who put in a whole lot more than just ten bucks. I'm talking a hundred bucks a pop and more."

James and I looked at each other. Thursday, Friday, Saturday, and Sunday. This guy could do up to half a million dollars. In four days.

Now I got it. James wanted to stick around and soak up everything he could. The good, the bad, the ugly. He wanted to learn just how everything in this operation ran. At the risk of our own safety, James wanted this education. Hell, I wanted this education. I finally figured it out. Stick with James, because it was an education.

"So Cashdollar could pay these two hot-shit entrepreneurs

some big bucks. What the hell does he care how much. Fifty, one hundred thousand? It may be pocket change to these young guys, but pocket change is good." Styles tugged on his hat, pulling it down almost to his eyebrows.

"They'd do it for one hundred thousand?" James was mesmerized.

"They would. Wouldn't you? Think about it, James. You're worth half a billion. It's tied up in stocks and bonds and whatever rich assholes do with their money. Maybe real estate and other stuff. Somebody offers you — maybe under the table — one hundred thousand dollars. Have you ever, in your wildest, seen that kind of money?"

Neither of us had an answer. Figures we'd never even pictured. Hell, we were excited about making four or five thousand dollars. One hundred thousand? We could probably own our entire apartment complex for less than that. Not that we'd want to. Our complex is a piece of crap.

"Pretty good money. And don't forget, my friends, this is a cash business. The rev and Mr. LeRoy can claim they only got four or five hundred bucks in the collection if they want to. They can pocket thousands in cash. And, as I said, pay the boys from *Meet and Greet* under the table. No tax consequences for anyone."

"So that's what he did? Cashdollar?" James was salivating.

"How the hell do I know, James? I'm throwing out the possibility. That's it." He paused, getting his thoughts together. "The word spreads. The rev, he's got a huge online business. I'd bet he gets a couple hundred thousand a week just from his Internet pledges. And when people hear that the *Meet and Greet* guys got rich because of Cashdollar? Trust me, the money gates are going to open wide. Remember the second half of that scripture, boys. *So that you can be generous on every occasion.* Generous to the rev."

"Holy shit." James was glassy eyed. He'd almost died and gone to heaven. "Internet. I hadn't even thought of that."

Daron opened the bottle and drained half of it. Our beer. Technically Brook's beer.

"He's got more arms than an octopus. This Thomas LeRoy, his finance guy? He's hooked into so many outlets, these guys are making millions in their sleep. Television, newsletters, the Internet, a radio network, a direct mail campaign — and LeRoy is working on a text-message campaign that they figure will rake in a cool million a year."

I was stunned. "How do you possibly know all of this?"

"I know, okay."

My God. A text-message campaign that would rake in a million by itself? I'd been thinking small time. I'd been thinking thousands, not hundreds of thousands. I'd never dreamed of millions. And today we'd been in the presence of billions. I couldn't get my mind around it. Billions. And the funny thing was, these two guys who started this huge Internet site, *Meet and Greet*, were maybe three years older than James and me. I finally got it. James was seeing the big picture. I was in the Stone Age. It was time to rethink my position. If James wanted to stay and learn, even though our lives were threatened, then we were going to stay and learn. Em would never get it. Ever. I had to live with that. But I got it.

"And the funniest part of this to me," Daron appeared to be winding up his delivery, "is that it's run by a handful of carneys."

James gave me a look. "That's what Skip said. I take it that's not a good thing."

Daron smiled at me, a look of respect. "Oh, I think it's a real good thing. If you're Cashdollar."

Dinner was huge. The crowd had worked up an appetite, and after six collections during two services, they still had enough money to pay ten bucks a head for our meager meal.

"I'll guaranfuckingtee you that was a record collection,

boys." Daron had probably called it right. "A record collection by anyone's standards. To come out of an attempted murder on a radio celebrity that the Lord had sanctioned, a death threat against the rev that the Lord was against, and then to bring out the two guys responsible for the business success story of the year? I'm tellin' you Skipper, James, people will be telling their great-grandchildren about that one. You were in the presence of greatness today. There is absolutely no question about that. If nothing else, I hope you appreciate how this is orchestrated. Every paper in the country tomorrow will have this story. And it's one hell of a yarn, isn't it?"

We agreed.

"It's fun to watch this guy work. He's just rakin' it in, and he finds new ways to do it every day."

During dinner, Daron stayed up near the front of the truck with James and I didn't see a whole lot of contribution. He smoked cigarettes, finished our entire supply of beer, slowed James down on a regular basis with his conversation, and twice asked me if I could speed up the ordering process. I was ready to kill the son of a bitch by the time the dinner shift was over.

Things weren't a lot different than they had been up front. There were long lines of hungry revival goers — angry people, pushy people, polite people, and people who just didn't give a damn. I called them The Starved Masses. All they wanted was a ten-dollar fix. And I gave it to them. With potatoes, peppers, onions, pickles, and whatever else they wanted. Even with our step-up, I had to lean down, sometimes almost falling from the rear of the truck, but I gave it to them. Whatever they wanted.

I used the grill and my cast-iron skillet, and the stench of fried grease, the raw odor of onions and peppers, the lard that we used to fry the potatoes, all came back to saturate my clothes, my apron, my skin, and my hair. The money was going to be good.

Getting the odor out was going to be tough. A shower would help get me back to normal, but there would still be a ways to go.

Daron smoked a cigarette and sucked on the last of the green labels.

And right at the end of the rush, right when I could see an end to the line and James and I had wiped the most recent sweat from our brows, right when I was actually trying to figure out about how many ten dollar bills we'd taken in, I saw them walking down the path toward our truck. The reverend Preston Cashdollar and his two deacons. And they seemed headed right toward our little hash wagon.

CHAPTER TWENTY-TWO

Daron came down to the back of the truck and watched as Cashdollar and his two bodyguards paraded down the path, waving at surprised members of the congregation. I watched an old lady using a walker grab Cashdollar's Bible-toting arm and hang on for dear life as she pleaded with him. One of the thick bodyguards immediately pulled her off as Cashdollar patted her on top of her thin gray hair and she moved on. Two middle-aged black men did a double take, then one produced a piece of paper and pen and offered them to the rev for an autograph. All the while he clutched the gold Bible, never letting go of it for an instant. It seemed to be the outward sign of his piety.

The two big guys on either side of him moved him down the path, never letting him spend too much time with any one person. The closer they got, the more I was certain they were headed for our truck.

I sensed, rather than saw, Bruce from the donut trailer leaning out, watching Cashdollar. When I turned and looked, he waved, as if nothing had happened between us. And, I have to admit, I was somewhat impressed with the fact that Cashdollar was mingling with the common folk. For all the talk about this man of the cloth, I had never thought about him going any farther than that sixty-foot platform inside the tent and his limo. James and I had seen the black Lincoln that deposited him behind the stage just minutes before the show, and that same limousine picked him up seconds after the last collection. I thought I'd even seen the limo that morning, down at South Beach. I had a very limited view of the man. Stages and limousines. The fact that Reverend Cashdollar would hang with the man on the street was impressive. Especially in light of what Styles had told us. The guy was in a league of his own.

James was staring intently. "Skip, is he coming over here?"

He was and he did. "Hello, boys." He nodded at us, a serious look on his face. His gaze lingered on Styles. James's friend seemed to wilt and I could sense some tension. Finally, Cashdollar looked at me. "I like to meet new vendors. You must be Skip Moore?"

I couldn't believe it.

"And you," he pointed up in the truck, "You're James. Good name, son. You know James was a disciple. Jesus referred to him as 'son of thunder.' He supposedly had a pretty bad temper." He paused. "I should clarify that. James had the temper, not Jesus." Cashdollar never cracked a smile.

"Thank you, sir. And thank you for stopping by. We were in the tent earlier and you were great. I mean, really, really —"

"Thank you, son. The *message* was great. Powerful. The *man* is weak. And the two young men who graced our stage today, that could be you and Skip in the very near future."

James's eyes got big, and he had a goofy grin on his face. Cashdollar nodded again. "I've been told you had some misfortune during your stay with us."

"Yes sir, but —"

"And Deacon LeRoy took care of you?"

"He did, sir."

"Good. I trust you won't have any other misfortunes. You see, it's obvious that this business isn't for everyone, is it?" He glanced once more at Styles, frowned, and his handlers moved him on down the row. I noticed he didn't stop at Crayer's donut wagon. He already knew who was in there.

Styles frowned. "'You were great, sir, really, really, really.' Could you have kissed his ass any more, James?"

"Daron, shut up." James pointed at him. "The guy is good. Damn it, he's very good at what he does."

"Yeah. He is. He also threatened you."

"What? He simply recognized that we'd had some set-backs."

"James," I watched Cashdollar heading down the path, "I took it as sort of a threat. Maybe I'm a little paranoid."

"Maybe you are pardner. Maybe he was trying to tell us we shouldn't come back, but did you hear what he said about—"

"We did. James, wasn't that a little over the top, that bit about the two of us being the next billionaire boy wonders?"

"Pard, I wouldn't be here, in this very spot, with grease on my apron, in my hair, in my clothes, and on my skin if I didn't believe it could happen. You've got to have faith."

"We've got two issues we're dealing with."

James was back on his pickle barrel, and he lit up a cigarette. "Pray tell, what are they?"

"One, you're buying into Cashdollar's dream."

"Tell me you're not."

I couldn't do that. Who doesn't want to believe that they will be blessed? "All right, when he said we could be the next *Meet and Greet* guys, I got a little jolt."

"See?"

Styles sat on the back of the truck, blowing smoke rings

from a small brown cigar. He'd pulled his hat down to his eyebrows and he was slowly nodding, taking in our banter.

"The dream is okay. We've all got to dream."

"Then what's the problem, compadre?"

"It's the messenger. Remember, you told him how great he was?"

"I did."

"And he said—"

"The *message* is great. The *man* is weak."

"Yeah."

"Yeah. He pretty much told you what he is. Weak. Personally, I think this guy is a scam artist, probably a crook, and we know of two murders, a drug overdose, and a shooting that may be attributed to him."

My buddy was quiet for a moment, sucking on his cigarette. "Fred Long, Cabrina Washington, maybe Michael Bland, and now Barry Romans."

"Can I jump in for just a brief moment?" Styles blew a puff of smoke at me. "Michael Bland, the full-timer... there's no question in my mind about an accidental overdose. There's no *maybe*. He was murdered, boys. *They* stuffed him with drugs. I'd throw his name into the mix of murdered bodies just for fun."

So we did. Just for fun. I was starting to wonder if there were more that we were missing. Cashdollar's little enterprise was littered with bodies.

"Okay," James processed it, "Michael Bland too. Three murders and a shooting."

"Exactly." I nodded to him. "You're back and forth on the issue, James. You want Cashdollar to be the answer, but I don't think he is. I think he's the problem. I don't want to think that, but I do. I think he's a crook. Isn't that one reason you brought Daron along?"

He nodded.

"And what was between you and Cashdollar?" I tapped Styles on the top of his hat. He looked up with a sleepy expression on his face.

"What do you mean?"

"The look he gave you? You, usually full of bravado, you backed up like you thought he was going to bite."

"We've met before. He was probably just trying to place me, you know."

"Bullshit. You said something back at the coffee shop about being warned by Bruce Crayer? You said that he tried to throw you out?"

"It was nothing, okay?"

I let it go.

"Skip," James was standing, talking with his hands, in full sales presentation, "I'm fascinated with this guy. With this place. The more I see, hear, smell, and taste, the more I want to know. I can't believe tomorrow is the last day. Hell, we're learning more here than we picked up in four years of college. Dude, this is a primer on how to go big time. If we take this business model and legitimize it, there's no telling how big we might grow."

I wasn't sure I could buy that, but then neither of us had done that well in college, so he could be right. I still wasn't sure how you took a revival evangelist and turned the concept into another business, but I'm sure James had given it some thought.

"James, I think you're riding with the wrong guy. You may be impressed with his business skills, but Cashdollar and company may be criminals. Doesn't that bother you?"

"Yeah, I want to know if he's a killer. I guess, the more I look into it, I want to know if you have to break the law to control your own situation."

"What?"

"I mean, when you get to be as big as this guy is you've got to control things. This guy is so much bigger than I realized. Does he have to manipulate things to keep them going?"

I stared at him. "Manipulate things? Break the law? We're talking murder here. Pretty severe stuff. Have you lost your mind, James? If he's killing people to keep the faith, then I want out right now."

"I know. Dude, I just want to get as much information as I can."

"Maybe Cashdollar should write a book. Answer all your questions."

James considered that for a moment. "It would be the next logical step, pardner. I'd stand in line to buy it, wouldn't you?"

Styles jumped down from the truck bed, stretched his legs as if he'd been working hard all afternoon, and pointed to the restrooms. "Got to get rid of some of this beer."

Our beer.

He walked away with almost a swagger. Over his shoulder he shouted back, "Oh, and by the way, James, your namesake, the disciple? He was doing Jesus's work when Herod cut off his head. Just for the record."

We watched him slowly walk to the building.

"We ought to get more beer."

James put his hand to his neck and stroked it.

CHAPTER TWENTY-THREE

We showered, and put on the same clothes we'd had on last night. James called Brook and begged off their date, Em called me and said she wanted to see some of the revival nightlife and James and I both decided that either Styles or Em could take us home tonight and bring us back in the morning. No matter how crappy our accommodations in Carol City, we wanted the comfort of a real bed — much more preferable than the bed of James's truck.

Of course, I had designs on a different bed. The night would be interesting.

"I'm playing cards, pard."

"For whatever reason, I don't think it's a good idea."

"Look, I want to learn whatever we can."

When I glanced down the path to the road that ran beside the campground, the police cruiser stood out like a sore thumb, slowly driving up the one-lane paved road that led to the parking lot, the tent, and the vendor trailers. No flashing lights on, but the car looked ominous nevertheless.

"What the hell do the cops want?"

James was not a fan of organized law enforcement. He had

vivid memories of the day they came to arrest his old man. They handcuffed him in front of his family, shoved him into the back of a black and white, and according to James, roughed him up after they got him to the station. I had no cause to doubt him. You know how some people blame everyone else and everything else for their predicaments? They act like it just couldn't be their fault? In the case of Oscar Lessor, it really wasn't his fault. His partner took the money from their business and ran, and Mr. Lessor was left holding the proverbial bag. He did the time for something he had no control over, and he came out a broken man. James never forgot it. Ever.

"Just a patrol, James. No big deal."

He'd seen the car and his fists were clenched.

I noticed Styles quickly ducking behind the truck, heading toward one of the concrete shelters that line the shore of the Intracoastal Waterway on the other side of the tent. He made a point of staying out of the view of the two officers inside the car. I guess selling stolen and counterfeit merchandise was against the law in Miami, and Styles was a little concerned about being recognized. And then I had another thought. We'd been with him since the Miami Airport. The three stolen airport bags were in his trunk, with who knew what else. Was there an all-points bulletin out for a Buick with three white suspects? Styles's Buick was in the parking lot, parked right by the road the cops were traveling. James and Styles weren't the only ones who weren't happy to see the cops. I had some serious concerns too.

The car stopped about thirty feet from us and two uniformed officers stepped out. I stood there about one second longer than I should have.

"You." One of the officers pointed at me and strode over to the truck. His partner stayed where he was, his hands on his hips, the sun reflecting off of his dark sunglasses.

"What?"

He glanced at the truck, and at James standing in the rear of the vehicle. "You work with the reverend?" He was about my age, cocky, and full of himself. I could hear the self-importance in his voice.

"We're vendors."

"So, you work *for* the reverend." Smug.

"What do you want? We have a license. Board of health, the whole thing." I signaled James who scrambled to bring it out. He obviously didn't want any trouble with the officers.

"Forget that. We need to talk to the reverend. Where do we find him?"

I breathed a deep sigh of relief. "He actually passed here several minutes ago. He was headed that way." I pointed in the direction they'd gone.

"How about a Thomas LeRoy?"

James climbed down from the truck bed and handed the license to the officer. The uniformed official brushed him off, and I saw that look in James's eyes. I prayed he would be cool about the situation.

"We're here because of a shooting at South Beach. Do either of you have any information about a Barry Romans? He's a local radio talk-show host. He was the victim of a shooting earlier today. Do you know anything about that at all?"

James stood behind the officer and stared hard at me holding up his hand and shaking his head.

"Uh, no. Reverend Cashdollar may have mentioned it during his service but —"

James continued to stand behind the officer, waving his hands and shaking his head.

"He talked about it? What did he say?"

"I don't remember. Just that somebody may have taken a shot and —"

"Did he talk about how it happened?"

"No. Definitely he didn't talk about how it happened."

He looked at me, the glasses reflecting my disheveled, worried look. After tapping the toe of his highly polished shoe for several seconds, he said, "Look, if you see either of them in the next half hour, tell them to come to this yellow tent." He surveyed the canvas monstrosity, taking in its size. "We want to talk to them. Understood?"

I nodded. He probably wanted to hear, "Yes sir." I couldn't do it. Especially not with James there.

"Do you hear me?"

Intimidation. For no reason at all. "I hear you. And while you're yelling at me, Reverend Cashdollar is still walking down there." I pointed.

The officer gave me a hard look through his tinted glasses, spun around, and walked down the path. His partner stayed by the car.

"Assholes. You don't become a cop unless you're an asshole." James whispered it. He glanced back over his shoulder at the other officer.

"What were you trying to tell me? Shaking your head, waving your hands?"

"Jesus, Skip, I know you better than you know yourself. You were going to tell them about Cashdollar's crusade."

"And what would have been wrong with —"

"All we heard was Cashdollar saying he didn't agree with Barry Romans' philosophy."

"Oh, I think it was a little stronger than that."

"Then you would have told them about his comments today and the death threat."

"I still don't see what would have been —"

"And because you were on a roll, you would have pointed out that Bruce Crayer just happened to be within a block of the shooting at the *time* of the shooting."

"James, damn it, you know I wouldn't have —"

"We know nothing, amigo. Once you start talking, they'll ask you questions all night long. They're liable to haul your ass downtown and arrest you on suspicion."

"Of what?"

"Whatever they want, pally. They can do it. 'You seem to have information, you come with us.' I'm telling you, the cops have the power. And they know it. In this country, in this city, you are guilty until proven innocent, and if you don't believe it, just deal with the cops."

"You've got it backward."

"Ever been there, pally? He was. My father is proof positive. Guilty. Until proven innocent. And even then, they find a way to fuck you."

I mentioned it already. Several times. James does not like law enforcement officials. The situation with his father had tainted his outlook on the police.

"Besides, we really don't know anything. Although tonight our luck may change."

"And what's going to happen tonight?"

"We're going to ask some questions, turn over some stones. I like the idea of this whole thing being kind of a mystery."

"Besides there being an attempted murder, besides there being a possible connection to a senator's death, and the death of a black girl, besides there being a drug overdose and a threat on Cashdollar's life, besides receiving a warning that we should leave, what's a mystery? And what do you think we can do about it? You, my friend, are crazy. We shouldn't be within ten thousand feet of this place."

He looked at me as if I hadn't heard a word he'd said. "Skip, for God's sake, we've been through this too many times already. Somebody blew out our tires. Somebody broke into the truck and stole five hundred bucks. Wouldn't you like to get to the bottom of this?"

"James, again I ask, what the hell can we do about it? I'll hang in here with you, but what can we do? We're not trained to deal with this kind of stuff."

"I've got some ideas."

"You're going to tell me what they are?"

"Daron has some ideas as well."

Oh, Jesus. Daron? His idea was to rip off the luggage from unsuspecting tourists. Daron's idea was to sell counterfeit watches and purses. This jackass's idea was to scam a hotel for free food and drinks. My idea was to cut bait and bail. Get the hell out of Dodge. "And if we try to do something and screw this up and upset someone, we may want the cops to be our best friends."

"Well then, my friend, the object is not to screw it up. Tonight, we will have to be like a midget at a urinal. Stay on our toes."

I had to think for a minute. It was from *Naked Gun*, but for the life of me I couldn't remember who said it.

CHAPTER TWENTY-FOUR

No one came up to invite us, but James decided he would attend the evening's card game. I gave James a stake, and stashed the rest of the cash in the locked glove box of Daron's Buick.

"I'd love to sit in on a game, but considering Stan and I didn't exactly leave on good terms, I probably need to stay away from the full-timers."

Daron had eased back into camp as soon as the patrol car left. I never saw Cashdollar or Thomas LeRoy interviewing with the cops, but I figured the officers must have gotten what they came for.

We all three sat on the back of the truck swinging our legs, listening to the crickets and night birds in a cacophony of sound. There was a glow coming from about thirty yards to the right, the light emanating from the small camper area, where the residents were watching portable televisions, building small campfires, or running generators for their lamps. The smell of wood smoke was in the air.

"I'm going to play, I'm going to drink some beers, and I'm going to win." James was having beer withdrawal. I thought maybe his buddy Daron would offer to run out to a carryout, and even buy the beer, but that hadn't happened.

"And what else are you planning?"

"I'm going to ask some questions. I'm sure the topic will be Barry Romans and the death threat on Cashdollar. I mean we've got some serious topics to throw around tonight."

"Ask him about our tires. About somebody stealing our money. About the threatening letter."

"Skip, fuck you. I can't just ask those kinds of questions. Come on, amigo. I've got to be a little subtle."

"You?"

"I can't just say 'who shot our tires? Who sent the threatening letter?'"

"I'm half serious." I was. "I asked Dusty last night."

"Did you get any answers?"

I ignored him.

"Besides, Stan said to only talk to him."

"Then fine. You're going to be with Stan? Then talk to Stan. Ask him those questions while he's fleecing you for all the money you've got on you." He kept saying one of the reasons we were staying, aside from the money, was to determine who was yanking us around. "James, you know as well as I do, if you want answers, ask direct questions."

"I should. I won't. I'll eventually get the questions answered, okay? But I'll do it my way. And nobody is fleecing anybody."

This whole adventure had been done James's way. I kept thinking maybe we ought to consider doing it someone else's way. I just didn't have the answer yet.

"Okay. I'll probably stop down later."

I saw Crayer leave his small tent in the village and slowly walk down toward Stan's pizza wagon.

"Maybe I could suggest we heard about Michael Bland's death and see what kind of reaction I get. Let's see if anyone talks about the drug overdose. And, I'm tempted to tell Crayer I saw him down on South Beach at the time of the shooting. What do you think he'd say to that?"

James shook his head. "Skip, your questions have already stirred these guys up. I don't think you can do that. That's practically accusing him of being involved. Try the subtle approach, pard. Take my lead."

"Yeah. Mr. Smooth."

He frowned.

"James, the more I think about it, the more I think Crayer might have been involved. I'm serious. He did not want to be recognized. As soon as he realized I was looking at him, he ducked."

"Skip," James gave me a grave look. "I love you like a brother, but don't fuck this up. We're in a position to make a lot of money. We're in a position to learn a lot about how a major business operation runs. And, we're in a position to find out if anyone in this group is responsible for multiple murders. Let it play out, pard. Okay? We'll get all the information we need. Just don't fuck it up."

"I'm confused." Styles looked back and forth at each of us. "What exactly are we looking for tonight?" He asked the question that really needed to be answered. "A little excitement? A chance to ruffle some feathers? Or are you two trying to point the finger at the rev's henchmen?" He pulled his hat down on his forehead. "If I'm going to be a party to this charade, tell me what you're trying to accomplish."

"Oh, I'd like to know if one of these guys is a murderer. I'd like to find out what makes this place tick, but what I really want to find out is who shot my tires out. I want to find out who stole our money. I want to find out why they don't want us back next year. I think Crayer was very clear about that, and I think the letter was very clear about that." James watched Crayer slowly walking down the path. "I don't want to walk up to these guys and start pointing fingers, but there's got to be a subtle way to get the information. That's what I'm looking for."

"Fair enough. I'll help you guys."

Styles had been such a big help up to now! As far as I was concerned he hadn't done anything. I asked the question that had been building up inside of me. "And how are you going to do that? How are you going to help us?"

"Look, if Thomas LeRoy paid for four new tires on your truck, he knows who shot them out."

"You think?"

"I'll guaranfuckingtee it."

"Maybe it's just that he doesn't want anyone to rock the boat. Maybe there was a concern that our complaining would upset church festivities. That would rock the boat, wouldn't it? He's buying new tires just to shut us up so we don't scare off the crowd. Can't afford to have a dip in the collection plate."

"You're right," Styles nodded. "They don't like anyone to rock the boat. And somebody has. However, Thomas LeRoy will try to smooth things over. But there's another side to this. LeRoy knows what happened. You see, there's nothing that goes on during this four days that he and Cash don't know about. Nothing."

"They know everything?"

"They do."

"Bullshit. They don't know everything."

"You're a naïve jackass, Skipper. These boys are pros. LeRoy and the rev both know what happened to you. And, they know who did it."

"Okay," I said. "Maybe they do know more than I think. Hell, they know that you're back in the camp, and I could tell by Cashdollar's reaction that he is not happy to see you."

"Well—"

"Why?"

"I told you. He thinks I was running a scam."

"It's more than that isn't it? What does Cashdollar know? What does Thomas LeRoy know?"

I thought he'd spill the information, but James jumped in.

"So how are you going to get that information?"

"The office."

"What office?" I hadn't seen an office.

"It's back behind the tent. A semitrailer with a padlocked door and steps leading up to it. We check out his office."

I'd seen it, but thought nothing of it. "That's an office?"

"It's the nerve center for everything that goes on around here."

I didn't know whether to believe him or not. He was an idiot and to trust him would be the dumbest thing we could do. I looked him square in the eyes. "And of course it's easy to just walk in and get all the information you want. I'm sure a business this size just closes at the end of the day and trusts the faithful not to break into the office. Come on, Daron, the place would have to be under lock and key and it would have to be guarded all night long."

Styles lit one of his small cigars and flicked the match at me. "No, you're wrong, smart ass. Actually they don't have the best security in the world, but it is guarded from midnight till six in the morning by — guess who?"

Who the hell would Cashdollar hire to watch his office?

"Come on, Skipper, James. Think." He blew a stream of gray smoke at me.

I thought. "One of the full-timers?"

"Give the Skipper a silver dollar."

"So your idea is?"

"I know the players. They're not the brightest guys in the world. I've got a plan. I can get by security."

146

"You can get by security? What? You've got a gun?"

Styles looked at me and gave me a sorrowful glance. "Skipper—"

"Don't call me Skipper. It's Skip."

"Skipper, I don't need a gun. I can find the information you're looking for. Actually it's quite simple."

What a horse's ass. "You can break into the office?"

"I can. You can be as sarcastic as you want, but I know something that you don't. I know something that very few people know."

That scared me. The fact that James had involved Styles scared me.

"Thomas LeRoy keeps an organizer."

"Yeah. I've watched him punch in the numbers. Stan the pizza man has one too." James had a smug look on his face. "So what does that prove?"

"They both keep all their notes on those organizers."

"Notes. Financial transactions." I was trying to hurry him along.

"Not just that. I told you. LeRoy also keeps track of every full-timer and the staff on that thing. He makes notes on people who work on the weekend revivals. You're in there I'm sure."

"So what's your point?"

"Both LeRoy and Stan download their organizers every night into a master computer."

"And?"

"That master computer is in the office."

"How is that supposed to help us?"

"I'm telling you, LeRoy probably wrote down the story about the tires, and if he did, he knows who shot them out. If he paid for the new ones," Styles pointed to the black beauties, "then he's got the info on who shot the other ones. My guess is, that person's going to have to pay Mr. LeRoy and Mr. Cashdollar back."

James's eyes rolled. It was obvious he was getting a little tired of his friend's arrogance and crazy stories.

I couldn't stand the arrogance either and verbally demonstrated it. "How do you know this? You were a one-weekend wonder. They asked you to leave the park. And now you claim to know more than almost anyone here?"

Styles hesitated, staring at his fingers. "I'm in that organizer."

James shook his head, obviously tired or bored with this conversation. "Let's move on."

"James, I can't tell you how I know, but I know. You get into that computer and you'll find out why they're after you."

We had one more day. Sunday. One more day and we could walk away with the kind of money James said we would make. The new tires were a gift. They more than made up for the old ones that were shot out. James made back the money that was stolen from us by playing poker. We weren't out anything, and by next year, I was hoping we wouldn't need to do this carney game again. So why didn't I just pack it in? Why didn't I just tell them I was out? Two reasons.

First of all, James is my best friend, and he wanted more information. He'd leveled with me. I knew up front he wanted information on how Cashdollar succeeded, he wanted the blueprint of success and neither James nor I had ever been this close to success before. He wanted to take advantage of that. James wanted information on who these characters were, and why someone had taken our money and shot out the tires. And, he wanted to know if anyone in this organization had the balls to commit murder. Multiple murders. And finally, I think James wanted revenge. Revenge on whoever had messed around with us.

Second of all, Em drove in at that exact moment, and I'd promised her I'd show her around. I should have jumped in her red T-bird, told her to head northwest, and said adios to Cashdollar and company. But I didn't. The world is full of should-haves.

CHAPTER TWENTY-FIVE

She looked great, in a pair of red shorts and white halter top, her blond hair looking just a little wind-blown. Styles couldn't stop staring as she stepped from the car.

"Jesus. She looks better now than she did in school, and in school she was —"

"She was what?" I glared at him.

"Smokin'."

She saw the three of us watching her and smiled. Maybe for effect, maybe for our afternoon delight, maybe because she'd really missed me for three months, Em walked over and planted a really juicy kiss on my lips.

"Em." James nodded.

"James." Frosty. I think if I left the two of them alone for a couple of hours, the freeze would thaw, would turn hot. I didn't plan on letting it happen.

"So," she smiled at me, her eyes shining, "what are the plans?"

The fading daylight caught her silhouette and I knew what plans I'd like to make. But there was James, and I had to help my partner. "You and I need to talk."

I took her hand and we walked up by the tent. She gazed at the yellow monster. "So this is where the magic takes place?"

"Isn't that usually a line from a rapper on TV when they take a tour of his house and they enter the bedroom? The rapper will say, 'and this is where the magic happens.'"

"I know. I've seen the shows." She looked into my eyes and I thought I might have a heart attack. "Well?" She squeezed my hand. "From what I hear, you get screwed in this tent too."

"Cute." The response and the girl. "There's some truth to the magic." I told her about the *Meet And Greet* boys, and I could see she was impressed. "And you should have seen James when Cashdollar dropped by and suggested that we could be the next billionaires."

"He really said that?"

"He did. However, he also asked us to leave and not come back."

"He told you to vacate the premise? I can't believe that. Come on, Skip. He really asked you to leave?"

"No." I was overly negative. And, I thought, for good reason. "He said 'obviously this business isn't for everybody.'"

She gave me a hard look. "Well, it's not."

She was right. It wasn't.

"It's just been a rough couple of days."

"And James wants to settle some scores?" Now a quizzical expression. She had a face that could change in a split second. And she could see right through me.

"Well, I think he wants to know who's threatening us."

"Skip, you're twenty-five-year-old guys. You've never been in a fight in your life to my knowledge." She paused. "Well, you got your asses kicked in that Cuban thing, but other than that—" She trailed off.

Asses kicked? We'd about got our lives snuffed out. The first of James's truck episodes. But that's another story.

151

Looking down the path that led to the nightly poker game she said, "You're new to the real world, and here you are playing with con men, felons, billionaires. A little scary isn't it? Don't you think you might be out of your league?"

"Maybe."

"There's no maybe about it. I'm just guessing here, but it seems to me these guys wouldn't even think twice about chewing you up and spitting you out if they thought you were in their way."

"Apparently they do."

"They do what?"

"Think we're in their way."

"Then leave. Right now. Pack up the truck, save yourself the five hundred dollars for tomorrow and go home. Or, better yet, stay tonight with me."

Now that was an offer worth considering. "I can still stay with you." God in heaven, she just made the offer. It's amazing how sex overpowers any other emotion. "But hold that thought. I sort of promised James that I'd hang around and see if I could find anything out."

Now she had the wild-eyed expression, that 'Skip, you dumb-ass' expression. I'd seen it before.

"What the hell do you expect to find out?"

And I realized, I didn't really have an answer.

"Come on. What do you think you're going to find."

"Well, if James has any balls, he's going to ask questions during the poker game. He's going to ask them if they know anything about the truck tires, about the money being stolen, and about the threatening letter."

"He won't. He doesn't have the balls, does he?"

"No."

"Then leave, Skip. We can go right now."

"I can't, Em."

"I should be pissed. I come back after three months, and it's the same old crap. You refuse to grow up."

"But?"

"But in a very strange way, I find it somewhat charming. Trust me, that won't last for long."

"Can it last just for tonight?"

"You really think these guys are crooked?"

"I think that Cashdollar and his crew may be responsible for three murders and another attempted murder this afternoon."

"Okay. So go to the cops."

"With what?"

She kicked at a loose stone, and walked away. Maybe ten feet. Then she spun around and looked at me. "Somebody has been following me ever since I dropped you off this afternoon."

"Following you?"

"I wasn't going to mention it."

"You weren't going to tell me? Why not?"

"Because maybe it doesn't concern you."

"And maybe it does."

"There's always that."

"What? Who?"

"A late model Cadillac."

"Now you sound like James."

"Please."

"Same car? Or did they switch? Are you sure you're being followed? I mean, maybe someone was just going the same way you were."

"Skip, I know what it's like to be followed. I've had several stalkers in my life."

I thought about that for a moment.

"You know, you almost get used to it. Some guys think it's their right to stalk a blond with a good figure. It happened in high school, it happened in college, and it happens now. It gets old, but I know when I'm being followed. I've been stared at, gawked at, ogled, and stalked. I know what it feels like, and I'm telling you with a great degree of certainty that I was being followed. No question about it, okay?"

I was working with the idea that other guys stalked her. How could I relate? "Because of us?"

"Two guys in their thirties, one black, one white."

"What does it mean? You think they're after you? Predators? They want to kidnap you?" I couldn't bring myself to say the rest of what I wondered.

"Could be. But I think it has something to do with you and James."

"So what do we do?"

"I don't know. I really wasn't going to tell you about it. But I do have the license number."

"Damn. You come back, and the first thing that happens is I involve you in —"

"In what? You don't even know what you're involved in."

I glanced over at the truck and James was watching us. The light from the sky had faded and he and Styles were standing by the truck, smoking cigarettes and apparently waiting for me to join them.

"So what are you, what are *we* going to do tonight?"

"Help Daron." I didn't want to tell her the rest.

"Help Daron what?" She knew something bad was coming. I could tell by the tone of her voice.

"You're not going to like it."

"I never do. However, it seems we've piqued someone's curiosity."

"Piqued?"

"I'd like to know why someone is following me. And I'd like to know why someone is threatening you."

"Well, we've got a plan."

She was getting impatient. "Skip, what is it?"

"Break into Cashdollar's office, go through Thomas LeRoy's computer, his files, and see if we can find any evidence."

"Jesus, Skip. You have lost your mind."

CHAPTER TWENTY-SIX

"We're not going to 'break in.' I mean, if we did breaking and entering, we'd do prison time." Styles tugged on the brim of his hat, finally pushing it back on his head. It seemed to me that the hat was an extension of his personality, whatever personality he had.

"I believe you either said that or certainly insinuated it." Making me look like an idiot in front of Em. To be fair, she already knew that.

"Listen, I understand what goes on back there. Usually, the security guy walks from midnight till maybe twelve thirty. That's it. He doesn't expect any trouble, he doesn't get any trouble. I would guess that the security man on the rev's office has never once — never once in all the time he's been doing this revival meeting — had to deal with someone who tried to break into the trailer. No money is kept in there. That's all taken to the bank and night deposited."

"So what are you saying?" James tapped his cigarette, knocking off the ash. I wished I had something to smoke, but Em frowned on it.

We all stopped talking as three people walked up the path, talking in low voices, and smoking cigarettes. A female voice laughed out loud, and when they passed, Daron responded.

"Whoever is patrolling parades back and forth in front of the office for half an hour, then goes into the trailer, stretches out on the office sofa, and spends the rest of the night sleeping. The appearance is of tight security, but whoever is in charge just crashes, leaves the door unlocked. It only locks with the padlock from the outside."

"You're kidding." I couldn't believe things were that lax.

"I'm sure it hasn't changed since the last time I was here."

"So you're suggesting —"

"That we wait until he's asleep, and we go in and see what we can find."

I studied him in the dim light. He was serious. "So, that's not a crime that will put us in prison?"

"Skipper, if the door is open, I consider it an invitation. If someone wakes up while we're there, we leave. Tell him we were looking for Thomas LeRoy. Tell him we were looking for a rent receipt."

"On LeRoy's computer?"

"It makes no difference. Here's a better idea. Have five hundred bucks on you and tell him you were going to drop it off on the desk for tomorrow's payment. Hell, he can't get mad if you were going to give them money."

He had a point.

Em rolled her eyes. "Boys, you could go to jail for what you're doing."

"Could." Daron smiled at her from under the brim of the hat. "Won't."

I realized I was dealing with a guy who walked out of airports with other people's stuff. Under the eye of Homeland Security, the airport cops, the TSA, and probably two or three other security companies I don't even know about. If anyone knew how to get away with shit, Daron Styles was the guy.

"I'm going down to play cards." James dropped the cigarette on the gravel and ground out the hot tobacco with the heel of his shoe. "You guys can handle the rev's trailer."

Was everyone crazy except Em and me?

"Skip? You okay with this?"

"No."

"We'll get it done. Look at the big picture, amigo."

"You've got money?" I thought I remembered giving him a stake. I still thought they would hand him his ass tonight, but there was no way to convince him. The game was fixed. I was sure of it.

"I've got enough, pard. I'll come back with another five hundred."

Daron shook his head. "They control the game, James."

"Last night, I was hot."

"You only win if they want you to."

"Bullshit."

Daron seemed to bristle. "Well, you live your fantasy. I've been in their games, and the full-timers don't ever let you win unless they want you to. Stan does some pretty impressive card tricks."

For the first time in my life I was impressed with Daron Styles.

James just smiled, flipped him the bird, turned, and walked down the path, whistling some tune. Whistling in the dark. The phrase was never more appropriate.

I wanted to say, "he's always right." But I didn't. The truth is James thinks he's invincible most of the time. And most of the time he is.

"It's about ten thirty, Skipper. We've got a couple of hours to kill."

I saw Em smile. I'm sure she was amused that Styles was calling me Skipper.

"So you think we can just walk into this trailer, and —"

"If we want to get a look at what's inside, that's the way to do it"

Em was tapping her fingers on the truck bed. An irritating rhythm.

"Just how are you going to break into this computer? On top of having someone with a gun inside the trailer, it seems highly likely that there's a code or password to get into the information you want."

She leaned in like she was trying to read his eyes, which were hidden under the narrow brim of his strange little hat.

"I've got it all worked out, little lady."

She didn't like that. I could tell by the steam coming from her ears. I don't think she liked the arrogance or the little lady quip. My turn to smile.

"How's that?"

He gave her a hard look. "I know the code. Took me a while, but I figured it out."

"You've done this before. What are you —"

"Skipper, I think it's important we get this information. Now if you don't want to know what's going on, I won't do it. If you want to find out, then just let me do my thing."

This guy was as cool and confident as anyone I'd ever met. And everything he did was illegal, immoral, and risky as hell. I was almost starting to see what James admired about him.

"What if we get caught? You haven't addressed that."

Styles reached into his shirt pocket and pulled out one of those little brown cigars. He took his time lighting it with a match.

"If we get caught, we cover."

And, as I pointed out, Daron Styles knew how to cover.

He'd been covering ever since I knew him. I pointed to Em.

"Tell him about the car."

"No. It's silly."

"You didn't think so a couple of minutes ago."

"What car?" Styles asked.

She shrugged. "Someone's following me."

"In a Cadillac."

"Does that have to do with this situation?"

Styles leaned up against the truck, flicking his cigarette butt into the dark.

"It didn't happen until I saw Skip this morning."

"You didn't recognize anyone?"

"No. I got the license."

"Give it to me."

She reached into her pocket and handed him a piece of paper. Without saying a word, Styles walked around the truck and I lost sight of him in a few seconds.

"What good is that going to do?" She looked up at me.

"I just think that everyone needs to put their cards on the table."

"Speaking of which, is James going to be all right by himself?"

"I'm sure he will be. There are six other guys down there. And when did you start worrying about James?"

"Skip, you told me there was a note that may have threatened your lives."

"I know. But I don't really think there's anything to it. It's a long way from shooting out someone's tires to killing someone."

She sat down on the wooden bench between the donut wagon and our truck. We didn't speak for a couple of minutes. Then, as quietly as he'd left, Styles reappeared, folding his cell phone and holstering it to his belt.

"FBI." He sat next to Em on the bench.

"What?"

"It's an FBI car."

"Em's car?"

"The car that's following her."

"Daron, why the hell is an FBI car following Em?"

"I have no idea. A guess, maybe. And I'm not supposed to know it's them, but there's no question about it. It's the FBI."

"As in the Federal Bureau of Investigation?" I wasn't sure that this made any sense.

"What do I have to do to convince you?"

Em spoke up. "Tell us why the FBI would follow me."

"I can only guess."

"Guess." I stared at him, tired of his games.

Styles pulled the hat down and peered out from under the brim.

"Three years ago, somebody gunned down a senator in Washington, D.C."

"We've been over that. Fred Long from Nebraska. Walking to a favorite lunch spot and somebody shot him. What does that have to do with Em?"

"Killing a senator constitutes a federal crime."

"And?" We almost said it together.

"It's federal, brother. That means the government gets involved. The FBI has jurisdiction and they've been watching this sideshow ever since."

Em looked at me for clarification.

"I told you, Em, there were rumors that Cashdollar was behind the killing of Fred Long."

Styles nodded. He was almost a shadow in the dark, but I could see his head bob up and down. "The FBI thinks it's more than a rumor."

"But," Em sounded totally confused, "why me? I've been gone for three months. I just got back."

"This shooting was three years ago." I waited for Styles to reply.

"It makes no sense." She sounded mad.

"Hey," Daron raised his voice. "You said guess. I'm guessing, okay?"

"Go ahead." I didn't want to stop him. Actually, some of what he was saying made sense.

"The Feds have been watching the rev's tent meetings for all this time. For three years. There were even some rumors that the FBI had planted an informant or two with the traveling troupe. The government thinks that the rev's rant on the senator was responsible for the murder. When I was here, selling my religious artifacts, there were subtle intrusions."

"Intrusions?" It was obvious Styles loved word games.

"Intrusions. The FBI kept monitoring the events. They'd occasionally send agents to record the services, interview people like Thomas LeRoy, stuff like that. It was pretty quiet, unobtrusive. But I think most of the people associated with this carnival know that they haven't given up. And, the FBI thinks that everyone who is new to this camp — this freak show — might be a link to the murder."

"New to the camp? Why wouldn't they look into all the old-timers? After all, this happened a while back."

"I think they're watching the old-timers, too. But if you're new, they're definitely interested in you."

"Why?"

"I don't know. Conspiracy stuff. Like maybe you worked on the outside, now you're working on the inside. Who knows what goes through the little brains these guys have? All I know is that the FBI watches anyone who works for the rev. I'm not guessing. That I know."

I studied his face in the fading light. I never knew how much to believe.

"Okay, but what about the shooting this morning? Somebody taking shots at Barry Romans? Explain that."

"Explain what?"

"That wouldn't be a federal crime."

"Doesn't matter now."

"Of course it matters."

Styles lit another brown cigar, the flame from his match dancing in the dark.

"Anything that might lead back to the senator's death is fair game."

"So the FBI can investigate anything they want to?"

"Son, they are the FBI."

"But why me?" Em looked at me. I shrugged my shoulders.

"Probably just curious. And you two were right near the shooting."

All this time I'd been thinking about Crayer being near the shooting. Em and I were there too. And Styles was telling me that a federal bureau was following my girlfriend because we had breakfast this morning? Or because I was new to the traveling freak show? Or maybe because she'd come back to town? It was too cryptic for me.

"My God, Daron," I was in awe of the situation we might be finding ourselves in, "you're telling me that it's possible I got Em roped into this because we are doing a three-day tent meeting? Selling burgers and brats is reason for the Federal Government to put a tail on us?"

"Friend," Daron stood up from the bench, "you asked me to guess."

"With some degree of certainy." Em spoke up.

"I have no degree of anything."

Truer words had never been spoken.

"All right," I urged him on. "You sound like you know one helluva lot about this for a guy who just spent one three-day meeting with these guys."

"Yeah, I know," he sighed. "But I don't want this to get out." He took a puff on the cigar and the hot tobacco burned brighter. "I had a visit from a guy when I worked here. On the last day he convinced me that I didn't want to work here any more. He suggested that if I had any outside relationships with the rev and his crew, I break it off with them. He suggested that his organization was looking into the possibility that I was involved in the Washington murder."

"That's crazy," I said. "They could easily check and see if you were in Washington at the time."

"Yeah."

"Well?"

"I was."

"Oh, shit."

"I'd been up there working the Georgetown area. Selling some knockoff bags and stuff. Actually, it was a pretty sweet deal. A bunch of us were making some really good scratch. We'd set up a folding table and two guys would do lookout. We could be gone in thirty seconds if we saw any cops or suits. Anyway, somehow they knew that I'd been in the D.C. area."

"So they threatened you?"

"I'd call it a threat. You see, I think they wanted me to know they suspected me. To see how I reacted. To see if I ran back to Thomas LeRoy or Cash, or whoever. I mean, it must have struck a chord with them—you know, me being in Washington, then me joining Cash and company."

And I wondered the same thing. Were we hanging with someone who could be a murderer? I wished James was back to hear this story.

"Once you quit, what happened? Did they keep checking on you?" Em was into it now.

"For a while. I'd see a car, catch somebody walking behind me. I didn't sell any knockoff shit for a couple weeks, because I thought they might arrest me for that."

I couldn't believe what I was hearing. "So it finally ended?"

"I think they realized I might be a lot of things, but I'm not a killer. Although, they desperately want to pin it on somebody."

"Well, neither of us was in Washington, D.C. three years ago." I'd never been there in my life. "We were still in school."

"That's not true, Skip." Em put her arm around my neck. "Daddy and I went to some hearings on contracting laws. It was in the summer of that year and I went along to keep him company. I'm pretty sure it was at the same time that the senator was shot."

"Unbelievable." I thought back, trying to remember Em being gone. Must have been a couple of weeks when we were out of touch.

"The car that followed Emily was owned by the FBI. I feel pretty certain that my visitor was from a government agency. Em, you and I were both in Washington that summer, so there's a good chance they're looking at you."

"You know, if I'd stayed away just another week, this crap never would have happened." She took her arm off my neck, stood up, and walked to the truck. She looked it up and down, touching it with her hand. "This damned truck of James's, it's already caused its share of problems hasn't it?"

"Em, it's not the truck."

"No. I know it. It's your roommate. I swear to God, Skip, he gets us into more hot water."

CHAPTER TWENTY-SEVEN

Em and I talked. It was late, and the feelings and the words came slowly. A little about where she'd been for the last three months. Mostly up in the panhandle, staying with a girlfriend. She was disappointed that I'd stayed with the security company. I couldn't blame her, I was disappointed too. We talked about her job with her father, and we talked about the future. Well, actually we discussed what tomorrow would bring. But in our relationship, it has always seemed to be one day at a time.

"How long are you going to hitch your wagon to James's star?"

I looked up and could see the stars, dazzling in the Florida sky. "I don't think that's fair."

"Skip, you're bright, you're intelligent —"

"I'm up to my ass in college loans. I have applied for other jobs, but with my grades and lack of experience, it just hasn't happened, Em." The same argument, the same answers. Emily is a rich bitch and she will never understand the other side of the tracks.

"And I'm still not sure what we're doing here. We could get into so much trouble."

I shrugged my shoulders. "Daron is the one going in. We'll simply stand outside and be the lookouts."

"Still—"

"You were followed by the FBI."

"We're to believe that scumbag, Daron Styles? Jeez, Skip, do you remember him in high school? He was a liar, a cheat—"

"Yeah. And you wouldn't believe what he's up to now."

"Don't even tell me."

I didn't. I would have lost my lookout partner if I had.

"The stuff he said makes sense. You know it, I know it. The fact that you really were in Washington, it's enough to be concerned that they're checking you out."

"Being checked out by the FBI—"

Styles came walking back from the Buick, carrying a shoe box. "Hey, Em. Know anything about Loeffler Randall shoes?"

"What?"

"About the value of Loeffler Randall shoes?" He opened the box and showed her these high-heeled somethings with a thin ankle strap.

"What are you doing with women's shoes?"

Styles looked at me and I frowned and shook my head. He hesitated, watching me closely. "Oh, nothing. I just sort of found them and wondered if they had any value." He waited for an answer, and when he got none he tossed the box into the truck. "Well, I'd say it's about time we stroll back to the trailer and see if our security guy has decided to call it a night."

I kept thinking about Dusty, the full-timer, the ex-school teacher, the gun-toting security guy from the other end of the path. Maybe they switched off and Dusty was security for the office.

Styles leaned into me, a little closer, and whispered. "Some really good stuff in those bags. Three, maybe four hundred bucks on eBay. Find out about those shoes. Okay?"

We acted like we were just out for a one o'clock stroll. Actually, I figured if anyone saw us they'd know in a heartbeat that we were there to break into Cashdollar's office. I was sweating, glancing in every direction, and wishing like crazy I hadn't involved Em. She was right. I got into some really bad scenarios because of my best friend. I mean, here I was doing what could arguably be called the dumbest thing I'd ever done, and not only was it sheer stupidity, but I was dragging Em right along.

"I hope you find something, Daron."

She sounded almost excited, like it was an adventure.

He whispered, softly. "He keeps a record. Of everything that goes on." Glancing back at me he said, "The incident with the tires? That will be in the computer. He may even write down why they shot them out, and who shot them out. I've just got to see if I can find everything."

"This record of things that happened," I whispered back, "I don't understand why he keeps it. And I really question whether it's that accessible. I mean if this stuff is damaging to Cashdollar, he's not going to leave it so you can break in and steal it."

"My friend, trust me."

"I don't."

"In this case, Skipper, I know what I'm talking about. He's got it all written down. And I told you, he's got Stan's notes too. I think he feels that he needs it as security." He paused for a long time, and we all stopped walking.

"Security?" I had to ask the question.

"I think he's afraid that the rev may take a hike. And if someone starts looking into the entire mess, I don't think that LeRoy wants to be involved. Any more than he has to be."

"He could bargain his way out, with a diary filled with this information?"

"Come on guys." Styles pointed his finger at me. "Can't you quit putting words in my mouth? I told you, I'm guessing."

Softly, she spat the words. "Bullshit. You said there might be information about you in this electronic notebook. You know exactly what they're doing. Don't you? You're not guessing."

"Yeah." I needed to stand up for Em. "Why the hell would he write about *you*, and what did he say?"

Styles was quiet. He sucked on his tobacco, my God he smoked a lot, and seemed to be pondering the situation.

"I told you that Michael Bland was a full-timer?"

Em gave me a questioning look.

"Yeah."

"Well, when he died of a drug overdose he had quite a bit of money on him. His winnings from the poker game."

I just wished he'd get to the point.

"So, I got word the next day that I was being accused of taking the money."

It all started to fall into place. The poker group had figured out that Styles was a scam artist, and it made sense that he would be the one to steal the money. But off a dead body?

"So, the next day, after the cops left, Stan, Henry, and Sailor came to see me. I had a little tent, and they pulled the flap back and asked me to come out."

"Threatening?" Em seemed to be more engrossed than before.

"Not at first. It was just after dinner that night, and I'd had quite a bit of business. I thought they were asking me to come down early to the poker game."

"That wasn't it?"

"No." Styles gazed at the trailer, as if anxious to get inside and find the fabled computerized records.

"What was it?" I needed to know. If I was putting myself on the line, I wanted an answer.

"I came out and they surrounded me. First of all, Stan said they were concerned about my background. I told him I was concerned about theirs too. That didn't go over too well. I could tell I'd pissed them off."

"Never pays to be a smart-ass when there are three to one."

"No. Then Henry, who is usually real laid back, says, 'Did you have anything to do with Michael's drug overdose?'"

"And you said?"

"Of course I said no. I'd seriously thought that his group, the full-timers, may be responsible."

Styles had been with the group for two days. He'd already figured out they were capable of murder? Then it hit me. In two days, James and I had come to the same conclusion. This could be a group capable of almost anything.

"So Sailor, who never says a thing, walks up and literally bumps my chest with his and says 'Where's the money?'"

"They thought you killed this guy and took his money?"

"I was the new guy. They didn't know me. The other vendors who weren't full time had been there more than once. The other guys were local, trusted, and the full-timers knew who they were. I was the one they didn't trust."

We were whispering, but getting louder. Em shushed us, putting her finger to her lips.

"Somebody may be guarding this place or listening. Let's keep it down."

Softer now. "Anyway, I tried to move away but they wouldn't let me. They kept crowding my space. They wanted to come in and search the tent."

"For?"

"What do you mean 'for'? For drugs and money."

"So what happened?" Em asked.

"I was getting a little noisy, hoping someone would come out of his tent or camper and scare these three guys away."

"Didn't happen?" I asked.

"No. Not right away."

"So what happened?" Em was in his face, asking her same question again, anxious to get to the end of this tense story.

"They told me they believed I may have had something to do with this guy's death. And they thought I probably lifted his cash. He'd been found not more than twenty yards from my tent."

"Did they threaten you?" I needed to know.

"That's when they said that this entire scenario was being recorded in Thomas LeRoy's electronic diary. His organizer. And that I should leave and never return."

"So you got thrown out by the vendors and the FBI? No wonder Cashdollar gave you a nasty look. Nobody wanted you back here."

"Yeah. But it's a free country, Skipper."

"It may be, but you certainly take advantage of it."

He smiled at me. "I'll admit it. I do."

We were all quiet for two minutes. I was even more aware that we were in deep shit. And James was down at the poker game, with these threatening people, probably losing his ass.

"So," Em wanted closure. "Did they ever find out who killed him?"

Styles shook his head. "No. There's never been anyone even suspected to my knowledge. Other than me, and they had absolutely nothing to go on when they looked at me. You want my guess?"

"If that's the best we can do."

"I figure it was one of the full-timers. He'd done something to piss them off. I'm not sure what, but they wanted him gone. This guy wasn't a drug user. At all. He very seldom even drank."

I tried to grasp the entire story. "And yet—"

"He died of an overdose. Somebody set him up. No question." I saw Styles pull his hat down over his forehead.

"Which one did it?"

"Skipper, I told you. This is all a guess."

"Who?"

"One of them who didn't show up at my tent. I think who-ever it was sent them up to talk to me."

It was obvious that he was getting anxious to go into the trailer. But not to find out if Em was in LeRoy's computer. Not to find out about the FBI. He wasn't going in to see who shot our tires out. Styles wanted to know what had been said about him regarding the death of Michael Bland. He wanted to know if Thomas LeRoy had actually accused him of being a murderer in the precious, tell-all computer diary.

"So, did they search your tent?"

"No. I'm not sure why. I thought for sure they'd come into the tent and tear it up. Maybe they were afraid the people around me would start to be suspicious about what was going on. Maybe they figured I would have covered up any evidence. I don't know. But they gave me the warning and walked away."

If they already knew who had killed Bland, they would have no reason to search Styles's tent. Whatever had happened, it had happened a long time ago and by now any evidence had probably disappeared. I asked the question casually. I didn't want to sound accusatory. "You never saw these notes that Stan and LeRoy took?"

"No."

"But you're sure they exist?"

"I'm sure."

"And you don't know for sure what these documents say about you?"

"This has nothing to do with me."

I didn't believe that for a minute. I looked at Em, in the dark shadows, and I could tell she wasn't buying into it either.

"I want to find out what they know about you two. And James."

"And you're not interested in knowing what LeRoy says about you?" Em called him on it.

"Maybe, a little."

"Uh-huh."

I realized something else had to be addressed. It was important. "Daron, one more question."

He was digging his toe into the damp dirt, his eyes watching the trailer. The padlock was hanging off the latch and the structure appeared to be open.

"Did you kill Michael Bland?"

He did a double take, snapping to attention. "Holy shit, no. Where did you ever come up with that idea?"

"I had to ask. I don't know for sure who I'm dealing with."

"Ah, I take a couple bags at the airport. I sell some stolen stuff now and then, but kill somebody? Are you crazy?"

I was glad I'd asked. Just by his reaction, I was pretty sure he was telling me the truth. Of course, with Styles, you never knew.

Em cleared her throat. She put her hand on my arm. "Daron, I have a question too."

"Shoot. But make it a short one. I want to get in there and see if I can find this thing." He seemed to brace himself.

"Okay. Here goes. Yes or no question."

"Those I can answer."

"Did you take his money?"

In the dark there were crickets, the call of a night bird, and the gentle lapping of water coming from the Intracoastal Waterway. In the distance I could hear a boat horn, a long mournful moaning sound.

"Daron?"

"Whose money?"

"Don't play with me. Michael Bland's money?"

Back to digging his toe into the moist earth. "Yep. I did."

CHAPTER TWENTY-EIGHT

When I was about twelve, I found a wallet with a couple of bucks in it. That was it. Two bucks. The wallet was on a park bench and I figured it had probably worked its way out of some guy's pocket. I didn't bother to see who the wallet belonged to, I just slipped the two dollars out and put them in my pocket. My first heist.

I remember the situation because about twenty minutes later I went back to the bench to put the two dollars back. I had a bad guilt complex and decided I needed to return the stolen loot. The wallet was gone.

"I've got to get into the trailer. Hell, we stand here and talk all night and it'll be morning before I get it done." Daron pointed to the trailer/office. "I'm going to get some answers tonight."

"You stole a dead guy's money?" I thought the park bench incident was bad enough.

"Look, I didn't say that. I'll fill you in on all of the details later. Right now, are you two going to stand guard? All you've got to do is give me a signal if someone is coming."

I wish I'd never asked the question.

Em shook it off. "What's the signal?"

"Start a conversation. Just pretend that you guys can't sleep, you're out walking and you start talking—loud, so I can hear you."

I looked at Em and she shrugged her shoulders. Kind of like, what the hell. We're here, we may as well pitch in. Like she was game for anything. I was still thinking about Styles taking the money off of a dead man. And the fact that the Federal Bureau of Investigation was checking out my girlfriend.

Styles put his finger to his lips and walked softly to the trailer. He stepped up on the wooden landing and the wood creaked under his weight. We all froze for a second. Then Styles gently tried the door. The moon gave us just enough light so we could see him ease the door open.

A soft light spilled from the entranceway and I could see a dim lamp burning on what appeared to be a small wooden table. I watched Styles look both ways, then he turned to us, gave us a thumbs-up, and pulled the door behind him, leaving just a small opening. Hopefully enough of an opening that he could hear us if we had to start talking. Loudly.

Em took my hand and squeezed it. Then she let go and motioned to me. We walked several yards from the trailer.

"You get into the damnedest predicaments."

"You were the one being followed by the FBI."

"I hope your buddy finds out why."

"Daron?" We were whispering, and my throat was getting raspy. You can't whisper too long before it irritates the vocal chords.

"Yeah. Daron."

"He's not my buddy. He may be James's buddy, but he's not mine."

She was quiet for a moment. "He took the money off of a dead guy? That's sick."

"It's better than killing the guy."

175

"I guess, but not by much." Em looked up and down the grounds. "There's no sign of anyone standing guard."

"No. Remember, he said the trailer guard usually crashes on the couch. He's probably asleep in there."

"And if he wakes up and finds Daron working on their computer?"

I didn't want to consider that.

"Styles will have to deal with it."

"And, Skip. What was the deal with the shoes?"

"The shoes?"

"Daron brings me designer shoes and wants to know the value? What was that strange scene all about?"

"Oh, yeah. That's another story."

"You're just full of stories, aren't you? You and your friends." She gave me an impish smile.

She was here because of me. I was here because of — probably James. And Daron was keeping the whole thing alive, with a bunch of stories that had a ring of truth to them. But with Styles, who knew?

"Tell me the story about the shoes. What's he got? A foot fetish? Come on, I've got time. What else are we going to do?"

"Um, it's not something you want to know about right now."

"No?"

"No."

"Don't do this to me."

"Em, I'll tell you later."

"Oh, I'll probably figure it out anyway. But if he asks again —"

"Asks what?"

"The value."

"Yeah?"

"The value of Loeffler Randall shoes."

I'd never heard the name. But I wasn't a student of feminine footwear. "Loeffler Randall shoes?"

"If he asks the value —"

"What?"

"About three hundred seventy-five dollars."

"Wow."

"They're quality shoes. Think *Sex and the City*."

Em cried when they cancelled *Sex and the City*.

"Okay, I'll give him the price."

"Maybe half that on eBay."

CHAPTER TWENTY-NINE

Em had fallen asleep, stretched out on the damp ground, cradling her head in her folded arms. I was sitting next to her, watching her, her diaphragm rising and falling with her soft breath. Her blond hair spilled over her arms and I thought about watching her all night long. I truly believe I could have. I was still wondering how I'd gotten into this situation. James was probably right. It was the questions I'd asked. And the fact that I knew about Cabrina Washington. I'd met the girl. For some reason, that meeting and my questions had triggered a response. Possibly my meeting and questions were the reason that we were all in a situation that no one seemed to understand.

There was no breeze, just the heat and humidity, and I could feel sweat running down my back. My T-shirt was wet, and there was a thin layer of perspiration on my face. I strained to hear any unusual sounds, but the droning of some insects, the call of an occasional bird, and Em's breathing were all I could pick up.

I may have dozed. I hope that wasn't the case. I'd like to think that I was a little more alert than that. I'd like to think that if I am asked to participate, I participate with everything in me, but the truth is, I may not be as reliable as I should be. Chalk it up to youth, or maybe too many beers during college. All I know is that Styles was standing above me, tapping me on the shoulder and I hadn't seen or heard anything.

"Hey, Skipper, let's get out of here."

It only took a second to shake off the cobwebs. I reached down and touched Em on the cheek. She shivered and opened her eyes. Even in the dark, I could see the first sign of confusion. Then she shook the webs off too.

"Come on."

"What did you find?"

"You're in the notes."

"What?"

"Back to your truck. Quick."

I was struggling to get up.

"I'm what?"

"You're on the computer. Look, there's a little explanation, but basically LeRoy thinks you and James are plants."

I couldn't figure it out. Plants? My mother had plants in the kitchen window. James had a fake palm tree that someone had given him, sitting in the living room window in our postage-stamp apartment. What the hell kind of plant was I?

"Plants?"

Styles extended his hand, I grabbed it and he pulled me into an upright position. "The full-timers think you and James are plants. They think the cops or the FBI planted you to get information on the murder of the senator."

No. Was he crazy?

"Are you crazy?"

"No. They may be crazy. I'm not."

"Daron, they can't be serious."

"Damn it, let's get the hell out of here."

"Plants?"

"Please! Move."

I was with him. The last thing I wanted to do was spend another night in this park. The sooner we debriefed, the faster we could get out of here and spend the night in a real bed. I realized it was late. James would have been back by now, the card game would have been finished a couple of hours ago. "Were you mentioned?"

"It's not important."

"Were you? Did Thomas LeRoy identify you as the guy who killed Bland? The guy who took his money?"

"Yeah. He did. He said they thought I was a prime suspect. Now, would you get your girlfriend so we can get out of here?"

Em staggered to her feet, and we stumbled around the tent, for all the world looking like two drunks trying to find their way home. And we hadn't had a drink. Not one beer.

I pulled her, hurrying her along. If someone was going to wake up and start screaming "thief," I didn't want to be anywhere nearby. We started jogging, and reached the far end of the tent. I stopped and took in long, painful breaths. Too many beers, not enough exercise. We caught our breath, and as we made the turn, I looked around to see if Daron was following. There was no one.

"Where's Daron?" Em slowed down. She glanced behind us.

"Daron?" I whispered in a loud, raspy voice.

There was no sound.

"My God, Skip. Do you think they found him?"

I ducked back around the corner of the tent, and quietly walked down the length, smelling the wet, stale odor of the large, damp canvas. I struggled to see in the dark, staring hard in the direction we'd come. In the distance I could see what looked like three people. The two on the outside appeared to be walking, the person in the middle was being dragged.

CHAPTER THIRTY

From the time I was probably six years old, I wondered what I'd do in the case of an emergency. Would I look out for myself? Would I step into the path of a bully to save a friend? When I was a little older I wondered if I would jump in the water to save a drowning child or stand there looking in horror as the body was washed downstream. And when I got much older, especially when I started dating Em, I wondered what I would do if we were accosted in a dark alley. Would I let it happen or step up and risk having a knife shoved in my ribs?

I don't believe too many people are ever put in that position. I was, once before, and I can tell you that every situation isn't the same. Em appeared at my back, and the two of us watched as the three people disappeared in the dark. I looked at her, tempted to start running, trying to save Styles.

"What just happened?"

"Em, I don't know. Somebody figured out he'd broken into the trailer?"

"And why aren't we trying to get him back?" She threw her hands up.

"Maybe because we know that if it's the full-timers, they have guns. Maybe it's because we don't know what the hell he's gotten himself into."

"Let's at least see if we can see where they're taking him."

Of course she was right. We walked quickly, trying to catch a glimpse of them, but the dark had swallowed any sign of the three.

"They could have gone to the camper village or one of the trailers or trucks. We have no idea."

I shook my head.

"It happened so fast. We didn't have a chance to see what happened." She took my hand and squeezed it again. "Skip, I've always wondered what I'd do in a situation like this."

"I understand. As you said, it happened way too fast."

"So, what do we do?"

There was only one thing to do. Find James. If Styles was in trouble, we were all in trouble. If Styles was on the computer, and we were on the computer, the situation was not good.

"We've got to get James."

"Are you sure that's a good idea?" Em questioned me.

"No."

"No, you don't think we should get him?"

"No. I don't think it's a good idea. Yes, we've got to find him." As far as I was concerned there was no choice. I needed to know if he was okay.

"James and I have our differences."

"I know, Em. I'm in the middle of many of them."

She smiled. I could see it even in the dark. "But I'd miss him if something happened to him."

I thought about it for a second or two. There was absolutely nothing we could do for Styles. But with any luck James had stayed late. Maybe he was still playing cards and they hadn't done anything to him. Yet. "Let's check the truck. The poker game should have ended about midnight. That's when they start with the security detail."

"What time is it?"

I strained to see my watch. "One thirty."

James wasn't in the truck.

"How about the card game? Maybe he stayed late? Had a couple of beers with the guys." I motioned toward the path.

We jogged down. I was feeling a lot of guilt leaving Styles to fend for himself, but I had no idea where they'd taken him. We were both out of breath in the short run to the pizza wagon. I'd preferred the exercise we'd had earlier in the day at Em's condo.

We slowed down as we got closer, and I noticed everything appeared to be dark. The poker table was empty. There was no sign of anyone, but a cigar still burned in an ashtray. Cigars go out if no one is puffing on them, so I guessed that someone, or a group of someones, had been there recently. Possibly they had gotten word that security had been breached. And if they knew that Daron had broken into the office and gotten into the computer, then anything was possible. They would probably know immediately that James and I were involved.

"This isn't good."

"So I'm asking again. Do you think James is okay?"

I rolled my eyes. "When it comes to James, I quit thinking a long time ago."

Em sat down on the one of the folding chairs, watching the smoke from the burning tobacco rise in a perfect spiral. "Daron says that these guys think you're working for the FBI?"

"He claimed that was in the notes on the computer."

"And the FBI was following me?"

"Again, that's what Daron said. I think it goes without saying that Daron can't be trusted one hundred percent of the time."

"But if he's right, if the FBI was following me today, and if you worked for them —"

"What? You're making no sense."

"Oh, my God. Skip. Maybe you're working for them."

I stepped back. Emily had lost her mind.

"Are you crazy?"

"No. I'm not. Who set this up? Who decided to take this job? Come on, Skip, who talked you into this?"

"You know who."

"Skip. Who convinced you to stay, even when someone shot the tires out of your truck? Even when you got a note threatening your life? Who?"

"You know who. But, Em it's—"

"No, no. Hear me out. Maybe he *is* working for the FBI. Maybe they offered him some good money to take this job, infiltrate the full-timers and see what he could find out. Wasn't that exactly what he was going to do tonight? He was going to ask questions and find out what was going on. Well? Wasn't that the plan?"

"Yeah, but—"

"No buts, Skip. Didn't he figure out that you needed Daron? Daron, who knew the inner workings of this organization?"

"Yeah, but—"

"Wouldn't it make sense that somebody like the FBI was behind giving him the information on Daron's history? The fact that Daron Styles had worked for Cashdollar?"

"I don't think—"

"That's just it. You said when it comes to James, you gave up thinking. Isn't that what you said? You said when it came to James, you gave up thinking a long time ago."

"I may have said that, but—"

"Damn it, Skip. *They* think you're working for the FBI. The full-timers think you are. How do you know that—"

"We're not. It's as simple as that. Anyway, think about it.

James isn't bright enough to pull that off without me knowing about it. He hates anything to do with law enforcement."

"And then, then the FBI starts following my car as soon as I hook up with you. What's that all about? Maybe they were outside the door when we —"

"You are crazy. In the last three months, you must have lost your mind."

Em stood up and took my hand. "I hope I'm crazy. Because this whole thing is very strange, and it sure has the feel of James pulling the strings."

CHAPTER THIRTY-ONE

James was my best friend. He'd stood up for me when I had problems, and I'd stood up for him. I had learned that I would put myself in jeopardy to save James. And I was damned sure that I'd put my life on the line for Em. But Styles? I don't think so. Although, as we walked back toward the truck, I realized he'd put himself on the line for us. Even though a lot of his motivation was to see if *he* was mentioned in the diary. There was some selfishness in his reasoning.

"What will they do to him?"

"Who? Styles? Or James?"

"You don't really think they have James?"

I didn't. I was sure by now he was back at the truck.

"If he asked all those questions, if they think he's part of the FBI—"

"Oh, God. He doesn't know that. James has no idea what Styles found on that computer." He needed to know. Desperately needed to know.

"It's not like we've seen him to tell him. Settle down. I'm sure he'll be all right."

She'd regained her composure and seemed to hold my hand even tighter.

There was a dim light on in the truck. We had a lamp that was powered by our generator and I could see it as we got closer. The giant tent stood black against the horizon, like a huge thundercloud in the nighttime sky. We walked a little faster.

"It looks like somebody's home."

A shadowy figure stepped out into the path and Em and I froze.

"A little late for a stroll, isn't it?"

Bruce Crayer.

"Where are you two headed?"

I could see his arm hanging at his side, and I was certain he was holding a pistol.

Em spoke up. "To Skip's truck. We were just going to get some things together and leave."

Crayer didn't move. Neither did we.

"You gonna take the truck? Are you pulling out for the rest of the show?"

I hadn't thought about it. If we took the truck, we could get out of Dodge and never return. If Em took me home, either to my place, or her place, James and I would have to come back and get the truck. And James had visions of selling more lunches and dinners tomorrow. Sunday. The busiest day of the revival meeting. And where the heck was James?

"No." I didn't want him to think I was considering cut-and-run. And I didn't want to introduce him to Em. We were in enough trouble already. I didn't want to give him any ammunition.

"So, did you hear what happened tonight?" Still standing there with his arms by his side. I was tempted to brush right past him. Keep on walking.

"What happened?"

187

"You don't know?"

Oh, I knew. "I wouldn't be asking if I knew."

He glared at me. "Somebody broke into the rev's office."

"Broke in? Like picked a lock? Broke the door?"

He hesitated. I couldn't see his face that well in the dark, but he seemed to be staring intently at me. Finally he muttered, "Something like that."

"Well, look. We've got to get our stuff and leave. The night's not getting any younger." I started to move.

"Did you hear what I said?"

"I did. I'm sorry."

Crayer was swinging that arm now and I was positive it was a gun. "Where were you half an hour ago?"

Where were we? Oh yeah. Playing lookout for Styles while he rifled through Thomas LeRoy's computer. "We just took a walk. That's all." I took another step.

"Hold it. I want to know where you were walking."

"I, we, um . . ."

"Who is the girl?" It was as if he'd noticed her for the first time. Again, I didn't want to give him any more ammunition.

"This is . . . my sister. She's just in town, visiting and—"

Em took two steps forward, letting go of my hand. Then she took a third step, now in Crayer's face.

"What? You're accusing us of breaking into someone's office? I think Skip just told you that we took a walk. A simple walk. Down the path, up the path. We were looking for James, but apparently the poker game broke up."

Crayer backed up two steps. I backed up two steps. All I could think of was Crayer raising that arm with the pistol. I was scared for Em, scared for myself.

"Have you seen James?"

He kept staring at Em, like he was trying to figure out her role in this caper.

"No. He played poker, lost a lot of money, and left."

Em stared right back at him. "If you'll kindly get out of the way, we'll get our things and leave. Please, step aside."

He seemed frozen in place.

"Now." Her voice was firm. Very firm.

And you know what? He did. He stepped aside.

Be bold. A lesson from Em. He'd stepped out of her way as she barreled past him, heading for our truck. I took several steps, then turned and stared at him. "I don't appreciate being accused of breaking and entering. And I want to know if you've got any idea where James is."

He scowled. "I told you. No. Actually, I was back behind the tent, going through the office. They think whoever broke in may have stolen something."

"Money?"

"I don't think so. We don't keep money there." A disgusted tone of voice. I think he was amazed that a woman had backed him down. "So you weren't back there? Right?"

"She told you, we took a walk."

He seemed to purse his lips, mumbled something under his breath, turned, and walked away.

I quickly walked to the truck, finding Em sitting on the rear of the bed. She was breathing heavy and when I touched her arm, it was damp with a layer of perspiration.

"You were something. You called his bluff. Way to go."

"God, Skip. He had a gun. He knows we were back there with Daron."

"You're shaking."

"What do you want me to do? He had a gun. I called *his* bluff? *I* was all bluff. I figured any minute he was going to either shoot me or grab me from behind in a chokehold."

"Didn't happen, babe."

She shuddered. "Where is your damned roommate?"

I didn't want to think about what might have happened to James. They'd nailed Daron and now James was missing. I wasn't sure what else could happen tonight, but so far our batting average was about zero.

CHAPTER THIRTY-TWO

When we were younger, we had a couple of run-ins with the cops. Nothing serious. It was more a case of somebody in uniform giving James and me a warning for acting like kids. One time we shoplifted some candy, and once we got caught sneaking a video camera into a movie theater. James was going to film the movie and sell videos. That didn't happen. Anyway, I knew James's feelings about the police. He didn't care for them at all. Sometimes we'd drive by a cop car and I could feel him bristle. He was careful to avoid them at all costs. Since he'd been an adult, I don't think he'd ever even gotten a speeding ticket. So it's hard to picture a situation where I'd ever call the cops or alert any law enforcement agency regarding James.

"Skip, maybe we should call the police."

"What? Why?"

She gave me that wide-eyed stare that she's perfected over the years. "Maybe because we saw Daron being hauled away?"

"Em, Daron broke into Cashdollar's office."

"To help *us*."

I had serious doubts about that. "It's a crime. We're going to call the cops and turn him in?"

"Skip, you told me, these guys are capable of killing someone."

"It's only a theory, Em. There's obviously no proof. If there was, they'd be in jail by now."

"Well, then, how about the fact that your roommate seems to have mysteriously disappeared."

I thought about that. Crayer said he didn't know James's whereabouts. And he'd apparently been on guard duty most of the late evening. I also thought about the fact that somebody had abruptly left the poker table. Probably after the game, since they seemed to start guard duty after everyone had played the game. But someone had left abruptly nevertheless. Somebody had gotten word that security had been breached. I could picture the half-smoked lit cigar in the ashtray.

"Well?"

"No. You know how James feels about the cops."

"So what do we do? If we don't call the cops, what do we do? Skip, Daron got hauled away and James is missing. Think about it."

I thought for a moment. We couldn't very well leave the grounds. James was here. And I did feel somewhat conflicted about Styles. Em was right. The guy found out some important information regarding our status. Crayer must have known that we were suspected of being FBI informants. Maybe that's why he let us go. And if they thought James was working for the FBI, what would they do with him? Hopefully they'd let him go too. But according to Styles, the last informant died of a drug overdose. And if I found James with a needle in his arm, I'd have a good idea where to start looking.

"Should we look for him?"

I thought about what she'd said. That maybe James had

actually signed on to work for the FBI, accepting money and putting us both at risk. James was a piece of work, and capable of just about anything, but first of all he wouldn't do that to me, and second of all, he wouldn't work for anybody in law enforcement. Couldn't happen.

"Yeah. Let's take another walk. We've got to do something."

She nodded. "You know, Skip, you're probably right. James would never work for the FBI. In any capacity."

It scared me when she mirrored me like that.

"That leaves the question, why was he so insistent in trying to get to the bottom of this. Is he just stubborn? Bullheaded? Somebody shot his tires out and tried to get him to leave and he's stupid enough to stay and get in their face?"

"Yes. On all accounts."

She thought about that for a moment. "And we're even dumber."

"I'm guessing."

"There's one more thing we need to address." She tugged on my arm as she jumped off the back of the truck.

"What's that?"

"We're blindly following James, right? You agree?"

"Not necessarily 'blindly.' I'd like to get to the bottom of what happened. Why they think we're working for the FBI. Why Cabrina Washington was killed. Why Crayer was in South Beach when the shooting occurred today."

"All right. Not blindly. But Skip, there's one other thing we're not dealing with."

"Probably more than one thing."

"Daron."

"While we're looking for James—"

"It's not even that. You don't trust Daron, do you?"

"Not at all."

"But he broke the law to help us out."

"True. I think he was helping himself as well."

"So now we're somewhat obligated to him."

"Sort of."

"What if he lied?"

"What do you mean?"

"You don't trust him. You know he's a scam artist. He's obviously selling stolen shoes and who knows what else, yet you blindly believe him when he says the car was FBI. You blindly believe him when he tells you that you're on the computer accused of being a plant."

"You think he made it up?"

"I think he could have."

"To what end?"

"Maybe he works for the full-timers. Maybe he's trying to scare you off. You know, it makes sense. It makes sense that the FBI would be following this little sideshow because there's a chance that someone here had something to do with the killing of a senator. That part makes sense."

I agreed. How the hell had we surrounded ourselves with these people and gotten into this situation? It was like a fantasy. A fantasy nightmare.

"But what if there really is an FBI informant?"

"It's not us. We've determined that James would never do that."

"What if it's Daron Styles?"

Now I hadn't thought of that.

CHAPTER THIRTY-THREE

They weren't going to get two of us without a fight.

"We're safe if we stick together." I wasn't at all sure that was true, but saying it made me feel better.

The first place I thought about was the big yellow tent. We walked in, trying to see anything in the cavernous canvas interior. It was almost two in the morning, the moon was behind a cloud, and there was no light inside that yellow monstrosity at all. He could have been there, but we wouldn't have seen him. The second place I thought of was the little camper village. Crayer had a tent there, and Crayer was on guard duty. That might be a perfect place to hide someone.

There wasn't much light there either, just the dark shadows of maybe twenty campers and tents set up along a row of trees. One of the campers had a dim lamp that set out an eerie glow, but that was it.

As we approached the area I heard a slow rumble, like a dog growling.

"Hold on," I whispered softly, my voice raspy and my throat getting sore. The sound was coming from a small camper, the windows open. I listened carefully and there it was again, a low rumble. And again. And again. Maybe a guard dog.

"Maybe we shouldn't go any farther." I could feel sweat running down my chest.

"Oh, for crying out loud. It's just somebody snoring." She pulled me away and we walked down to Crayer's tent.

We walked past four poles and a tarp where someone had piled some canned goods on a table, two more tiny aluminum pull-behind trailers that looked about the size of our bedroom in Carol City, and three brightly colored tents. Mint green, burgundy, and a powder blue.

As we got closer to Crayer's tent, Em squeezed my hand tighter. "He's out here somewhere."

"James?"

"Your friend, Mr. Crayer."

"Yeah."

"I suppose he might find us."

"We're not breaking any laws."

In her soft voice, whispering, she said, "That doesn't seem to make any difference, does it?"

It was possible. The village was in an open area, the big revival tent back to our left, but in the dark, Crayer could come out of nowhere and I did remember that he carried a gun. I was constantly aware of that fact.

CHAPTER THIRTY-FOUR

Crayer's tent was an ugly military green. It was medium sized compared to the other tents, and small compared to a couple of the larger camper/trailers. The flap was pulled down and tied off on the front. Not much of a lock, but I figured that the people in the village watched out for each other. There had to be some valuables in each abode, and the inhabitants probably kept a sharp eye out for anyone who looked suspicious. Hey, I sell security systems. I understand how it works.

"This is it?"

"This is it. I've watched him go back here several times." My throat felt raw. I was anxious to speak in a normal voice again.

Em kept her hand in mine. While I wasn't exactly thrilled with the situation we found ourselves in, I was pleased that she was keeping so close. There was something about being in a dangerous situation that seemed to foster intimacy.

"The flap is tied down."

"Couldn't be tied down from the outside if he was on the inside."

Even in the dark I could see her smile. "Good point, kemo sabe."

"But, that doesn't mean that someone isn't inside."

I felt her grip tighten. "Daron? James?"

"Can you keep a look out while I check inside?"

"Yeah."

"Em —"

"What?"

"No falling asleep."

She let go of my hand and punched my arm.

I leaned down and untied the two strips of canvas. Slowly I raised the flap. Behind it was a see-through mesh cover closed by a zipper. It was too dark to see beyond. I slowly unzipped the mesh and parted the halves.

"Do you see anything?" She spoke in a hoarse whisper.

"Too dark."

"Let your eyes adjust."

I did. There was a little moonlight and starlight from the outside, as well as a soft light coming from a trailer parked near-by. As I stared into the tent, my eyes started to adjust. Not great vision, but I could make out a cot and sleeping bag. They were empty.

I stepped inside. The tent was too small to stand up, and I could make out a couple of bags, probably containing clothing and personal effects. That was it. A cot and a couple of bags.

I stepped back out, zipping up the mesh.

"Big disappointment."

"You were seriously hoping to find one of them?"

"Would have been nice." I tied the canvas strips down, duplicating the knot that Crayer had used.

She grabbed my hand again. "So where do we go now?"

"Let's try the truck one more time. I keep thinking that James would go there when he couldn't find us."

"If he's capable." I felt a tremor in her hand. "Oh, God, Skip. I'm sorry. I shouldn't even think things like that."

We walked back toward the truck, keeping an eye out for any of the security guys.

"Skip, they could have taken James and Daron off the grounds."

"Could have."

"If they're afraid of a backlash from Cashdollar's congregation, they certainly wouldn't do something to them here, would they?"

"Something?"

"I don't know. Beat them up or—"

"Or kill them?" As soon as I said it I felt her shudder.

"They wouldn't. Not here."

I thought about it. They had call girls visit the poker group. They played high-stakes games of chance, although I questioned whether there was much chance in those games, and Cashdollar preached against intolerance by being intolerant. But murdering someone on his own campus? Would they kill James or Styles?

"Forget I said it." She tugged my arm, hurrying to get back to the truck.

"You know the story about my first revival meeting?"

"You've told me."

"And the day after?"

"Something about the seventeen-year-old girl?"

"The something was they found her dead body in plain sight. Probably in this same area, so I don't think they have a problem killing people right here on the grounds."

We walked in silence. The tent loomed in front of us, a huge mountain of a structure. I could see the truck, sitting on its four brand-new tires. Maybe James would be there. Maybe Daron would step out and everything would be back to normal. Well, nothing was going to be normal again.

"I've got to use the toilet." Em nodded in the direction of the portable johns.

"Go behind the truck."

"I'm not going to go behind the truck. I'll just be gone a minute."

"Em. It's not safe. For either of us. Just go up by the tent. I won't watch."

"You couldn't see anything anyway. I'm going to the Porta-Johns. I'll be able to find my way."

"Em—"

"I'm going." She started walking.

"I'm right behind you." I took two steps in her direction.

"Go back and see if James is in the truck. I'll be all right."

I turned and walked to the truck. The moon was in and out of the clouds and when it was hidden the night was black. It took that moment to hide, and I wished with everything in me that I'd followed her. I shouted out in a coarse whisper. "James."

There was nothing. No response.

I looked across the way, and Em was gone from sight. No James. No Em. Five feet from the truck I decided to walk back to the portable restrooms and stand guard for Em. I turned, took a step, felt my foot hit something solid, and pitched forward. It was the last thing I could remember until I started to drown.

CHAPTER THIRTY-FIVE

There's a form of water torture that soldiers use on the enemy when they want to break them and get important information. I think it's called waterboarding. It has something to do with blindfolding the enemy, and then pouring water on his face. I'm not sure I have it all down, but I'd always heard that when you can't see anything and water is in your face, you can't shake the sensation that you're drowning. While it's not supposed to be dangerous, it is supposed to be very scary.

I can now tell you first hand, that when you can't see, when everything is pitch black, and when someone is pouring water in your face, you feel like you're drowning. I can tell you first hand that it is very, very scary.

I came up sputtering, gurgling, coughing, and swearing.

"My God, man. Are you all right?"

I was not all right. I wiped at my face and my hand came away, dripping. Water and something thick and slippery. I brushed at my forehead and winced from the pain. It was a gash, not too deep, but it hurt. Man did it hurt.

The light hit me in the eyes, and someone was wiping my face with a cloth.

"Don't move. Let me clean the cut out."

I was sitting, the cut stinging as someone dabbed.

"Man, I thought you were out for good." Daron Styles pressed hard on the wound. "Can you put your hand up there and hold the cloth in place?"

I reached up and held the cloth against the bleeding laceration. "What the hell happened?"

The light played around my face, then dropped to the ground.

"You tripped."

"On what?" My head ached, and I had that dizzy, sick-to-your-stomach feeling that you get when you've had too many beers.

"The suitcase. When you wouldn't respond I got a pitcher of water from the truck and threw it on your face."

"What the hell?"

"Hey, it worked. I didn't know if you were alive or dead."

The throbbing inside my skull was killing me. "The suitcase? One you took from the airport?"

"Yeah. I went through one of them in the car and found this flashlight. I brought the other one over here to the truck and was going to look through it using the flashlight. I only set the suitcase down for a minute to go take a leak. You picked that time to stumble over it."

I kept the cloth tight against my head. "What the hell are you doing walking around? We saw you being dragged away from the office trailer."

"No, you didn't."

Closing my eyes, I tried to concentrate. Styles had been there, then he wasn't. Two people seemed to be dragging someone from the trailer. And Em and I had both seen —

"Where is Em?"

He shrugged his shoulders. "You're the only one I've seen."

"We've got to look for her. And James."

"Slow down, Skipper. You need to take it easy for a minute."

I tried to stand, putting weight on my one hand while I pressed on my slashed forehead with the other. It didn't work. I was too dizzy. I'd been in that shape before, but for an entirely different reason.

"I thought you were with her."

What was I going to say? Here was a guy who'd given us all kinds of information, and I didn't know if any of it was true. He'd said Em was being followed by the FBI. He'd said that we were in some notes kept by the hierarchy of Cashdollar's empire. I saw him being dragged away after the break-in and here he was as if nothing had happened.

And Em thought *he* might be an FBI informer. I, on the other hand, thought he might be the killer. He'd already admitted to taking money from a dead man, Michael Bland, after the man had overdosed. And who knew if that was even true? He might have given Bland the drugs. I seriously didn't think it was out of the question. It was hard to think things through with my head aching.

"Look, I'm sure she's all right."

I wasn't so sure. "How long was I out?"

"I was gone only three or four minutes."

His light played on the ground and reflected off the suitcase. It was open and clothes lay scattered on the ground.

"How you feeling?"

"How do you think I feel. You leave this crap here in the dark —"

"Man, I am so sorry."

I wondered. One of James's favorite movie quotes came to mind. It's from a movie called *The Ten Things I Hate About You.*

The quote is short and simple: "You can't always trust the people you want to." Right now, Daron was the only person in the world I wanted to trust. And I couldn't. He might be the enemy, and I wasn't ready to take that chance.

"Look, tell me where you last saw Em, and I'll go look. Okay? I mean, this —" he swept his free hand as if to include my position on the ground and his spilled suitcase full of somebody else's underwear and who knows what else, "this is my fault. Let me go find Em." He swung the light up, blinding me again.

"Get the light out of my eyes."

"Sorry."

"Where do you think she went?"

I didn't want him within ten feet of her.

"Skipper —"

I wasn't going to tell him anything.

"Just tell me."

"She's right here." The voice was over his left shoulder, and as he swung around, the light bounced off her golden hair. "And what the hell happened in the five minutes I've been gone?"

CHAPTER THIRTY-SIX

"Apparently I can't leave you alone for five minutes." She shook her finger at me. "Skip, how do you get into so much trouble?"

Normally her cute sarcasm would charm me. This time it didn't. For the second night in a row, I was spending time in some godforsaken campground, lying on the grass and wondering if I was ever again going to visit my crappy bed in Carol City, or ever feel the sting of a razor to shave off almost three days of growth on my face. "I work at it, okay."

"Em, this is all my fault. Mea culpa. Mea culpa." Daron tugged on the brim of his hat.

"Seriously, what happened?" The sarcasm was gone. Em was now all business. Gruff and ready to take on reality.

"Skip tripped. Hit his head on a rock." As simple as that.

"Tripped on what?"

"Oh. My suitcase." He motioned to the opened luggage, his flashlight playing on women's underwear — a couple of bras, some panties, and what appeared to be a teddy.

"*Your* suitcase? Just one more thing about you that makes me very uneasy."

Styles seemed to bristle. "What makes you uneasy? I've put myself at risk tonight to help you guys, to find out what's going on here, and you have the nerve to say that?"

I tried again to stand. Em reached down, offering me her hand, and I slowly rose. The dizziness seemed to have gone, and although I was just a bit lightheaded, we walked to the truck. Em lifted the latch, raised the door, and we hoisted ourselves up to the bed, sitting with our legs dangling over the edge. Styles sat on the dew-damp grass and looked up at us.

"You came out of the office, took us around the tent, and you disappeared."

I slowly removed the rag from my head. The white cloth was damp from the blood, but it felt like the flow had stopped.

"I can explain that."

"Let's hear it," Em said.

"I went into the office and it was just like I said. The guard was crashed on the sofa."

"Who was on duty?" I wanted to know.

"Dusty. He used to be a schoolteacher. Math or some science."

"I know him."

"Anyway, he's asleep in the other room. So I sat down at the computer." Styles lit a cigar and when the first smell of tobacco hit me, I could feel my head start to spin. I grabbed the edge of the truck bed and Em grabbed me.

"You okay?"

I wasn't sure. I took a deep breath, more oxygen than smoke, and felt better.

"I turned it on, waited for it to boot up, made sure the speakers were unplugged—"

Em interrupted. "So it's all supposed to be on the computer? I thought he and this Stan kept stuff on their organizers."

"They do that too."

"And where are the organizers? In a safe?"

"No. I guess they keep them on their persons. There isn't any safe. After each service, an armored car pulls up around back and takes the offerings to the bank. No money spends any time here at all. At least that's the way it was three years ago. I imagine they've got the same policies in effect."

I could feel the skin on my head start to itch. The last thing I could do was scratch.

"So, you turned on the computer?" I was doubtful if anything he was telling us was the truth.

"I did."

"You've never seen this computer before? And you were able to just go in and find all of this information?"

"It's a long story, son, but I have been on that computer before."

"And inside that office before."

"Yes."

"And you're not going to tell me why?"

"I don't think it's any of your business. But I can tell you that no one was any wiser, and yes, I did figure out the password."

I had no idea how you ever figured out passwords. You go to movies and see people get like three chances before the program locks up, and these hacks put in things like birthdays, anniversaries, the name of a kid, or a pet, and sure enough, on the third try they get it right. I wasn't that inventive. I used ABCD. That was it. Of course, I had nothing in my computer or my cell phone that had any value whatsoever.

"I had the idea. Just had to look it up. Thankfully there was a Bible on the shelf above the desk."

Em raised her eyebrows. "A Bible?"

"A Bible."

"And you looked up what?"

"Seemed like the only logical password they would use. I just had to make sure I got it right. 2 Corinthians 9:11"

"And?"

"It opened right up."

I had to admit, it was brilliant. I'd never have thought of it. "So what did you find?"

"I had to root around, sort through a bunch of stuff, but he's got pages full of anecdotes, events, and stories about things that have happened everywhere the rev has been."

Em was being her cynical self. "So it was that easy? You just walk away with all the information? Just like that?"

"You calling me a liar?"

"I just find it hard to believe."

"Let me finish my story. Then you can poke it full of holes. Okay?"

She shut up.

"I knew that LeRoy and the pizza guy kept notes. I don't think even the full-timers know all that's in them. So I'm going through all these pages, and sure enough, there my name is."

Em was leaning forward. I hoped she didn't get so engrossed that she'd fall off the edge of the truck. "And mine?" she said.

"No. But James and Skip are mentioned. He simply sidebars their names with 'FBI informants' and a question mark."

"So they don't really believe that? They're not one hundred percent sure?"

"Skipper, if they were *one hundred percent* sure, you'd really *be* an informant, wouldn't you?"

He had a point.

"They're looking into it, son." He flicked his ash and for a brief second a spark burned in the night air.

"So what else?" I needed to know who the heck I saw being dragged away from the office.

"I'm reading and not paying attention."

"And?"

"And I hear a slight rustling. I turn around and Dusty is standing there with his gun pointed right at my—" he paused, glanced up at Em, then continued, "groin. I thought he was going to shoot my balls off."

"Dusty caught you?"

"He did."

"And why didn't he shoot your balls off? I think I would have." Em glowered at him.

Styles took a mouthful of smoke, let it trickle slowly from his mouth and smiled. "A former school teacher doesn't have the balls to shoot someone else's balls off. I knew that going in."

"Taking a chance, aren't you?"

"He's a school teacher, for God's sake. Mug—I would have been worried about. Crayer? Don't have much history on him so I'd be careful. Stan, you never know, but this guy, this Dusty, was a school teacher."

"What happened?"

"He says something lame, like 'what do you think you're doing here?' "

I remembered his bail-out answers. "And you said you were looking for Thomas LeRoy."

"You remembered? Of course. I told him I was going to talk to LeRoy about giving you guys a break on your rent tomorrow. You know, on account of the rainy day you had yesterday."

"So he just let you walk out?" Em couldn't quite believe it.

"No. I'm sitting there in front of the computer, on Thomas LeRoy's personal page, and I guess he didn't believe me."

"So what happened." I was tired of the slow delivery.

"I picked up the lamp from the table and hit him as hard as I could."

"He never fired? Never tried to stop you?" I couldn't believe it.

"Son, he was a school teacher. He didn't believe it was going to happen. And I hit him with a ton of thunder. As hard as I've ever hit anyone."

"Wow." Em was in awe. "So he's the one they were dragging across the grass?"

"I believe it was Dusty. And when I saw two of them coming toward the office, I figured he'd signaled them with a cell phone before I bashed him. I headed out in a different direction. I didn't want to involve you two."

"Do you think he's told them about you?"

"Hard to tell. My guess is he didn't know it was me until after he called them. Even then, I'm not sure he knows me. It was several years ago, and with the hat and stuff, I looked different. I only saw Dusty once or twice anyway. I think he just told them someone was breaking in. And I hit him hard enough to put him out for a while."

"That hard?"

"Maybe hard enough to kill him."

"Daron. You don't even want to think that."

"I hit him so hard my hands still ache. I seriously don't think Dusty will be turning me in any time soon."

"So that leaves one more big question." I talked softly. Not so much because I was afraid someone would hear, but because if I talked above a whisper, my head started throbbing again.

"Yeah." Em nodded.

Together we said it. "Where's James?"

CHAPTER THIRTY-SEVEN

It was almost three thirty, and we still had about three hours of dark.

"We can take advantage of the dark or we can wait until daylight and see if we can find him."

Hundreds of crickets rubbed their legs together in a mind-numbing nighttime roar. I wondered how people could even sleep with the noise. I wondered if James was sleeping.

"Or we can call him on his cell." Em pointed at my phone clipped to my belt. I hoped the battery was charged. I hadn't been home in so long, I had no idea if it would work. I'd never considered calling James. We see each other often enough that I don't think about calling. I pulled my cell from my belt and pushed the two digits for instant dialing. In two seconds I could hear the phone ring. Once, twice, then I heard the obnoxious ringtone of his phone coming from the back of the truck. Some hip-hop rhythm by a group I didn't know.

"He left the phone behind." Em jumped down from the truck. She looked back at me, and in the dark I could see her attempt at a smile. "How do you feel, scarface?"

It wasn't funny. I could feel the beginning of a scab, but I didn't want to touch it. I didn't follow her, and stayed sitting on the edge of the truck bed. I wanted to sit for a while longer, and make sure I wasn't going to be sick.

"Daron. There are a number of things about you that bother me."

"I appreciate your candor, Skipper. I've always thought you were somewhat of an asshole and that bothers me."

I ignored the comment. "If we can get on the same track here for just a moment—"

"Okay."

"You said you took the money off a dead man? Can you explain that?"

Styles pushed the hat way back on his head, and in the dim light I could see that the long hair on the sides and back of his head compensated for the deep receding hairline.

"I never said that."

Em walked over to Styles, still sitting on the ground. "You said it. I heard you say it. Skip heard you say it."

He slowly stood up, this time lit a small cigar and leaned against the truck. "Skip, I'm truly sorry about your accident. It was my fault. Not intentional, understand, but my fault. When I am at fault, I will admit it. To the right people."

"And we're the right people?"

"In this case." He turned and pointed the lit end of the cigar at Em. "You accused me of being dragged away from the office. You saw it with your own eyes, but it wasn't me."

"Oh, for crying out loud, Styles." Em was pissed. "We both heard you say you took the money off a dead man."

I was surprised. She was raising her voice, but Styles kept his low-key, barely above a whisper. "I never once said that."

"I heard you, Daron." I was afraid she was going to wake up the little makeshift village.

"Nope." He sucked on the cigar. Watching him, I wanted a cold beer in the worst way. Beer and a good smoke just go together. I would have taken the cold wet bottle and applied it to the cut on my head, then I would have sucked the golden beverage down my throat in two or three gulps. James has always maintained that there's very little a couple of cold beers won't cure.

"Yep." Em just shook her head, apparently in disbelief of Styles's audacity.

"Look, little girl. Let's get it right. You asked me if I took the money from Michael Bland. I finally admitted I had."

"And?"

"I took it, because he offered it. Before he keeled over from a drug overdose."

Em took a step back. "What?"

"Bland came up to see me about an hour before they found his body. We'd talked, and I think he knew that I wasn't exactly on good terms with the full-timers or with Thomas LeRoy."

"He came to see you?"

The crickets seemed to get louder the closer we got till dawn. He raised his voice slightly to allow for the noisy insects.

"He did."

"And what did he say?"

"That he was a full-timer, but he didn't condone some of the things they did."

Em smirked. "He said this to you. Someone he'd known for one or two days?"

"I think he knew they were going to kill him and he didn't know who else to turn to."

"Why did they want to kill him?"

"So he hands me this paper sack."

She asked again. "Why did they want to kill him?"

"And he says 'these are my winnings for tonight. Over eight

hundred bucks. If something happens to me, get it to my sister in Coral Gables.'"

"And you did?"

"Yes. I hate to admit it. It goes against my reputation as a slimeball."

As charming as he appeared, there was no proof that any of what he said was the truth.

"Daron, I asked you twice. This is the third time. Why did they want to kill him?"

"The truth?"

"No," I said. "Lie to us."

He was quiet for a good thirty seconds. I thought maybe he'd fallen asleep on the ground, but then I saw the ember at the end of his cigarette glowing brightly.

"I don't know for sure."

"An educated guess, Daron. Come on." Em was her sarcastic self.

"You've called me a liar all night long. You questioned the computer files, you questioned the FBI reference, you questioned why I was hauled out of the trailer, and you accused me of taking money from a dead man, even though I never once told you that. Why should I tell you my thoughts on Michael Bland or anything else about this traveling sideshow? Why?"

"Because my best friend may be in the same situation. Because James is missing and I want to figure out who is behind this. Why did they want to kill Michael Bland?" I needed to know. Desperately.

"Because they thought he was a plant."

"Jesus."

"Was he?" Em had kneeled down, almost on eye level with Styles.

"He might have been."

"What makes you think so?" I couldn't wait for this answer.

Styles tossed the cigar away and I could hear it hiss as it hit the damp grass. "Remember I told you that someone, maybe from a government agency, told me to leave and not associate with these bozos? Someone who knew I was in Washington? You remember I told you someone gave me a warning?"

I remembered. Another story in a long line of questionable crap from Daron Styles.

"Well, Bland was the one. Warned me. Wouldn't say any more than that. Told me I could be a suspect in a murder."

"He knew you'd been in Washington? The same summer that the senator was shot?"

"There was a brief mention of it. Like, 'look, I know you were in D.C. when Fred Long was murdered. These guys here know it too. You could be a suspect.'"

"And what does all that mean?"

"I don't know, Skipper, but it happened. And then he gave me a phone number to call if anything happened to him."

"So? It could have been the phone number of his mother? Maybe his sister? Ex wife?"

"No."

"How do you know?"

"I called it."

"And?"

"They answered 'FBI. Miami.'"

CHAPTER THIRTY-EIGHT

We were juniors at Samuel and Davidson University in Miami when the FBI appeared on our campus. Twice. The first time, we heard about it through a friend in the business school. Some crazy freshman sent an e-mail to the White House, saying he wished the president would die in office. And he sent it out over the network at Sam and Dave U. I doubt if there was much investigation, other than why the kid was that stupid. They found him in about two hours.

Two suits drove onto campus, went directly to the kid's dorm room, arrested him, picked up his computer as evidence, and no one at the university ever saw him again. I don't know if they charged him or let him off with a warning, but as far as I can tell he never came back to Sam and Dave. James's theory is that the kid is in solitary confinement at a secret prison a mile underneath Washington D.C. I just hoped that James wasn't joining him.

The second time the FBI showed up, it was in the form of a semiattractive woman recruiter. She had blond hair, kind of swept up, and she set up at a job fair and I picked up a brochure.

I talked to her for a while but I think they were looking for someone with a lot better grade point average, and probably someone with a little more motivation. I just thought it would be cool to have a job where you wore a suit and a shoulder holster. They wanted someone with a business and accounting background. It never would have worked.

I guess I shared a healthy, or unhealthy, fear of cops and officers of the law, just like James, even if they used attractive women as recruiters. I'd seen what they could do. So I figured that if the FBI was really tailing Em, if they really did have a plant on the park grounds, and if Thomas LeRoy really thought that James and I were plants, things were pretty serious. I was even more worried about James. As far as I knew James was on the grounds. But where, I had no idea. No idea at all.

Em looked at Styles with uncertainty. They stood, leaning against the truck, warily watching each other. "So you're saying that this guy trusted you with the information that he worked for the FBI?"

"Look, I'm telling you what I know."

"And you know about the FBI? You can get license plates tracked, you know about FBI plants? Excuse me for questioning this, Daron, but you seem like the least likely person to have any knowledge of the FBI."

"Yeah. I would normally act offended, but I know what my reputation is. And I've fostered it to a certain extent. You probably have every right to question my qualifications. I'm very close to the core of this situation. And I'll tell you why. But I don't want this to go any further. Do you understand?"

I couldn't wait to hear this one.

"Do you know what I do for a living?"

Em stared back. "As far as I can tell, you steal suitcases and try to sell women's shoes."

She'd figured it out.

"No. That's a sideline. I sell knockoff stuff. Basically from the trunk of the Buick."

"Knockoff stuff?"

"Louis Vuitton handbags, I've got 'em. Coach purses, you can't beat my price. Fendi, Chanel, Versace, they're my specialty." He talked with his hands. Dramatic, like a cheap hustler. Which I guess he was. "All cheap imitations. Although," he paused, "they're not as cheap as they used to be. These knockoff companies are getting pretty damned good, and a good fake costs a little more than it used to. You take the Emporio Armani sunglasses, I mean—"

"What the hell does this have to do with the FBI?"

Styles dropped the sunglasses story. "More than you think. The FBI investigates intellectual property crimes."

"What kind of crimes?" I had no idea what he was talking about. When someone mentioned intellectual I was usually lost.

"Intellectual property crimes. Trademark and copyright infringement."

Em nodded. "So you, selling knockoff purses—"

"Purses, watches, DVDs, perfumes."

"You could get arrested by the FBI?"

"I could."

"For a couple of purses out of your trunk?"

"The cops are involved too, and they're a bigger worry. But, the FBI is in charge of that shit, and when they are trying to bust one of the big warehouses where we get our stuff, or they're trying to track down some importers and arresting people at the port authority, then I'm in a lot of trouble. They can take me in, arrest me, get me a federal conviction if they think it helps their case."

"Really?" I had no idea I was dealing with a Federal criminal. I thought he was just a two-bit crook. I wondered if James knew. It would elevate Styles in his book.

"Yeah. You'd think they'd all be working on terrorists, but

there's some of 'em who work the DVDs and watches and purses. So I'm always looking over my shoulder. If I see a suspicious car, there's a friend of mine who can run the plate. If I see a suit approaching my stash, I wrap it up, real fast. I can be gone in about twenty seconds. I have a healthy respect for the cops and especially the FBI."

"I didn't realize you had job hazards like that."

"That and shoplifters. I hate those people. No respect for what I go through to get the merchandise in the first place."

Em looked up under the brim of his hat. "I suppose you could go legit. Get a real job? No?"

Styles turned his head and ignored her.

"So you think they killed Michael Bland because he was an FBI informant." This was getting to be very surreal.

"I do."

"And this Bland, he trusted you to call the FBI. What were you supposed to say?" I couldn't imagine trusting Styles with anything.

"We never discussed it."

"What *did* you say? When they answered 'FBI Miami' what did you tell them? That he'd died. That you suspected he was killed?" Em was on the same page as I was.

"I said 'wrong number,' and I hung up. Are you kidding me? I can't have anything to do with those people."

It was obvious that Styles was not going to be a help from this point on. He was paranoid, possibly with good reason, and he'd told us most of what we needed to know. If it was true. And I still wasn't sure if any of his stories had one element of truth.

"Guys, if these people here think that James and I are FBI, what's to stop them from doing the same thing they did to Michael Bland?" I tried to figure out how they would give James and me a drug overdose.

"Nothing. Nothing would stop them." Styles walked a

couple of steps from the truck then turned. "There is nothing stopping them from finding a way for you two to have an accident. Or, just shooting you."

Em patted my leg. "You know, Skip, we've given them a great reason to shoot you."

"What's that?"

"Somebody broke into their office. I suppose in the course of trying to find the culprit they might have to shoot—"

"My God. Have you both lost your minds?" This just wasn't registering. "I've played cards with these guys. While I wouldn't trust any of them, any more than I'd trust Daron, I don't think they are murderers." Really.

"Well, there's a chance you could be wrong." Daron kept his gaze steady, looking at me through narrow slits. "And I think we should all be worried about James. Let's make that the primary focus. James. I don't want to find him this morning with a needle sticking out of his arm."

James would be proud. He'd elevated himself to a top-tier position, and he'd had nothing to do with it.

"I can tell you with some certainty, that someone on the full-timer roster is a killer. Bland was killed to protect that person's identity. He apparently had information about the senator's killer."

"You don't know that. Not for sure."

"Skip," It was the first time he'd called me Skip instead of Skipper so I figured he was serious, "Michael Bland died not twenty feet from my tent. It wasn't an accident, it wasn't that he accidentally took too many drugs. Someone *fed* him too many drugs. And I have a good idea of who it was. A newcomer to the group. Someone who was brought in to get rid of the plant. They knew Bland was the plant. And remember, they think you are a current plant."

"Who was it?" I had my favorites, but I wanted to hear it from him. "Who fed him the drugs? Who was brought in, because whoever it was, they're still here? There aren't any new full-timers are there? And whoever it is might be planning my demise."

"I'd rather not say."

"Come on, Daron. Who do you think killed Bland? If we know who to look for, we might pull James's ass out of the fire. Jesus. I've just told you that my life is on the line. James's life is on the line. And you can't give me a hint?" I couldn't believe I said it. My best friend was in a whole lot of trouble, I was in a whole lot of trouble, and I had no idea how to save us.

"I'm sure you've figured it out. I can't get any history on this guy, but he's on the top of my list."

I knew nothing about Sailor. I knew nothing about Stan. I knew, surprisingly little about Crayer even though we'd talked. He said he'd made a lot of donuts in his day. That was about all I could remember. No history. Henry was a former tool and die maker, Dusty was a schoolteacher, and Mug had three felonies. I had no idea how long Mug had been with the group, but my money was on him. It made sense. Unless you knew that Crayer was in South Beach when the radio host was gunned down. Unless you knew that Stan seemed to run the full-timers. Almost like a mafia organization. Unless you figured that Sailor was quiet, lurking in the background. And then there was Dusty. Styles figured he was a schoolteacher and couldn't be involved. But I wasn't sure. And what about the tool and die maker? I knew nothing about him.

"I've figured it out." I turned to Em. She looked at me with wide-eyed expectation.

"Who? This is great."

"After working it over in my mind, I've got it."

Styles shook his head. "I don't believe you know squat."

"Wrong. I've narrowed it down."

"Ahhh." Styles smiled a sly smile.

"One of six."

"Smart move, Skipper."

"But one of those assholes has James."

"But there's Cashdollar or LeRoy. So let's narrow it down to eight." Styles pulled one of those brown little cigars from his patterned shirt pocket and struck a match. The ember glowed in the dark. "Can I say something that is the truth but won't set well with you and your beautiful girlfriend?"

I nodded, looking at Em. She nodded. Anything at this point. Anything that would help us find James.

"I don't want to upset anyone, but three years ago, in those three days I was here, a lot of shit happened."

Lies or truth, I knew that a lot had happened three years ago when Styles sold his trinkets.

"And I still remember all of the players here. Stan, Henry, Crayer, Sailor, Mug, and Dusty. And of course, Michael Bland, may he rest in peace."

"Get to the point." My head was aching and every time I raised my eyebrows I could feel the stiffness in my forehead where the blood was drying and the skin was already trying to knit.

"Somebody killed Michael Bland. If that person suspects James is trying to find him, and he has James as a prisoner, there's a good chance he'll take care of him too. And if he takes care of him —"

"Oh for crying out loud." Em was exasperated. "No one is going to 'take care' of anybody. James is probably having another beer with one of the vendors. And if all of this crap is true," she shot a disapproving glance at Daron, "if they believe that Skip and James are with the FBI, then there's an easy way to fix it."

My eyes snapped open, causing my forehead to wrinkle, causing me to wince in pain. "And what is that?"

"Convince them that you're not."

CHAPTER THIRTY-NINE

The idea had merit. Go down and tell them that we know what they think. But there were a couple of problems with the concept.

"All we know is that Thomas LeRoy suspects you." Styles had jumped up into the truck and was sitting on James's upside-down pickle barrel. "We don't know that the full-timers even have a clue."

"Although you think they do."

"I think they *probably* do."

"So what's wrong with just marching down to Stan's or going over to Crayer's tent and telling them that they're crazy. Telling them there's no way in hell that we're associated with any law enforcement agency."

"Number one, they probably wouldn't believe you. If you worked for the FBI would you admit it? No."

"I'll give you that one."

"Number two, they may not even be suspicious."

"I know. But we think that they are."

"Number three, they are going to want to know how we

know. And it's going to come out that I walked into the rev's office and rifled through LeRoy's computer notes."

"They know somebody did."

"They also know somebody smacked their security guard and probably gave him a concussion. I don't think I want to admit to that just yet."

We were all quiet. I could smell the lingering odor of fried burgers in the truck, mixed with the scent of dew-dampened grass and trees. And when I breathed deeply I thought I could pick up the scent of the water flowing in the Intracoastal, a briny, iodine smell that reminded me of the expanse of the ocean and a sandy beach somewhere in the Caribbean. I'd never been somewhere in the Caribbean. I just hoped that I'd live long enough to take the trip. Maybe to the Bahamas or the Virgin Islands.

"There's one other thing to consider." Em had been taking it all in, and I could tell she had a different angle. "They think you're plants with the FBI? Well guess who the FBI thinks I am."

"They think you are somebody who was involved in the killing of a United States Senator. You were in Washington at exactly the right time. And now you show up here."

"And you were there at the same time, and now you're here." Em was smug.

"So, some of us are suspected killers, some of us are suspected informants, and the truth is, nobody is anything."

"Except you." I couldn't let him just skate on that statement. "You're guilty of breaking and entering and assault, my friend."

"Yeah. But we got the information, Skipper. It's on Thomas LeRoy's computer, and that's exactly what we were going for."

"And in the meantime, my good friend is missing. I think it's time we make a truck to truck, trailer to trailer, and tent to camper search." I gingerly let myself down off the truck bed.

"At four in the morning?" Styles didn't sound like he liked the idea.

"Hey, we've got a good chance of finding everyone home."

"Good point."

There was no way I was letting Em out of my sight, and I think Daron was a little concerned about going out by himself. So, while we could have covered a lot more territory if we'd split up, we decided to all three go together. At least that was the plan.

We were halfway on our walk to the village when Daron suddenly remembered he'd left something back at the truck. He wouldn't say what it was, just that he had to go back. We offered to walk with him, slowing us down even more, but he refused and I watched him trek back toward the truck till he was swallowed in the dark.

"That can't be good." Em took my hand.

"He'll be fine. He's gotten himself out of more jams than anyone I know."

"Skip? I don't trust him."

"He's never given you a real reason to."

"Again, everything we have heard tonight has come from him. The story about this Bland, how he trusted his money and his story to Daron. And the stuff about the FBI and the guys who were following me. All Daron's story."

She had a great point. If he was lying about any of it, we were on a wild goose chase. And what purpose would it serve for him to lie?

"There's one thing that we know is true." I looked up at the sky and could see the stars, clear and bright. Early-morning light was still a couple of hours away, and the inky black sky showcased the fiery balls of gas as they sparkled through the atmosphere.

"What's that? What's true? I'm confused and I'd like to know one thing that's true. Tell me."

"James is still missing. And the longer he's missing, the more worried I am."

CHAPTER FORTY

Styles had disappeared. We gave him five minutes, then another five, and finally we walked back to the parking lot to see where he was. The Buick was gone.

We walked back to the village, and I checked my cheap Timex. It was going on four a.m. I could hear the faint sound of a radio or CD player, very soft, playing a Kenny Chesney song, and I remembered the tailgate party before his last concert in Lauderdale. Em and I had driven up, set up in a big parking lot, and ended up playing beerpong with a couple of college kids and some kid's sixty-year-old mom.

I struggled to pick up the lyrics as we walked. Something about sitting around, wasting another day while he drinks another beer in Mexico.

"Where do we start?" Em surveyed the tents and campers. "We already know that he's not in Bruce Crayer's tent."

"Yeah. If I knew which one was Stan's I'd look there."

"Stan lives here too? In the village?"

"I assumed he does. These guys are nomads. I don't imagine they have much of a home base. Even though they're full time with Cashdollar, I think they do carnivals and county fairs when he's not traveling."

"You could make a living like that?"

"Em," I was whispering again. I didn't want to wake everyone in the village, only one unit at a time, "there are thousands of these events. James did a search on the Internet and there are two hundred fifty-four counties in Texas alone. Like sixty-seven in Florida, maybe eighty-eight in Ohio, and everyone of them has some kind of event. And these things go on every day of the year. In every state in the Union. I mean, we could travel fifty-two weeks a year and never run out of places to go until we're ninety years old."

She was silent. Then, "You're giving that some thought?"

I laughed. Silently. "No. It's one of those things you just say when you're putting it all together. We were just talking, that's all."

"Well," she spoke in a hushed tone, "I'm not coming along if you do. If you ever do decide to travel as junk-food vendors, you be sure and let me know how it all works out. Okay?"

I didn't always say the right thing around her. But right now, I was just hoping that my junk-food partner would still be around for tomorrow's meal.

"I'm still not sure what you have in mind. Do you want to go up to each of these places, wake them up, and ask if they've seen James? Is that the plan?"

"Unless you've got a better one."

"This seems so stupid and so pointless."

She was right. And what was I going to do? Actually say, "Have you seen this guy, he's kind of scruffy at the moment, old T-shirt, jeans, hasn't been home in a couple of days."

We approached the first small, aluminum camper. It was banged up, and two propane tanks were hung on the back. The dim light from the moon gave it an eerie silver-yellow glow, like maybe a ghost lived there. Someone had strung a laundry line from the camper to a scrub pine. A set of men's underwear, a couple of T-shirts, and some cargo shorts hung on the line. As we got closer, the music got a little louder. Someone in the trailer had the radio on. Inside me, I rejoiced. Maybe someone was actually awake and I wouldn't have to wake him. I did a quick look around, half expecting to see Crayer, with his pistol in hand.

On the radio Chesney had been replaced with Willie Nelson and Toby Keith singing "Whiskey for My Men, Beer for My Horses."

"You're going to knock."

I was getting my courage up. And I was going to knock, but I heard rustling inside, like someone getting up and going to the bathroom. And then you could hear a stream of water, like someone using the toilet. These little campers offered not much in the way of privacy.

"Give them a minute."

"Skip, this is embarrassing." She backed off and stood about thirty feet from me. I can't say I blamed her.

The noise stopped and for a moment there was just the crickets and the country music. Then there was a loud belch coming from inside the camper. I mean loud.

"My God, you can hear everything that goes on in these things." Em was whispering from thirty feet away, but I could hear her. I hoped whoever was inside couldn't.

I softly walked up to the wooden stoop and stepped up, cringing. In another few hours it wouldn't bother me at all. It would be daylight, and everything would be fine. But in the middle of the night, it just didn't feel right. In another few hours, who knew what would have happened to James.

I looked back and the darkness nearly covered Em. I could barely see her nodding her head in encouragement. I knocked lightly. There was no answer. I tapped again, just using my index finger on the door. Nothing.

I knew someone was inside, and there could be no question they heard me. So they chose not to answer. I wouldn't either. How stupid to answer the door in the pitch-black of the night-time. I glanced back one more time at Em. This time she'd disappeared into the gloom. There was nothing else to do but try again. Or give up before I got started.

I gave it one more try. A little louder this time. The songs switched and now Carrie Underwood was singing. "Save me from this road I'm on, Jesus take the wheel." I thought about saying a little prayer right about then. I needed someone on my side and figured it couldn't hurt. Just as I started to step down from the wooden platform, the door creaked open. The first thing I thought was that it desperately needed some oil. Slowly the door opened, the creaks giving a spooky sound and feel to the old camper. It was like an old horror movie.

I couldn't make out the shadowy outline of the person behind the screened entrance. Whoever it was opened the door and started to exit. "Excuse me, I hate to bother you this early in the morning, but—"

In the softest of whispers, the person interrupted. "Hey, pard. I was just coming to find you. Let's get out of here."

James carefully pulled the door closed and we stepped down to the ground.

CHAPTER FORTY-ONE

He heated some coffee in the pot on the grill, and we sat on the edge of the truck bed, waiting for the sun to come up. Another hour, hour and a half. It had been another night with no bed, and in this case, no sleep. Em rocked back and forth next to me, and I'm sure she just kept repeating over and over to herself "what the hell did I get myself into?"

"I'm touched you guys were looking for me," James was slurring his words, and my guess was that it was more from alcohol than lack of sleep.

"You're touched, period."

"Hey, Skip." He was weaving a little and I hoped he didn't fall off. "Amigo, Tonto, pard, I couldn't just say 'I've got to check in with my roommate.' Come on, Dude. I'm a grown man."

"I hear you."

"Well, I may not feel like one all the time, like now maybe, but I can make my own choices." He belched.

"Point taken."

"James," Em spoke up. "If Skip had been missing, if he hadn't shown up in three or four hours under these conditions —

under conditions where your lives had been threatened, where someone had taken a gun to the truck and stolen your money —"

"What? Was your question?" There was no question. He was drunk.

"Would you have gone out looking for him? Wouldn't you have been upset if he didn't report in?"

He nodded for a while, and I got up and took the coffee pot off the grill. I poured some into his blue mug and handed it to him. I still don't know if coffee actually sobers you up or if it just makes for a wide-awake drunk, but it seemed like a good idea. The only one I could think of.

James took a sip of the hot beverage and looked at Em. "Yes. To all of your inquiries."

"What were you doing in that camper?" Em was back on the James conspiracy kick. I could tell by the tone of her voice. Maybe he was FBI. Maybe he'd been playing a game of charades this weekend.

"I have a perfectly logical explanation."

We'd been quiet on the walk back to the truck. I was in shock, Em seemed furious, and James was drunk, so no one had much of anything to say.

"Let's hear the explanation." I couldn't wait for this.

"Skip, I had an opportunity I couldn't pass up. I lost a couple bucks in the poker game, and —"

"How much?"

"Oh, I don't know. I think I owe them maybe seven hundred dollars."

"What?" He was dangerous. "Honestly? Seven hundred?"

"Pardner, wait till you hear the rest of this. It gets better."

It had to. He was blowing our profit margin. He'd spent all of the stake, and then gone in debt for another seven hundred.

"So we had a couple of beers after the game, Stan and Mug and I. Some of the guys went up to do their security duty, and then it was just me and Stan. And he gets out the hard stuff."

"The hard stuff?"

"Your old buddy, Jack. Remember, you and Uncle Buzz? Stan brings out a bottle of Jack Daniels and pours me a glass. So we're sipping Tennessee whiskey and he's telling me about the business." James glanced at Em, never picking up on her disdain. "Em, did you know these guys can net two or three hundred thousand dollars a year if they really work at it?"

I shook my head. "No, Em. We're not thinking about it. It was just idle conversation. Seriously."

"We're having a great conversation, just the two of us, and Crayer comes running down to the pizza wagon."

"Yeah. He was on security tonight."

"Stan drops his cigar in the ashtray and tells me he's got to go for a minute. He tells me he'll meet me up by our truck, so I headed up that way. Pretty soon he comes back. He's not very happy. I thought maybe it was you guys breaking into the office, but he doesn't say anything."

"Had to be what it was."

"Well, then, he invites me to his trailer. Wants to know more about you and me, pard. Wants to know what makes us tick. If we have any side jobs that we do. Then he wants to know why you asked so many questions. And he keeps digging."

"And what are you telling him?"

"First of all, I'm figuring out that he drinks too much. Jesus, he polished off half the fifth by himself. And he's the one starting to get tanked. I didn't tell him much of anything. He asks if we ever worked for the government. Can you imagine? The government? He wants to know why we decided to work this weekend for Cash. He calls him Cash, like they're old buddies."

"And you told him."

"I did. There was nothing to hide."

"And what else?"

"Now get this. I start asking him about the full-timers. I'm thinking here, pard. I figure that if he's getting a little sloppy, I need to take advantage of it. I asked him, just like you told me to, if he knew who shot my tires out."

"And he said?"

"He was gonna look into it. That's good, eh?"

I kept my mouth shut.

"He reaches into a small dresser he's got, and pulls out a semiautomatic pistol. He said it was a Smith and Wesson 39. I don't know guns, but it looked pretty impressive. He says "this little beauty isn't a tire popper. It's a people stopper. When I'm on security detail, when I'm on the road or in some strange town selling pizza, this little guy is my best friend.""

I nodded. "Yeah. I imagine it's a little scary to be on the road these days."

"He called his Smith and Wesson a people stopper, Skip. Said it's his best friend. Said his Smith and Wesson is the only real friend that he's got. That scared me."

It scared me too. It didn't surprise me, just scared me.

"Then, I told him we'd been robbed. And he laughed and said it was probably one of the guys just giving us an initiation. See?"

"James, so far it doesn't sound like you found out anything."

"Oh, that's where you're wrong, pally. So then I asked him about his organizer. I told him I'd seen Thomas LeRoy with one, and Stan pulls his out, proudly, saying it was the same exact one. He and LeRoy would share information and stuff."

Em sat forward. "What kind of stuff?"

"Well, financial stuff. What vendors had paid up. If there was trouble, like the tires being shot out. And then he told me that he keeps track of all the full-time vendors because sometimes these guys have to meet with Cash, he calls him Cash, and Stan needs to know where all of them are at all times. He's got to be able to get ahold of them when there's a problem, or Cashdollar needs to find out if they can show up for a revival meeting or other stuff."

I'd poured coffee for Em and myself, and I could feel the warm beverage steaming its way through my veins. My head ached and I wished I had some aspirin, but aspirin thins the blood and I figured it was important for my blood to stay thick so the scab on my forehead could form. I don't think strong coffee affects the blood, and the caffeine actually made me feel much better.

James seemed to be a little more clearheaded. He was rolling with his story. "So, I'm thinking, dude, I say to him, prove it."

"Prove it?"

"Show me where everyone was, or will be. So he motions me over to this little table where we've been sitting and drinking, and he punches in a couple of numbers and there's a list of everybody. Henry, Mug, Sailor, Crayer, Stan, and Dusty. Then he goes to one year ago, and there is a list of where they are. Henry and Mug are in Iowa at some convention. Sailor is in Key West, and Dusty is working in Michigan."

"Crayer?"

"I knew you would ask. Crayer is in Washington, D.C. at some street fair, selling his donuts."

"So he's got them all accounted for." I thought it was a neat trick, but it was nothing like the story I had to tell James.

"Oh, I poured him another drink, and he gets two beers and now we're doing shots and beer. And he isn't done with the organizer. He says 'now look. I can go back to whenever you want, and these guys will always be in my system.'"

"It's a good system, but what does it prove."

"Stay with me, amigo. So I said, can I see the organizer. And he hands it to me. Just like that. He's so proud of this thing. And

I punched in the day that Fred Long was shot in Washington. He couldn't see what I was doing."

"Whoa."

"Yeah. That's what I was thinking."

"And?"

"Everybody is accounted for. Mug is in maybe Oregon. Dusty is in Ohio, Henry is in Georgia, I think, and Sailor was in Key West."

"You said everyone was accounted for."

"They were. So I change the screen, and go to hand it back to him and he's passed out at the table. Skip, I actually drank this guy under, man. I could have walked out with the organizer or anything else he had."

I took a swallow of the bitter coffee, and clapped him on the back, gently. Every move I made reminded me I had a head injury.

"He didn't have much, but I could have."

"James," Em was terse. "You said everyone was accounted for."

"Yeah. I did."

"It's a game he plays, Em. I'm sure he'll tell us before the sun comes up."

"I'll tell you right now, pard. I kind of thought maybe you'd figure it out yourself. Stan and Bruce Crayer were in Washington, D.C."

We were quiet for a minute. I thought about the ramification.

"Doesn't necessarily prove anything, does it? Crayer as much as admitted he'd been there. Remember? He told us he was there when the senator was killed."

"Nope. Doesn't *prove* anything. But it means there were only two people in the full-time group that had the ability to kill the senator. *If* a full-timer committed the murder."

I leaned back on my elbows and saw just a hint of color in the sky. It was probably my imagination. "So Stan and Crayer were in D.C.?"

"They were."

"So was Styles."

"Styles didn't kill Senator Long."

"You never know. Em and I have some thoughts on who he might be."

"Oh, come on." James sounded put off.

"And Styles, Crayer, and Stan weren't the only ones in D.C. on that weekend.

"Who else?"

"Em."

"No shit?"

"No shit."

"Hey, Skip."

"Yeah, James."

"I drank that son of a bitch under the table."

"Hey, James?"

"Yeah, Skip."

"You owe that son of a bitch seven hundred bucks and I don't know where you're going to get that kind of money."

CHAPTER FORTY-TWO

The three of us sipped at the coffee and listened to early morning birds chirping in the trees that lined the parking area. I could hear a little more water traffic on the Intracoastal Waterway and the South Florida humidity was already building, even before the sun surfaced.

We told James about the FBI and, even though he seemed a little confused, I think he got the gist of it. Somebody thought we worked for the FBI, and somebody else thought the FBI was after us. We told him about Styles being mentioned as a suspect in a murder and theft, and the entire story about Michael Bland.

"And you could even think that I'd work for the FBI? Dude." James, in his drunken state, was still miffed.

It was just about five a.m. and we'd slowed down. I'd been up for a long time, and we still had lunch and the evening meal to serve. I decided on a quick shower in the block building, and Em had decided to go home.

"I'm taking off, Skip. I hope you guys will be all right."

"I'd love to join you." I really wanted to.

"You'd join me in a good sleep, and that would be about it."

"And I could use one of those." Trying to figure out how safe James and I were. That and where his buddy had disappeared to. I may have mentioned that Daron Styles was good at getting out of jams. He'd just disappear.

I grabbed a towel and an old bar of soap and eased myself off the truck.

"Watch your face." She walked me to the building. "Don't want to touch that cut or get it wet."

We watched the black limousine as it slowly drove up the road, past the vendors' trucks and trailers. The parking lights were on, but no headlights, as if the driver didn't want to telegraph his presence. Em and I stopped to watch it as it reached our truck.

"What's that all about?" She was whispering again.

"I don't know. Cashdollar is the only one I know with a limo."

The car turned left in front of our truck and drove through the grass and disappeared around the side of the yellow tent. I saw the license plate. CSHDLR1.

I motioned to Em, and we quickly walked to the truck. James was standing in the shadows, his eyes cast in the direction of the departed vehicle.

"Did you see who it was?"

"Yeah. It was Cashdollar and LeRoy. And a couple of bodyguards. A little early for those two."

"Want to take a little walk?" James looked at me.

"Back to the office?"

"That's what I'm thinking. Just kind of ease our way back there, just taking a walk. I'd like to see what they're up to."

Em grabbed my arm. "You've skated on all kinds of problems tonight. Don't put yourself out there. I'm serious, Skip. They already think we were involved in the break-in."

James gave me that look. Are you a man or a mouse?

I shrugged my shoulders.

"Then I'm out of here." Em shook her head in disgust and walked toward her car, shaking her head.

"Come on, pard." Still some alcohol in his bravado. "Let's just see what they're up to."

"Let's leave it alone, James."

"They think we're FBI, amigo. As funny as that may seem, they killed the last guy who was FBI. Don't you think we should find out if we're going to live or die?"

"My guess is die." He stepped out from behind the donut trailer, the gun pointed right at me.

"Bruce?"

"You keep asking questions and fucking around with this operation, somebody is going to kill you."

He kept coming, the gun never wavering.

"Look, I'm all for just leaving right now. Let us get our food straightened up and we can be out of here in twenty minutes. Right, James?"

James was frozen, not moving and not talking.

"You broke into the office, you stole files from the computer, they've taken Dusty to the hospital in serious condition, and kid, it's time to put a stop to it. You've fucked up this operation for the last time. Comprende?"

"Look, Bruce —"

"No, you look. You've screwed this whole thing up. In the short time you've been here, you've gone totally overboard. To put it bluntly, I'm tired of your interruptions."

He stood toe to toe with me. He pressed the barrel of the gun into my stomach and I closed my eyes. I sincerely thought my time had come. The Lord's Prayer came to mind and I remembered the first line. *Our Father, who art in Heaven.* I couldn't remember anything else.

"Mr. Crayer?"

He spun around, and Em swung the cast-iron frying pan as hard as she could. In the dim light I could see her damage. Crayer swung around, facing me. The front of his face was a grotesque configuration of broken nose, smashed lips, bloodied gums, and broken teeth. His hand dropped the gun and he staggered several steps, finally falling on his face. She'd saved my life, and all I could think about was how much Crayer's face had to hurt.

CHAPTER FORTY-THREE

"Out of the frying pan, into the broiler." James came alive.

I recognized the quote from the movie *Moonglow*. I was surprised he'd recovered so quickly.

"Jesus Christ, Em, where did you come from?" James was his old animated self.

I reached out and she backed away. "I was by the truck. Skip's frying pan was handy so I grabbed it. Are you aware of what just happened?"

"Em. Thank you. I don't know what else to say." I wanted to hug her.

"You might say 'I hope you didn't kill him.'"

"He was going to kill us." I was still in shock.

"I don't know that. And I've never done that much damage to anyone in my life."

"Thank you for doing it." James seemed stone-cold sober.

I kneeled down and took Crayer's wrist in my hand. I wasn't sure how to do it, but I knew if you pressed your finger on his vein you could feel a pulse. There seemed to be one.

"I think he's alive."

James walked over and put his hand on my shoulder. "Dude, what was that all about?"

"I don't know."

Em dropped her weapon on the ground, staring at the victim as she spoke to me.

"Well, give us your best educated guess. I'd really like to know what caused his reaction. Can you tell me?"

"Crayer is a full–timer. He's concerned that we're investigating who killed the senator."

James nodded. "Investigating who killed the senator, Michael Bland, the Washington girl, and whoever took a shot at Barry Romans."

"They figured we broke into the office. They don't know how much we learned, but they decided it was enough that it was time to kill us." Kill us? It just didn't sound right. "Anyway, that's my guess." I didn't have much of an imagination.

"I think you're right." James stared at the prone figure. "Crayer's in charge of this full-timer group. He is fed up with Skip's questions—"

"My questions?" James was quick to blame everyone else. "Come on. You asked Stan all kinds of questions tonight."

James held up his hand. "No need to argue. They think we're after them, and there must be a reason to be after them. There's some guilt. And my guess is that it involves murder."

Em was watching us with that disgusted look on her face. "My God, I almost killed someone tonight."

For the first time, I could tell she was shaking. I reached out and she pulled away again. "Please, don't touch me. I just need some time to adjust."

James looked away, staring at Crayer's reclining form. "Let's move the body. It's almost daylight and people are going to wonder why a guy with a bloodied face is lying ten feet from our truck. My guess is, it won't be good for the business."

"If we put him inside his truck and cover him with a blanket, he should be okay for a while." I didn't have any other ideas.

"If he wakes up, he's going to sound the alarm. And, my guess is, he's going to really be pissed."

"So what do we do?"

Em had stopped shaking and was watching the two of us, her eyes going back and forth. I could hear the wheels turning in her head. "If you were smart, you'd drive out of here right now."

I nodded. "She's right."

"You don't think they can find us? Thomas LeRoy has our addresses."

"Then you've got to call the cops. Because without protection, these guys are going to come for you." Em was right.

"And, I hate to say this," James hesitated, "you, too."

I could see her biting her bottom lip. "Yeah. I'm in this too, aren't I?"

"You are."

"You know, not too long ago I could just call Daddy."

I nodded.

"But sooner or later you have to grow up." She pointed to Crayer's body, his chest rising and falling with regular breathing now. "Let's get him into his donut truck, find something to tie his hands and feet, and go confront the reverend in his office."

James stared at her with a look of respect and a little bit of fear. "Just like that? We're going to confront these guys? With what?"

Em reached down to the ground and picked up the hand-gun. "With this."

Now this was a side of my girlfriend I'd never seen before.

We worked together, not an easy thing to do, pulling and tugging the body of Bruce Crayer. There was no blanket so we covered him with some old rags from the truck.

Fifteen minutes had passed. "I still think we need to see what Cashdollar is up to." James was focused on the reverend.

"I still think you're an idiot." Em had earned the right.

"Em, thank you. I don't know if Crayer would have pulled the trigger, but if you hadn't come along, we could be dead now."

She listened to James and gazed at him with an impassioned look.

"But, we just keep getting in deeper and deeper. Think about it. Styles almost killed Dusty. You almost killed Crayer. It's going to be hard to just walk away from this place. Know what I mean?"

"Your point is?" I'd never seen this cold side of Em before.

"My point is, I want to know what else is going on. I'm going back to the office and see if I can hear or see anything at all."

She was silent. This girl who had surprised me with her courage and strength. She nodded. "You're right. We're too deep in this thing. We need something that can get us out."

"You want to walk back with us?" I was surprised.

"I don't want to. I need to."

CHAPTER FORTY-FOUR

We walked back along the tent. Em had the gun. My fantasy of wearing a shoulder holster and working for the FBI was thwarted by my girlfriend. Go figure.

"Exactly what are we going to say to Cashdollar?" James, who wanted all the answers, had no idea what to ask.

"Damn it, we're going to ask him why we're being targeted." Em was riding high on adrenaline.

"With a gun in our hand?"

"Jesus Christ, Skip, somebody almost killed you. I think we ought to have some protection."

I couldn't argue with her. But I was getting dangerously close to suggesting the cops get involved.

We kept close to the yellow canvas, walking slowly. I don't think any of us knew exactly how to handle things.

"Technically," James said, "we beat the snot out of two of the full-timers. I suppose they have a right to be somewhat upset with us."

"Technically," Em replied, her voice dripping with sarcasm, "*we* didn't."

"No. *Styles* put Dusty in the hospital. That wasn't our idea." I agreed with her. "And if it hadn't been for Em and the skillet, we might not be here right now."

We turned the corner and I could see the trailer. The Cadillac limo was parked on the side and the door was wide open, a soft light emanating from within. Em stopped about thirty feet from the trailer, apparently losing some of her courage. James and I stopped too. Without the gun, or even *with* the gun, we didn't feel like bursting in on the scene. As we huddled by the tent, the first shot rang out.

The explosion, like an M-80 firecracker, scared all three of us, and the bullet hit the metal Cadillac body, ricocheting off the car.

"Jesus." James dove to the ground, and I stood there, frozen in place, not totally understanding what was going on.

"Skip." Em grabbed my hand and together we fell to the ground.

Then a second shot was fired, and a third. I heard the crunch of glass and a loud bang.

His head buried under his arms, James whispered loudly. "Was that the Caddy?"

I raised up and looked. The big car listed to the right, the windshield a spider web of cracks. "Somebody shot a tire." Trying to keep my voice as soft as possible.

He slowly raised his head and looked at the damage. Not more than three feet from me, he grimaced and whispered. "Not to worry. Thomas LeRoy will buy him a brand new tire."

The next shot sounded louder than the others and I wondered whether the shooter had moved closer to us.

Then everything was quiet. I could smell the acrid odor of gun smoke and realized we were probably way too close to the action.

No one came out of the trailer. No one set foot out of the car.

"Should we see if anyone is inside? Someone may be hurt." Em's voice barely rose above a whisper.

We didn't go. We waited for somebody else to make the next move.

James raised his head, staring at the Caddy. He whispered. "Damn. It's a waste of a fine car."

We waited what seemed like minutes. I could feel my heart racing, thankful that we'd stopped in time. Another ten or fifteen steps and we would have been in the path of the bullets.

Light no longer streamed from the Cadillac. It appeared that one of the shots had taken out whatever light source there had been. Finally we saw movement in the office doorway and a large silhouette appeared, highlighted from the back by a faint yellow light. I couldn't tell for sure, but it appeared to be Cashdollar. I wanted to crawl under the tent and hide, but it was impossible. Whoever it was turned his head and scanned the surroundings. How he didn't see us is still a mystery. Apparently he had only one focus. The limousine.

"Are you sure we have to do this?" The big voice. It was Preston Cashdollar.

"We've talked about this. I think it will help the situation." The voice from inside the trailer sounded like Thomas LeRoy. I wondered where the bodyguards were. Especially when someone was shooting up Cashdollar's car.

The big man walked down the wooden steps, apparently not afraid of another barrage of gunshots. A burly man in what seemed to be a gray suit stepped from the shadows beside the trailer. In the dim, early morning light, it appeared to be one of the bodyguards we'd seen yesterday.

"Are you ready, Reverend?"

"As ready as I'll ever be." Cashdollar stood by the door of the Cadillac. "Don't mess this up."

"No, sir."

"Laying flat on the ground, my head slightly raised, I watched in horror as the man raised a pistol, aimed it at Cashdollar and pulled the trigger. From only fifteen feet away he couldn't miss. Cashdollar grunted, staggered, and fell to the ground. I heard Em gasp. I lay there in shock, trying to figure out how we were ever going to explain this to the authorities.

With my head just slightly raised, I couldn't tear my eyes from the scene. Thomas LeRoy stepped from the trailer as the light from the office trailer highlighted his frame.

"Give me the gun, Walter."

The shooter handed the gun to LeRoy. I could see the deacon more clearly as he walked down the steps. He had on a jacket, maybe a tie. Formal attire for early in the morning. As he took the gun, I noticed he wore gloves.

"Two more steps, Walter, and we should be done. Go see how he's doing."

The bodyguard, Walter, walked over to Cashdollar, on his back on the ground. He leaned down, touched Cashdollar's face. "You all right, rev?"

Thomas LeRoy, division head of financial affairs, walked up to Walter, raised his arm and pulled the trigger on the pistol. I watched the gun jerk in his hand as the bullet hit the bodyguard in the side of his head and he went down like a ton of bricks. In the dim light I could see blood and brains spattered against the limo door. I thought I was going to be sick on the spot.

CHAPTER FORTY-FIVE

We were almost burrowed into the ground. I don't believe I will ever grab onto anything as tightly as I grabbed the earth beneath me. Terra firma. It was the only thing giving me any protection, and there wasn't much of that. All LeRoy had to do was turn around and I don't know how he could have missed us. Thank God, he didn't. I don't think I heard a breath from the two people next to me. Not one.

I didn't even look up. I heard LeRoy's voice, soft and low. "Cash, where did he hit you?"

Then the deep resonance of Cashdollar's voice. "Upper thigh. Didn't hurt that much."

"I'll get you up into the trailer, then I'll take care of the rest. Can you walk?"

There was grunting, and the rustling of clothes. Twice I heard someone cry out, then the sound of footsteps on the wooden entranceway, and finally the door to the trailer closing.

We waited, none of us saying a word. I could feel the wet grass pressing against my face, soaking through my T-shirt and jeans. The cut on my head throbbed, and with every breath the still morning air and the heavy humidity were thick in my throat. Then I heard the sound of the door opening and LeRoy walking back down the wooden steps. It had to be LeRoy. I doubted if Cashdollar was walking on his own. If the deacon walked toward us, if he took two steps in our direction—he didn't. The footsteps went in the other direction. Toward the far end of the tent, the slap of his shoe leather growing fainter and fainter. Then there was no sound at all. And suddenly, as if they hadn't been there before, I heard morning birds, calls and answers, the crickets that had been strangely silent, and the sound of running water inside the trailer.

I slowly raised my head. The trailer door was closed, but I couldn't see a padlock. I assumed that Cashdollar was still inside.

"Let's get the hell out of here." James was up on one knee.

Em lifted her head and the two of us gently stood up. The red sky cast a rust-colored light on the grisly scene in front of us. Sprawled on the ground, next to the Cadillac, was the body of the burly bodyguard. The side of his head was covered in blood, the thick red substance spattered on the side of the limo. One of his legs was bent at a strange angle and his eyes were wide open in total surprise as he stared at the sky.

Beside me, Em grabbed my hand with her free one and shuddered. The pistol clutched in her hand, we turned and walked as fast as we could toward the end of the tent and back to our truck, all three of us strangely silent. My headache and the sharp pain in my forehead were totally forgotten.

As we rounded the tent, we made a dash for the truck.

"What just happened? Somebody please tell me." She was shaking.

I shook my head, trying to put the events back in sequence and see if any of it made sense.

"The big guy tried to kill Cashdollar." James spoke for the first time. "The bodyguard must have put five or six rounds into that car. If the reverend had been in the Caddy, he'd be dead.

I nodded. "But he wasn't."

"And apparently he's going to be all right."

"I can't believe we saw it. And LeRoy, shooting the body-guard. My God." Em looked back at the tent, now an orange color as the early presunrise light highlighted the yellow canvas. Behind that temporary temple, that massive church made of stiff, heavy cloth, was a dead man and a wounded religious icon.

"We've got to be careful who we tell this to." James opened the back of the truck and the sliding metal door rattled and shook as the small steel wheels rolled the door up. The sound seemed to bounce down the row of trailers and trucks.

"It was almost staged. I mean, the way it all played out. Like somebody scripted it. Am I the only one who saw it that way?" Em watched the two of us, waiting for a response.

"Whoa. What about Crayer?" I glanced at the donut trailer.

"Oh Jesus." Em looked into my eyes and I could see this was all catching up to her. "Skip, we should go. Now. Let's leave the truck, and the three of us get out of here."

"You hit him pretty hard. We should at least see if he's alive."

"He was going to shoot us. I had to do something."

"If you hadn't hit him, we probably wouldn't be here right now." He surprised me. I can't ever remember James actually giving Em much credit for anything and he'd thanked her twice tonight.

"I didn't know what else to do." Em shrugged her shoulders.

"I know this sounds strange," James sounded hesitant, "but there was something that struck me about what we saw behind the tent."

"Strange?" Everything about what we saw had been very strange, sick, and perverted.

"I said that. Scripted, staged."

"No, man. Something wasn't there."

"What?" Em didn't like James's drawn-out explanations any more than I did.

"Something Cashdollar has with him morning, noon, and night."

"James." He was starting to piss me off.

"Think about it. What does he always have with him?"

I thought about it for a moment. Cashdollar was always dressed well, worked a crowd well —

"What are you talking about?" Em threw her hands up.

"You've never seen Cashdollar, in person or in pictures, without his gold Bible. Am I right?"

We both thought for a moment. Even going back ten years ago with Uncle Buzz, I remember that the preacher, who turned out to be Cashdollar, carried a Bible tightly clutched in his hand. He never, ever let that gold Bible out of his sight, and almost never out of his touch. When he came down to our truck, he carried the gold Bible. Tonight, or rather this morning, there had been no sign of the gold Bible.

The three of us looked at each other, wondering what it all meant. We'd just witnessed an attempted murder, a killing, and we'd all three been involved in bashing someone in the face and taking his gun. And here we were, standing behind the truck that was supposed to make James and me wealthy beyond our wildest imaginations.

We couldn't ignore the situation, since we'd become part of it. It was very iffy to take the story to a higher authority, and I didn't think the three of us were strong enough to take matters into our own hands. There weren't any other options I could think of.

As the sun made its first appearance of the day, breaking a brilliant tangerine orange over the horizon, we heard the sirens. They were in the distance, but getting closer. I had a good idea of where they were headed.

CHAPTER FORTY-SIX

"*You* look." Em stood back from the truck.

James watched from a distance. Halfway between our vehicle and the donut wagon.

Crayer's pink apron was draped over the counter where he served the fried dough, as if he'd just taken it off. I walked around Crayer's trailer and noticed the door to the inside was ajar. I should be the one with the pistol. Something to defend myself. I kept thinking that someone who had been smashed in the face with a cast-iron skillet would not be in the best of spirits. And I'd already witnessed a death this morning, and I wasn't looking forward to another one. Especially mine. But Em held the gun. James had looked at the weapon and said it was almost identical to Stan's Smith and Wesson.

I eased the door open. James and I had lifted him up the two metal stairs that led to his wagon and had put him on the floor. Then we'd tied him with some sort of plastic rope we'd found in his trailer. Now, he wasn't there. I stopped for a moment, thinking I was mistaken. Could we have moved him somewhere else? I looked around the inside of the small trailer. Nobody. No body.

Someone had found him and moved him, unless he'd regained consciousness, found a way to cut the plastic rope, and walked away. For some reason I doubted that had happened.

"Well?" Em asked in a hushed voice.

I turned around and shrugged.

"What?"

James echoed the line. "What?"

"He's not here."

Now they said it together. "What?"

I climbed down. The sirens were nearing the causeway. My guess was we had two or three minutes before they would enter the park, a couple of minutes before they reached the big yellow tent.

"What about Crayer's tent?" James asked.

"What about it?"

"Maybe somebody cut him loose and he went back there."

"Then that's the last place I think we want to be." Em still gripped the pistol, and in all of the confusion and fear, there was something strangely erotic about Emily and a gun. Don't ask me to explain it.

I don't know what possessed me, but I suggested the *last* place we wanted to be. "I think we need to know if Crayer is okay. If that means going to the tent—"

"He tried to kill us." Em raised her voice. "If he does die, it was self-defense."

"We need to know." I didn't argue with her very often, but this time it seemed important. "In a couple of minutes there are going to be cops swarming over this place and maybe FBI, and it just seems to me we've added one more layer of complication. We need to get our act together."

"Then you go." She handed the pistol to me, handle first.

I took it, feeling the heft. Cold steel and plastic inserts in the handle. It was important. We'd been through a lot during the night and I needed some closure. At least on Crayer.

"Are you really going by yourself?" Em gave me a questioning look.

"I'm going. I need to see if he's alive." I pushed the pistol into my belt and pulled my T-shirt down over the bulge. I had no idea why I was so adamant about Crayer's tent, but I was. I needed to know if he was dead or alive. I turned and walked toward the camper village, and nobody tried to stop me. I believe they felt a sense of guilt too, and we needed to know if we'd been involved in killing someone, self-defense or not.

The flap on the tent was pulled down, but it wasn't tied. A couple of early risers walked by me, nodding, as they headed toward the portable restrooms. I wasn't sure of the etiquette when approaching a tent. Obviously you couldn't knock. Did you shout out? "Hey, Bruce, sorry about bashing your face in. Can I come in and see how you're doing?"

The early light cast my long shadow as I approached the small green tent. I patted the pistol, wondering if I'd ever use it if needed. Flip the flap? Shout out? I was five feet from the entrance, wondering if I should even bother.

"Bruce? Crayer? Are you in there?"

No sound.

"Bruce?"

There was a rustling. Something was moving inside the tent. My hand brushed the pistol, as if I had a clue what to do with it. At best, it would look impressive to someone. It might frighten someone off.

I stood there for a moment, then gathering all the courage I had, I raised the flap. The rustling stopped and I froze. Now what?

"Bruce?"

The gauze was unzipped and as I leaned down, it parted. Daron Styles stuck his head out. "Hey, Skip. So you're looking for him too?"

255

CHAPTER FORTY-SEVEN

When my father left home, things sort of fell apart. It's not that they'd been going so well before then, but my working mother and little sister seemed to hang out in their own world, and I was left to figure out what was left of mine. James became the brother and the family that I never had. And because he became such an important part of my life, I forgave a lot that James did because he was family, the only real family I know. So, in some perverse way, I have to forgive friends of the family. Like Daron. Thank God there aren't too many of them.

"Where the hell did you disappear to? You break into the trailer, almost kill someone, then leave Em and me to cover it up?"

The sirens were much louder now.

He glanced over his shoulder, tugged the brim of his hat down low and put his finger to his lips. "Could you say all that a little louder? Maybe they didn't hear you over by the Intracoastal."

I lowered my voice. "So what happened to you? You just walk out on us?"

"I told you I've got a friend who gives me heads-up on the FBI."

"Yeah. The friend who runs license plate numbers and tells you when there's going to be a raid on your dealer's warehouse. That friend?"

"Let's just say I needed to visit her. The friend. Okay?"

"At three in the morning?"

"Hey, I got the information I needed. That's all that's important."

"There's a lot of stuff that's gone down since you left."

"Let's walk." Styles looked over his shoulder one more time.

"Walk? Christ, if you only knew what I've been through tonight—"

"Softly, Skipper, tell me what's happened."

"You hear the sirens?"

"Couldn't miss 'em." They were across the causeway and must have pulled into the campgrounds by now. In thirty seconds they would be in the parking lot.

"One of Cashdollar's bodyguards tried to kill him, and Thomas LeRoy killed the bodyguard." I started shaking, the kind of shaking that you can feel in your hands, so if you're holding a drink you're afraid you're going to spill the whole thing.

"Tried to kill the rev? Where did you hear this?"

"We saw it, man. We saw it." And I still couldn't get the picture out of my head. Walter's brains spattered on the car.

"Jesus. Is the rev alive?"

"It appeared he's okay."

We'd reached the aluminum camper where James had drunk Stan the pizza man under the table. A proud moment for my friend. The door hung open, and I could see what looked like a green couch or chair inside. Someone was slouched in the chair. I gestured at the trailer. "Stan's place."

Styles looked up and stopped. He took two steps backward, then climbed the two wooden steps leading to the entrance.

"Daron, what the hell are you doing?"

"Come here, Skip." The sirens were ear piercing as they pulled into the parking lot. There must have been three vehicles, and they all shut down at once, the screaming sirens giving off that long, lonely wail when they finally die.

I glanced over at the parking lot and could make out an ambulance and at least one cop car.

"Skip. Up here."

The last thing I wanted to do was see Stan. Still, I climbed the stairs.

"Seems there's a lot of this going around this morning." Styles stood there, looking at the slumped body of the pizza man. Blood stained the green fabric chair, and a pistol lay on the linoleum floor beneath his outstretched hand.

After what I'd seen so far, I should have been shockproof. I wasn't. It appeared he'd put the barrel of the pistol into his mouth and blown the back of his head off. I closed my eyes and stepped out of the trailer. It was all I could do to keep from heaving.

Styles walked out, and stared for a moment at the vehicles in the parking lot. "A little too late for this one. Put the Glock into his mouth and bang."

I walked away, Styles following. I needed to put some distance between myself and that picture. We walked to the edge of the trees that bordered the small village. I thought about walking even farther and never going back.

"Skip, he killed himself. It happens."

"There would have to be one hell of a reason."

"You never know. It might be something very simple."

"What was that you said back there? He put something in his mouth. The gun, right?"

"Yeah."

"You didn't say 'gun.'"

Styles studied me. "What did I say?"

"You said he put the 'gunk' or something in his mouth."

"The Glock."

"What is a Glock?"

"A nine-millimeter pistol. It was a Glock on the floor. Model 26, I think."

"How do you know that?"

"I've been around guns."

"And a Glock isn't a Smith and Wesson?"

He gave me a surprised look. "Two different animals. Why?"

"Because James was here earlier, in Stan's camper, and Stan's gun was a Smith and Wesson."

"Maybe he's got a couple of guns."

"No, I don't think so. I don't believe that Glock was Stan's gun. He told James that his Smith and Wesson was the only real friend that he had."

CHAPTER FORTY-EIGHT

They were waiting for us as we trudged back to the truck.

"We were about ready to add you to the list, amigo." James threw his arm around my shoulder.

"So here's the guy who ran out on us." Em gave Styles a look that could kill.

"There was a good reason."

"First of all, what's up with Crayer?" James was anxious.

"No sign of him. At all."

"Dude, we need to find him. Em and I've been talking. He's the only one who can seriously implicate us in this whole mess, and that's only because Em acted in self-defense. Where would he go?"

"Self-defense?" Daron was puzzled. It struck me that I'd never asked him why he was in Crayer's tent in the first place.

"He was threatening us with a gun. Em hit him in the face with a frying pan. And I mean, she *hit* him. We put him in his donut wagon, but when we got back he was gone."

Styles pushed the brim back. "That's two we've taken out of commission. Dusty and Crayer."

"And—" I coaxed him.

"And *three* that are out of commission. One, permanently."

"Who?" James needed to know.

"Stan. We found him in his trailer, the back of his head blown off."

Em grabbed my hand and looked in my eyes for confirmation. "Oh my God. Who killed him? I'll bet it was the bodyguard. He must have shot him before he tried to shoot Cashdollar."

"Appears to be a suicide." Styles sat on the wooden bench and lit up a cigarette. He shook another out of the pack and offered it to James. "Gun was on the floor where he dropped it."

James took the cigarette and leaned against the truck. "Man, I talked to him not more than three hours ago. In that trailer."

"Skipper told me."

"I even saw the gun. He was proud of it."

"The Smith and Wesson."

"Yeah."

I jumped in. "Daron says this one's a Glock."

James turned his hands palms up. "A gun is a gun. It still can kill people, right?"

The commotion was centered around the office/trailer. They'd pulled the ambulance around back and I assumed that Cashdollar had first dibs. After all, he was still alive. Two detectives in sport coats and bad haircuts talked to a handful of people who were milling around the scene, but no one claimed knowledge of anything.

Em was still holding my hand and I liked it. "Skip, how much trouble are we in if we don't say anything?"

"I don't know. But I'm sure LeRoy and Cashdollar will tell the story. I mean, the guy tried to kill Cashdollar."

"And that gave LeRoy the right to walk up and shoot Walter in the head?"

I rolled my eyes. "Em, how do I know? I'm still not sure of exactly what we saw."

The news had hit radio and television because there was a line of traffic that backed up to the causeway and beyond. The worse the news, the better the attendance. We'd heard it on the truck radio. It was brief and incomplete, but the basics were in place. Preston Cashdollar had been shot early Sunday morning at Oleta State Park. He was in good condition. One of his bodyguards was found dead outside his office trailer. As an aside, the story stated simply that a worker at the campground was found dead in his trailer. A worker. That's what we were too. Workers.

The press was salivating. You can never have too much bad news. I was just glad that we—Em, James, and myself—were being left out of it.

James sat on the driver's side, Em sat on the passenger side, and Styles and I stood on the ground as the newscaster finished his report.

"And finally, on a related note—" I think we all held our breath, "—radio talk-show host, Barry Romans, died early this morning of gunshot wounds he suffered yesterday morning while walking not far from Ocean Drive. Reverend Preston Cashdollar had been highly critical of Romans' political stands, and there were rumors that the shooting may have been related to Cashdollar's criticism of the radio celebrity. Again, talk show host Barry Romans, forty-eight years of age, dead of gunshot wounds."

CHAPTER FORTY-NINE

We'd gone in early and still were relegated to the rear of the tent. They were packed in and hundreds of people were left outside to listen to the speakers. The morning service was delayed until nine thirty and I found out later the park had to shut off attendance due to the overflow crowd.

The morning ministry was conducted by a young black guy who lacked the power and the punch of Cashdollar. He opened with prayer, and given all that had gone on, given the fact that we were still relatively unscathed, except for my forehead, I closed my eyes and said thank you. I didn't know what else to do. He then read scripture. I looked it up later and it came from the book of Matthew. The message didn't surprise me.

God greatly rewards those who trust in him fully,
often beyond what they could imagine.

The three of us sat in the tightly packed tent, noticing the police officers stationed at the end of several aisles. I don't know if they thought there might be more gunplay or what, but I was hoping we'd seen all the dead bodies we were going to see for a long, long time.

The first collection was taken, and I couldn't even fathom how much money was put in the plates. The worse things got, the more money Cashdollar and crew seemed to collect.

The minister thanked the congregation, and moved behind the center podium.

"My friends, we are gathered to worship the Lord. To thank him for our bountiful blessings and to ask him to help us build more followers from this foundation. Most of you are here because you are believers. You are followers. You understand the need to give so that you may receive. However," he paused, taking a long time to switch gears, "however, many of you came today to see what all the commotion is about."

There was a rumble in the enclosed area. Murmuring, some nervous laughter.

"Last night, there was," and he paused again, as if he was searching for the right word, "there was a lot of activity on our campgrounds. We feel you should know what happened, and we have asked someone involved in that activity to talk to you. On behalf of Reverend Cashdollar and our collective family, let me introduce Deacon Thomas LeRoy."

LeRoy stepped out from the side of the big stage and walked to the center. From any distance, the man cut an imposing figure. From his closely cropped hair to the brilliant shine on his shoes, the man moved with style and grace. Maybe even more than Cashdollar, Thomas LeRoy was in charge. Confident to the point of being cocky, he surveyed the assembled masses. The minister handed him a wireless microphone and LeRoy stepped to the edge of the sixty-foot structure.

"Early this morning, as you have undoubtedly heard, Reverend Preston Cashdollar was shot behind this tent."

The murmuring grew in intensity, the assembled people talking to each other, acknowledging their ignorance of the shooting.

"Please, let me continue." He waited, letting the voices die down. When he was in total control again, he continued. "The Reverend is in good condition, and was not seriously wounded."

A light applause grew, and within thirty seconds the crowd was on its feet, applauding, stamping their feet, shouting amens, and whistling. Cashdollar was their guy, and they wanted a speedy recovery.

When it died down, after two or three minutes, LeRoy continued. "Sadly, Walter Bradley, one of the reverend's loyal friends and bodyguards, was killed in the gunfire."

"There's a spin." James looked at me with a puzzled expression. "Is LeRoy going to admit killing him?"

The crowd murmured again. I doubted if any of them knew Walter.

"Yesterday, Reverend Cashdollar told this assembly that there was a threat on his life. This morning, someone acted on that threat. We now know who that person is. It is a man who we trusted for many years, a man who many of you know."

Em leaned over. "Is he really going to tell everyone that Walter shot Cashdollar?"

"This morning, we found the body of the killer."

The suspense continued. The buzz under the canvas was audible. This is why they'd come. I half expected another collection before LeRoy told them it was Walter who'd shot Cashdollar.

"The body of Stanton Barnes, a food vendor on our grounds, was found in his trailer, where he apparently took his own life. Although all the evidence is not collected, we feel that the same gun used to shoot our Reverend Cashdollar, the same gun that killed Walter Bradly, Reverand Cashdollar's trusted bodyguard, and possibly the same gun that was used to kill, yes kill, Barry Romans, was the gun that Stanton Barnes used to take his own life."

"Stan?" James threw up his hands. It made no sense at all.

CHAPTER FIFTY

"Is anyone going to address this?" Em stood in the rear of the truck, cleaning off my grill and the frying pan. "We just heard a story that we know isn't true."

James took a deep breath. "Em, we're the only people who know that it's not true. And what if we report this and they don't believe us?"

"We can't just let it go." She paused, then, "Oh my God. You're right. What if they don't believe us? They don't listen, and Thomas LeRoy starts looking for us."

"As it is, nobody knows that we know." I was still trying to wrap my brain around the situation. They were blaming Stan for shooting Cashdollar and killing the bodyguard, Walter. If we told the truth, there was a good chance LeRoy and company would come after us. "Nobody knows, Em."

"But we do, Skip. We're not going to be able to live with ourselves. We have got to tell someone."

"There are two things I need to tell *you*." Styles was separating paper plates and cups as the four of us worked in the truck, getting the meat ready, cooking up the onions and peppers, and getting ready for one heck of a rush. There were more trucks, vans, and SUVs than I'd seen all weekend. Three trucks with satellite dishes on the top and station call letters on the side had pulled up next to us. Three cop cars were parked up by the tent, and three armed officers stood duty by the exit as people filed out from the morning service.

"First of all, I found out who the FBI plant is."

I about dropped the spatula. "You waited this long to tell us?"

"My informant told me this morning. And the good news is, it's not you."

James put a thin coat of oil on his stove-top grill and started the first burgers of the day.

"All right, smart-ass, who is it?"

"Crayer."

"No." Em was helping me with the vegetables.

"Yes. But he's not FBI."

I had a hard time following him. Most of the time. "He is or he isn't?"

"He works for them. He's not an agent. Apparently, they brought him in right after the senator, Fred Long, was murdered. Maybe three years ago. It's been his job to infiltrate the group and see what he could find out."

Em turned pointing her finger at him. "The man put a gun in Skip's stomach and said he was tired of our interfering. He threatened to kill him. That's what somebody from the FBI does?"

"My guess, okay?"

"Make it a good one."

"I don't think he was threatening you with your life. I think he was trying to get you to either shut up or leave."

James looked up from the grill. "Why?"

"For the same reason you've known since you got here. You

asked too many questions. You were stirring things up. Son, Thomas LeRoy and the guys thought *you* were FBI plants. And you were about to upset the apple cart. The real FBI plant needed some space and you weren't giving him any."

"What cart?" I was lost.

"My informant says that Crayer was close to proving somebody in the organization killed senator Fred Long. Very close. And you guys came in and got everybody paranoid."

Em touched my arm. "That's my Skip. Scaring the hell out of people."

"So, Crayer decided to get rid of you."

"But you don't think he was going to kill us?"

"I have no way of knowing."

I had a hard time with it. This group, with millions of dollars at stake, couldn't figure out who the FBI plant was? Styles could figure it out in one night?

We saw the crowd, staring at the parking lot, talking loudly and waving, pointing, pushing, and shoving to get closer. The four of us jumped from the truck and tried to see over the ever-growing crowd that was spilling from the yellow tent. I watched Styles working his way through the crowd, as if he was on a mission. James, Em, and I stayed back, watching from a distance.

A big black limo was slowly making its way up the small road, inching along as the crowd parted. People were reaching out and touching the car, and it kept coming, up near our truck, then around the tent. For just a moment, a brief second, I saw the Florida license plate. CSHDLR 2.

"Skip?" Em grabbed my arm, squeezing it tightly. "We can't just accept that story."

"I know. I know. We should be talking to the police right now, telling them our version but this whole thing is surreal. It's —it's—"

"Bigger than we are?"

"Yeah. I'm overwhelmed. I mean, what are the three of us supposed to do? I mean, if we had a little experience in these matters—"

"In these matters? That could be the dumbest thing you've ever said. Ever."

"Em. Let's serve some food. We'll figure it out." I'd said dumber things before. She just wasn't there.

We'd started taking orders, and they were coming fast and furious when Styles appeared, climbing up the fold-down steps onto the truck.

"Hey, boys and girls, the rev is back."

"You saw him?"

"Got out of the limo back at the office. They've hauled that other car away. Anyway he gets out with a cane, and what looks like some padding on his leg. Couldn't tell for sure under the suit."

"Well, I'm glad he's okay." Em flipped some onions onto a bun, leaned down and handed a burger plate to a lady with bleached blond hair and flabby arms. "Guys, LeRoy is blaming Stan for shooting the bodyguard. We have got to do something."

Styles ignored her. "Something strange behind the tent. I've seen the rev enough to recognize it when something is different."

"What's different?" I loaded up three plates, the works, and stooped down to a lady with two little kids and thirty dollars in her hand.

"He got out of the limo and something was missing."

James shouted it out while he flipped three burgers in one toss. "The gold Bible."

"Give that man a cigar."

Em brushed her blond hair from her face, the heat, humidity, and grease from the grill giving her a little problem with her sexy coiffure. "How does that matter? Is that a big deal all of a sudden?"

Styles was rummaging around in our refrigerator, pulling out cold beef patties and making a mess on the truck bed. Finally I saw him pushing everything back into our refrigerator, and he stood up, a green bottle in his hand. The son of a bitch had hidden a green-label beer in the back. He glanced at Em. "It could be a big deal." He forced the cap over the edge of the grill, smacked the top with his hand, and the beer cap snapped off. Styles put the bottle to his lips and drained half of it. He could have offered to share.

Em gave me a wide-eyed look. She didn't have to forgive James's friend. I did.

"Why?"

Styles tugged on the brim of his hat. It came down almost to his eyebrows. "Instead of looking *for* something, look for something that's *not* there."

It actually made sense. It was thinking outside the box. Instead of seeing what *was* there, see what *wasn't* there. The gold Bible was conspicuously missing.

"I don't see what—"

Styles jumped in. "Skip, I've got an idea. Cashdollar is going in for the evening sermon. He'll kill." He grimaced. "Sorry for the pun. This will be the biggest collection sermon of his career."

"What's your idea?"

"You and me, we're going to be actively involved in this sermon."

"And how is that going to happen?"

"Trust me. When it starts, I'll let you know."

"Hey," the voice was below the truck bed. "There are about one hundred people in line here. Are you guys going to serve or do we have to go to the pizza place?"

Em looked down, and smiled at the man. "Yeah. Please go down there. And let us know how that works out for you, okay?"

I was piling on the toppings, serving the burgers, and Em was right beside me, doing the same.

"Working for Daddy is a whole lot easier." She wiped sweat from her brow.

"So you appreciate what I do for a living?"

"I think you're dumber than hell. But hey, I'm attracted nevertheless."

I spun around, in a rare second of free time, and shouted back to Styles. He was just finishing his beer. "Daron, you said you had two things to tell us. Number one was that Crayer was an FBI plant."

"Oh yeah. It may not mean anything, but Cashdollar had a meeting with the Congressional Black Caucus in Washington, D.C. The same day that Fred Long was murdered."

CHAPTER FIFTY-ONE

The crowd had grown. How that was possible, I have no clue, but the spillover factor was unbelievable. Where there had been two thousand people, there were now three or four thousand. If the fire marshal had appeared, we would have been closed down. People were parking at restaurants and gas stations up to a mile or so away and walking down to the park. The state of Florida would have been proud of their park, but the natural beauty, the river, and the Intracoastal Waterway was not what the crowd was coming to see.

The buzz was out that Cashdollar had made it back for the last event of the weekend. I couldn't fathom how much money the man would collect tonight.

"It's going to be a night to remember, Skipper." Styles smiled, a sly look on his face.

Even more satellite trucks lined up inside the camper village, and a Fox News affiliate had a camera positioned outside the tent. Local news stations were lined up inside and camera flashes popped every quarter of a second. Standing on the ground, looking up at the truck, I saw James pose every once in a while.

"So, when do we go in?" I wanted a decent seat.

"We don't."

"Daron, Cashdollar is making his debut. Less than twenty-four hours after being shot, he's going to preach. We should be in there."

We were probably already in trouble for not telling the authorities what we'd witnessed. I wanted to see Cashdollar's spin on the event.

"Skipper," I hated that name, "everyone will be in the tent."

"Yeah? You think?"

"I'm banking on it, son."

"And we're not going?"

"No."

"So not everyone, just—"

"Almost everyone."

And the crowd continued to file in. Past our truck, past the police armed guard, through the opening in the canvas. And they filed and they filed and they filed.

Finally, with three hundred or more people outside the entrance, and several hundred lined up on the road past our truck, Crayer's donuts, and the rest of the vendors, the sermon started. The speakers blared outside the yellow tent and the choir started singing. It was going to be one hell of a night.

"Ten minutes, son."

We stood there as LeRoy spoke. "Today," the voice echoed from the speakers, "in the last twenty-four hours, Reverend Preston Cashdollar was shot. No one knows the reason, but a threat on his life brought a serious threat to this ministry. God steps up, brothers and sisters. God works miracles. Tonight, it gives me a great honor to welcome back our own, the Reverend Preston Cashdollar."

The crowd erupted, screaming louder than I'd ever heard. They shouted out hosanna, whistled, cheered, and screamed. In the midst of the greatest commotion I'd ever witnessed, including a John Mayer concert and a Dave Matthews show, Daron grabbed me by the elbow and pulled me away.

We fought our way around the outside of the tent, bumping into people every second. Finally we had rounded the left side of the big monstrosity and we were standing in front of the office. The first thing I noticed was the padlock wasn't on.

"I'm going up." Styles gave me a cold look.

"You're crazy."

"You said it yourself, son. Everyone will be inside the tent, seeing if miracles really do come true."

"And what do you want me to do?"

"Come on up with me."

"Look, man, I don't know what you're looking for, but the last time you were in there, you almost got killed, and you almost killed someone."

"Won't happen this time, Skipper. Everyone is inside big yellow. The last thing they're going to worry about is someone inside their trailer."

He walked up the wooden platform and twisted the handle. The door opened, and he stuck his head in.

"Come on up, buddy. Nobody here."

I'd been through a lot. I didn't understand most of what was going on around me, but for some reason that escapes me today, I figured at this point I had nothing to lose. I put my foot on the stair and walked up to the landing. Styles was standing there, waiting for me.

"Nobody here but us chickens, Skipper."

In my high school history class we had a chapter or a page or maybe just a paragraph on Napoleon Bonaparte. The French general had a quote that I memorized, not because I understood it, but because I thought it was cool. Now, I understood it. And it made perfect sense. *Men are moved by only two things. Fear and self-interest.* I think that talk-show host Barry Romans said the same thing. Fear and self-interest. And I was in agreement. That quote pretty much summed up the last three days.

CHAPTER FIFTY-TWO

I walked in and the desk was directly in front of me. The computer that Styles had hacked into was sitting, totally exposed, on top of the desk, and to the right was a set of filing cabinets. No safe. Because the money was picked up as soon as it was collected. My bank took five days to process and cash a check I deposited. Cashdollar could get an instant credit. James often said it. You've got to have money to make money.

Styles was pulling open drawers and clawing through files. "We're going to find something. Start looking."

I had no idea what I was looking for.

"Skipper, go into the other room. See what you can find. I'm going to hack the computer."

A narrow entrance led to the second half of the trailer. It appeared to be more of the living quarters, and as I walked in I saw two vinyl recliners, a flat-screen television, a bar, and two bookshelves. There must have been thirty or forty bottles of booze behind the laminated wood bar. I felt like pouring myself a drink. Or two or three. And again, I didn't have a clue as to what I should look for.

I walked behind the bar, a narrow area with a sink. I shot a quick look over my shoulder, imagining what would happen if we got caught.

The crowd noise from the big tent outside was muffled but loud, and I caught myself listening, straining to hear any sound that wasn't contained in that tent. At the first sign of anyone discovering us, I wanted to be ready to bolt. A large cabinet was beneath the wall-mounted flat-screen television and I opened the right door. There were dozens of DVDs. The titles that caught my eye were several movies that James and I considered our favorites. *Dumb and Dumber, Bill & Ted's Excellent Adventure, Midnight Cowboy,* and *Talladega Nights: The Ballad of Ricky Bobby.* The second shelf contained more of the same, but a couple titles I'd only heard about. *Star Whores, Laying Private Ryan,* and some others I couldn't believe had been invented.

From the muffled cheering, I was sure that Cashdollar had been announced, and had probably taken the stage. I looked behind the furniture, still not sure what I was looking for. A three-tiered bookshelf was set into the rear wall, and I glanced at several of the titles. Most of them were what I would consider religious works. *The Record of Christian Work, Paul: A Work In Progress, Institution of the Christian Religion,* and others.

I scanned the three shelves and turned to the outer room. I can't say what caused me to look back at the shelves, but there, on the top shelf, was a gold book. A Bible. I slowly walked back and, stretching, I reached as high as I could and pulled down the large volume. It felt surprisingly light in my hand. The roar of the congregation grabbed my attention.

"Daron."

"Skipper." I walked to the other room.

"Daron, you've got to see —"

He didn't even look up. "Here, on the computer. Man, the other night I didn't look deep enough. Listen to this —" He looked up for just a brief moment. "LeRoy writes this shit. I can't believe he keeps this on record."

"What? What did he write?"

"Listen. You're not going to believe it."

I listened.

"The crusade has led us to this. Fred Long. Enemy combatant killed in the war. Michael Bland, enemy combatant. Killed in the war. Barry Romans, enemy combatant, killed in the war. Walter and Stan, trusted sacrificed soldiers."

"Jesus."

"Jesus. Anyone could copy this. Download this. The man is crazy. I can't believe it. I fucking cannot believe it."

I shuddered and my hands were shaking. We both looked at each other, realizing the implications.

"Skip, we need some more evidence."

"Christ, you've almost got a signed confession. Daron, we've got to get out of here. This is bullshit."

"Give me something else."

"Did you hear me?"

"Try to find something. We need to nail these guys."

"Why?"

Styles ignored me. "Look, here." I tentatively walked behind the desk. There on the screen was a short paragraph, a note that LeRoy had written to himself.

Daron Styles. Reason for Bland's overdose. $800 in cash that came up missing. Styles killed Bland for the money. When feds start getting warm, give them information on Styles.

"That's why."

And if they thought we were spying on them, they'd find a way to turn over information on us. James, Em, and me. Em had possibly killed Bruce Crayer with a frying pan and, if they had a clue about that, we could be in big trouble. So, like a dumb-ass, I decided to listen to Styles and look for whatever I could find.

Walking back into the living area, I listened carefully. Every quiet moment from the tent made my heart jump. Every eruption of applause caused me to catch my breath. My hand caressed the cover of the golden Bible. I hoped it would calm me a little, but it didn't. The cover on the book was leather and it had been dyed a deep gold. The letters on the front were raised and simply read, THE HOLY BIBLE. Was it Cashdollar's book? It was beautiful, almost awe inspiring, but our brief conversations about the book and its importance as to what had happened to us seemed insignificant. This was the real deal.

"Hey, Daron." I shouted in a coarse whisper. He needed to see this.

No answer. It occurred to me that he'd left. I wouldn't put it past him to leave me, if he thought there was the least bit of trouble. And he'd just uncovered a boatload of trouble. I glanced at the doorway. There was no sign of him.

Running my hand over the gilt-edged pages, I realized I was holding something of true beauty.

"Hey, Daron." Nothing. Then a sound outside the trailer. Maybe footsteps or a shovel turning over dirt.

I flipped open the first couple of pages and rested on Genesis. Chapter 45, verse 18 should have been one of Cashdollar's slogans. *Ye shall eat the fat of the land.* I opened the book partway and I swear my heart stopped. I coughed to start it again. The hollow shape of a handgun was cut into the pages. The shape was there. The gun was not.

CHAPTER FIFTY-THREE

For at least a minute I gazed at the perfect shape of a handgun carved out of the pages in the book. I tried to grasp the situation. Cashdollar, carrying the book everywhere he went. Cashdollar, carrying a gun, even to his revival meetings. Cashdollar, being in Washington, D.C. the same day that Senator Fred Long was shot, carrying his gun-toting Bible. Who would ever question a minister with a Bible? Who could ever question his intentions, question his geographic location, question his reason for anything? For God's sake, the guy was Preston Cashdollar. Beyond reproach.

Finally, I walked into the main room, the book in my hand. "Daron," he sat in the small swivel office chair behind the desk, eyes staring, his life having oozed from the deep, blood-red gash in his throat.

Deacon Thomas LeRoy stood next to him, an eight-inch knife in his hand. "Ah, Brother Skip. So you are one of the culprits as well?"

"Jesus."

"Praise him. He is why we're here."

I tried to catch my breath. Styles was dead.

"Put down the book, brother."

"You killed Daron?" It wasn't registering.

"He broke into our office. And, we have suspicion that he may have murdered a gentleman who used to work for us."

"Michael Bland?"

"You see?" LeRoy, held up the knife, waving it in the air. "Mr. Moore, it's obvious you're involved as well. When I call the police and tell them that you broke into our office — that you both may have committed murders, well —"

"Murder?"

"Bruce Crayer, Mr. Moore. I think someone in your little band may have killed him."

It was tough, grasping the situation. Styles was dead. And LeRoy was blaming me for Crayer's possible death. All of this in a matter of seconds. I closed my eyes for a brief moment and tried to regroup. Not more than two minutes ago Styles was reading a list of the sins of Thomas LeRoy, LeRoy's startling accusation regarding Styles, oh my God, Styles, and now —

"You killed Walter, the bodyguard." I blurted it out. He'd never admit to that.

LeRoy shook his head slowly. Almost as if he disapproved of my statement. "Walter was a soldier in the war."

I stood in the room, physically frozen, with the Bible clutched tightly in my hand. "A soldier?"

"Let me explain. In Christ's work, in the Lord's mission, all is fair. Our mission, the Cashdollar crusade, is to destroy the oppressor."

"The senator? Fred Long?"

He captured me with his cold gaze, and he tapped the blade of the knife in his palm.

"And Barry Romans?"

I tried to look into his eyes, to see if I was getting through.

They were lifeless. And the steel blade kept beat to a silent tune.

I couldn't help myself. I had to keep going. "And this has nothing to do with the amount of cash you receive? Come on. Every time you pull one of your stunts, your donations go through the roof. You and Cashdollar figured out that when people die, you make money. A lot of money. Am I right?"

I was shaking. Styles was four feet from me, blood running from his neck. To make it worse, his eyes were open, as if he was taking this all in. It was all I could do to keep it together.

"You broke into our office, Eugene." The guy had done his homework. He even knew my given name.

I tried not to look at the lifeless body of Daron Styles. I had to keep LeRoy going. The longer he talked, the better my chance for living. Goddamn James. He'd put me in a life-or-death situation, and I silently swore I'd never, ever, do anything he suggested again. I had to pin this guy, and I did just that.

"Do you know we saw you? Saw you shoot Walter in the head?"

He was quiet for a moment. The sheer bulk of the man kept me on one side of the room. While his tailored suit, the flawless way his jacket hung from his frame, was impressive, I still realized he was probably six foot four and weighed 230 pounds, and I was sure he could toss me around the room like a sack of potatoes. That and the fact that he had a sizeable weapon in his hand made me decide to keep the desk between us.

"There are agencies that are against the reverend. They'd like to bring him down. It was time to disarm those agencies."

Disarm? "So you made up the story about Cashdollar's death threat? It was all a way for you to lay the blame for the murders on someone else." I felt the perspiration soaking my T-shirt, beading on my forehead, and running down my face. And LeRoy, looking very cool.

He stared at me, still tapping the knife blade in his palm.

"Made up? I can tell you that every day of his Christian life, the reverend has had death threats."

That was probably true. He'd pissed off a lot of people.

"You had the bodyguard, Walter, shoot him in the leg. Just to make it look like the threat was real. Then, you shot the bodyguard with Cashdollar's gun. We saw it, and we bought into it. We thought you were killing the guy who shot Cashdollar to protect the reverend. It was all smoke, wasn't it?"

It struck me again. Like Styles had said, you can see something plain as day, and not see it at all. Like watching two men drag Styles from the office when it wasn't Styles. Like hearing Styles say he took the money from a dead man, when he never said that at all.

"And then, then when you laid it on Stan we knew the whole thing was a set up."

"Should I applaud?" Tap, tap, tap. "Should I congratulate you?" Tap, tap, tap. "Should I confess to whatever you are suggesting?"

"No." I tried to give him the same cold, calculating look that he was giving me. "You don't have to." I held the front cover of the book and let the gold Bible fall open, the cut-out shape of the gun hanging down for anyone to see. I would bet my last beer that the shape fit a Glock nine-millimeter gun perfectly and, until this morning, I didn't even know what a Glock was.

"Strong words from someone who just broke into our office. I think you need to pray that God accepts your soul, brother Eugene."

"Do you understand what I said? Until you got up in front of your congregation and said that Stan had killed the bodyguard, we were buying into the whole thing. And now what are we supposed to do?"

"Die." He took two steps toward me, the knife in front of him.

"Wait." I needed to stop him.

He hesitated.

"Did Stan have anything at all to do with this?"

LeRoy smiled. For the first time.

"Stan? Stan wouldn't have understood any of it. In case you hadn't noticed, he wasn't the brightest bulb on the circuit. Stan and the full-timers were loyal only because of the money. When we wanted them to help us with a project, I would call Stan and he would get them all together. They were paid quite well. Money, women —"

"He was a stooge?"

LeRoy shook his head. "A soldier. Not a very bright soldier, but a soldier nonetheless."

"You made it look like suicide. You used Cashdollar's gun. His Glock. So Stan appears to be the master criminal who killed Fred Long. The guy who shot Barry Romans."

"He was a soldier. We needed him to do his part."

"His part?" I watched LeRoy's eyes. I'd always heard that you can tell what someone is going to do if you watch his eyes. But all I could see were black pupils that stared directly back at me.

"This is getting tedious." He took a step toward the desk and I backed up. "Stan will be accused of the murders. It was necessary for the ministry."

"You're crazy. Do you know that? You're bonkers — off the chart." I had to try to get him off balance. Somehow I had to get out of that door.

"There are agencies that were looking for Senator Long's murderer. We just handed them their killer."

"The FBI?"

"Are you part of that agency?" He raised his voice. His eyes grew wide and I knew I'd tapped into the true secret. The guy was a raving lunatic.

I had him going. Because of Styles, I knew more than he could possibly imagine. "No. I'm not a part of any agency. But you've got notes on your computer that suggest you think I'm FBI."

Outside I could hear a roar and I realized the service was still in progress. The noise, the confusion, would cover up any sound of my death. I assumed LeRoy was counting on it.

"Brother Eugene, you are about to join your friend, Daron Styles."

He took two more steps around the desk as I backed up.

"You guys poisoned Michael Bland, the FBI informant. You did, didn't you? And you're going to point a finger at," I felt sick to my stomach and kept my eyes focused on LeRoy, "Daron Styles. You're going to blame him. And *you* killed Cashdollar's girlfriend? Ten years ago."

He pursed his lips and shook his head. "Little Cabrina Washington. No. I didn't. But that's in the past, Eugene."

"Cashdollar? He did it? Tell me. He strangled Cabrina Washington? And Cashdollar is the shooter, am I right?"

He came around the desk. "I sent you a friendly note. I told you to move on or you might be a victim, but apparently you and your friends don't take a hint."

"You stole our money?"

He stared at me. "Eugene, I have money. I have no need of yours."

Damn carneys.

"There is nowhere else for you to go. You and your friend here have caused enough problems. It's time to put an end to them."

The trailer door slammed open and he spun around. The wind, one of the full-timers, it didn't make any difference. A momentary distraction was all I needed. I was about to save a life. Mine. I reached under my T-shirt, pulled out the gun that had been digging into my gut for four or five hours, pointed it in the general direction of Thomas LeRoy, and pulled the trigger. Twice. He went down and didn't get up. I hoped I hadn't killed him. I remember whispering a silent prayer. And then, I hoped I had.

Em stood in the doorway with her mouth hanging open. Finally she looked at me, her eyes as big as saucers. "Oh my God, Skip, I can't believe you did that."

"I can't either."

She was shaking. I was shaking. I dropped the pistol on the floor and stumbled to her, hugging her as she sobbed. I may have sobbed too. It was an emotional time and I can't account for my actions.

CHAPTER FIFTY-FOUR

The cell phone rang. "Hey, dude, Cashdollar is on the radio." James was at work boiling the crab, and listening to an all news station.

"And what's he saying?" I looked down and saw I was on empty. I still had about five miles to go to my next appointment, and I couldn't remember a gas station anywhere nearby. I couldn't afford gas, anyway. Sales were slow, and we'd pretty much gone through any profit we made at the revival meeting.

"Same shit. He says he was not aware that Thomas LeRoy was working behind his back. He says he is astounded that LeRoy and possibly Stan were going around killing people without his knowledge."

"So he's not going to help defend LeRoy?"

"Doesn't sound like it. According to the interview, when LeRoy gets out of the hospital, he's on his own."

"And Cashdollar gets off, no questions asked?"

"Amigo, there's no proof."

"The gold Bible, James. Jesus."

"You know what they said, pard. No Cashdollar fingerprints on the weapon or the Bible. And you know they found that second gold Bible, *with* Cashdollar's fingerprints, and *no* pages cut out to hold a gun."

I knew it all. It had been front-page news for a week. Cashdollar had been on Larry King just last night. I also knew that Cashdollar was guilty as sin.

"James, let me know what else he says." The radio in my used Prius had crashed two weeks ago.

"Will do. Eventually, LeRoy is going to go after Cashdollar, but it could take a long time." He paused. "Pard, have you heard from the cops?"

I hadn't. Not since that night, and five hours of being interrogated. I did have an attorney. Em's dad stepped up and hired a guy to represent me if there were any charges. So far, there hadn't been. "Since we were taken in for questioning I haven't heard anything, James. No news is good news."

"Solid. And the pistol?"

"The last I heard, nobody had ever registered it. And Em's and my fingerprints were the only ones they could recognize on it."

"Not Crayer's?"

"They claim that any other prints were not identifiable."

"Man."

The phone beeped. "James, hold on."

"Hey, you."

"Em."

"Are we on tonight?"

"Yeah. Something very cheap, okay?"

"You bring a bottle of wine. I'll provide the entertainment."

I liked the sound of that.

"Skip?"

"Same question."

"Same answer. I haven't heard a thing about Crayer. No one knows where he is or even who he is."

"It bothers me. A lot."

"I know. I'll see you tonight." I pushed the button and James was back.

"What do you think, James? How did he do it?"

"I don't have the answer, bro. Just a guess."

"Yeah, you and your friends have some pretty good guesses."

He was silent for a moment. "I think the rev walked up to them, pulled the Glock from the Bible and shot them. Put the Glock back in the Bible and walked away. As simple as that."

"How about your tires?"

"LeRoy. I'd bet on it. Trying to scare us off."

We were both quiet. Finally, I said it. "I really came down on you about Styles. I'm sorry. He turned out to be a stand-up guy. Really."

"Amigo, I still don't understand. He normally wasn't the kind of guy who just jumped into other people's problems with both feet."

"Yeah. I was thinking the same thing. But he did."

"He did. And I miss him. Hey, I've got to go. There's a line of people waiting for food, and you know how that is."

I did.

Two days later I got a call from an unidentified number. I'm one of those guys who picks up anything. I've been sorry once or twice.

"Is this Eugene?"

"It is."

"Eugene," the voice was soft and sexy, "I was a —" she paused, "a friend of Daron Styles."

"Yeah."

"You may receive a phone call regarding him in the next several weeks."

"I was there when —"

"I know. There are going to be more questions. They're going to ask you about his contacts. Please, you and your friends, simply say that you were casual friends and there's absolutely nothing else you can add."

"Casual friends?"

"That's right. Eugene, it's very important."

"If you were his friend, I need to tell you that I misjudged him. What happened to him should never happen to anyone."

"Eugene. Please. You were casual friends. Nothing more. That's all you should say."

"I'll do it."

In the movies, on TV, in books, the ending always ties up the loose ends. It doesn't seem to be that way in real life. At least for me. I'm still waiting to see if I'll be charged for shooting LeRoy. I'm still waiting to see if Bruce Crayer surfaces. I'm still waiting to see if Cashdollar gets away with murder, and I'm still waiting to see if Em and I will survive. I keep remembering my uncle Buzz, saying we're all waiting for the next revival. I wish that was the only thing I was concerned with. Actually, I don't think I could ever visit another revival meeting. And I mean ever.

I saw Cashdollar on TV that night. I think it was Fox News that interviewed him. His ministry was skyrocketing. They showed him in front of a large gathering. The banner was behind him.

YOU WILL BE MADE RICH IN EVERY
WAY SO THAT YOU CAN BE
GENEROUS ON EVERY OCCASION.

I'd donated to that cause. I'd bought into the concept, just a little bit, and I still didn't have more than five bucks in my pocket and four beers in the fridge. Cashdollar's ministry. The stuff dreams are made of.